Three Brothers, Two Plots and a Monk

Three Brothers, Two Plots and a Monk.

The everlasting

Chronicles of Brother Hermitage

by

Howard of Warwick

From the Scriptorium of
The Funny Book Company

The Funny Book Company

Published by The Funny Book Company
Crown House 27 Old Gloucester Street
London WC1N 3AX
www.funnybookcompany.com

Cover design by Double Dagger. Cover image public domain.

Ebook ISBN 978-1-913383-68-8
Paperback ISBN 978-1-913383-69-5

With gratitude for corrections of the quill:

Mary

Also by Howard of Warwick.

The First Chronicles of Brother Hermitage

The Heretics of De'Ath

The Garderobe of Death

The Tapestry of Death

Continuing Chronicles of Brother Hermitage

Hermitage, Wat and Some Murder or Other

Hermitage, Wat and Some Druids

Hermitage, Wat and Some Nuns

Yet More Chronicles of Brother Hermitage

The Case of the Clerical Cadaver

The Case of the Curious Corpse

The Case of the Cantankerous Carcass

Interminable Chronicles of Brother Hermitage

A Murder for Mistress Cwen

A Murder for Master Wat

A Murder for Brother Hermitage

The Umpteenth Chronicles of Brother Hermitage

The Bayeux Embroidery

The Chester Chasuble

The Hermes Parchment

The Superfluous Chronicles of Brother Hermitage

The 1066 from Normandy

The 1066 to Hastings

The 1066 via Derby

The Unnecessary Chronicles of Brother Hermitage

The King's Investigator

The King's Investigator Part II

The Meandering Chronicles of Brother Hermitage

A Mayhem of Murderous Monks

A Murder of Convenience

Murder Most Murderous

The Perpetual Chronicles of Brother Hermitage
The Investigator's Apprentice.
The Investigator's Wedding
The Investigator's Kingdom
The Boundless Chronicles of Brother Hermitage
Return to the Dingle
Murder Can Be Murder
Murder 'Midst Merriment
The Innumerable Chronicles of Brother Hermitage
How Many Monks?
No Murder Here.
Not Another Murder.
The Everlasting Chronicles of Brother Hermitage
What Dead Body?

Brother Hermitage Diversions
Brother Hermitage in Shorts (Free!)
Brother Hermitage's Christmas Gift

Audio
Brother Hermitage's Christmas Gift
Hermitage and the Hostelry

Howard of Warwick's Middle Ages crisis: History-ish.
The Domesday Book (No, Not That One.)
The Domesday Book (Still Not That One.)
The Magna Carta (Or Is It?)

Explore the whole sorry business and join the mailing list:
www.Howardofwarwick.com
Another funny book from The Funny Book Company
Greedy by Ainsworth Pennington

Three Brothers, Two Plots and A Monk

Caput I: Knock Knock

There was a knock on the door.

Cwen, having just promised Hermitage that there wouldn't be a knock on the door so soon after the last investigation, had the decency to look surprised.

She even appeared to be genuinely worried that her utterance had had some mystical effect and brought this event to pass.

'Ooh,' Wat said in mock fear of her new-found powers. 'It's true what they say about old mothers.'

Cwen pointed at him. 'I am not a mother yet, and if you call me old again, there will be another much harder knock, a lot closer to your head.'

Wat held his hands up in surrender 'You couldn't make the visitor a bearer of great wealth, could you?'

Cwen snorted and got up to go and see who this perfectly normal caller was and what their ordinary business would be.

'Most likely Ern, wanting you to pay the tavern bill,' she said. 'Come to take some of your existing wealth away.'

Wat did not look happy about that.

Hermitage was too stunned to react at all. Thoughts along the lines of "surely not" and "it cannot be", were elbowed aside by "here we go again."

He didn't want to think highly of himself, in fact, he never did, but he thought that this continual punishment by murder investigation was a bit much.

He had not led a sinful life. He had taken the cloth at an early age and devoted himself to service and the work of the scriptorium before being appointed the King's Investigator.

Surely, he deserved some reward for his commitment, not to be constantly embroiled in the sins of others.

It was not for him to say what he deserved and did not deserve, naturally, but he wondered about the trials of Job for a moment. Of course, he wouldn't be so prideful as to compare himself to that faithful servant, but Job never had to investigate a murder for King William of England.

And that is what this knock would be, there was no doubt.

No one came knocking at Wat the Weaver's door unless it was for him. And no one wanted him unless there was some murder to be investigated.

Passing trade did not wander up to a tapestry workshop on a whim. No one saw the place and thought, "Oh, yes, I've been meaning to order a tapestry for my castle. I wonder if anyone is in?"

And the people of Derby kept their distance, none of them wanting to be seen at Wat's door, even though his tapestries these days were entirely proper and decent.

As the ability to think straight slowly returned, Hermitage reasoned that this caller would not be a Norman noble or a king's messenger. They would not bother knocking.

The conquerors considered that everything in the country was now theirs to do with as they wished. That included walking through any front doors that took their fancy, if not kicking them down.

Official callers for Hermitage's services did not ask politely.

And if this was unofficial, it might simply be some local with a problem for resolution and not a murder at all.

Several people in the town seemed to have got entirely the wrong idea about Hermitage. Either they didn't know what a King's Investigator was at all, which was entirely reasonable as he was the only one, as far as he knew, or they thought it was some cure-all for anything to do with death.

Apparently, the passing of old man Kernik had been expected for some time, perhaps that was the cause of the knock.

But then, the deaths of everyday life were handled without him. Mistress Goodby and the priest were capable folk. Well, Mistress Goodby was.

More calm spread through him as he thought this might simply be some traveller on the road who was seeking directions.

After all, there was a Norman camp on the field opposite and no one in their right mind would go near that place for anything.

Or it was simply someone from that camp, asking to borrow a cup of oats or something.

He told himself to not to get so alarmed at the slightest disturbance. Not everything was about him.

Cwen reappeared in the room bearing a puzzled expression.

Hermitage raised his eyebrows in enquiry as to who this harmless caller had turned out to be.

'It's for you, Hermitage,' she said.

Well, that just showed that optimism was a complete waste of time.

'Oh, Lord,' Hermitage prayed for release. 'Not so soon?'

Cwen shook her head. 'I don't know what they want, but they're a bit odd.'

'They?'

'Two of them. Official-looking types. All proper and correct, if you know what I mean.'

This did not bode well.

'Are they coming in?' he asked, looking over her shoulder

to see if anyone was close behind.

'No.' That seemed to be part of Cwen's puzzle. 'They say they will wait upon you.'

'Wait upon me?' Hermitage had never had anyone wait upon him in his life. Well, he had, at the monastery in De'Ath's Dingle, but having people wait upon you in that place was not a pleasant experience.

'You mean they're just standing at the door?' Wat asked.

'That's it. And they look like very well-to-do people.'

Now Wat's eyebrows rose. He liked to meet well-to-do people.

'No, they do not want tapestry,' Cwen said. 'They want Hermitage.'

Hermitage wondered if he could stay where he was and leave them to wait, maybe for so long that they went away.

'Did they, erm, mention what it was they wanted at all? Apart from me?' he asked nervously.

'Murder, you mean?' Cwen got straight to the point. 'No. They just bowed a lot and said they sought audience with Brother Hermitage, the King's Investigator, and would wait upon his pleasure.'

'This is a first,' Wat observed. 'Having someone politely ask you if you'd mind investigating their murder for them. It almost sounds as if you could turn them down. Not today, thank you.'

'I don't think they've come about murder,' Cwen said.

'Really?' Hermitage's hopes rose, despite the fact that they knew better.

'We know what murder's like, we've dealt with enough of them,' Cwen explained. 'These two do not have the smell of murder about them.'

'The smell?' Wat asked.

'You know what I mean. They're not nervous and worried, they aren't fearful or scared. They're not in a panic. Neither are they demanding and difficult. It's as if they've come on a matter of everyday business.'

'What everyday business could anyone have with me?' Hermitage asked. 'What are they, anyway, Norman?'

'Saxon,' Cwen replied. 'Which is part of their oddness. How many well-to-do Saxons are there any more?'

'Fighting men?' Wat asked.

Cwen shook her head. 'More like, erm, Hermitage.'

'More like me?'

'Yes, you know, parchment and quills and the like.'

'Scholars?'

'I didn't like to ask.' Cwen sounded quite embarrassed.

'Learned men,' Hermitage clarified. 'I assume they are men?'

'Yes, definitely that.'

'Hermitage,' Wat waved an arm towards the door. 'Why don't you simply go and see what they want? It doesn't sound like they've even got a murder. Or if they have, it's not a very urgent one.'

Hermitage would much rather sit here and discuss the men at the door for a few more hours than go to the door and see the men.

'Could be they're here for your work.'

'My work?'

'You know, the post-Exodus prophets.'

Hermitage was so surprised at this that he forgot all about the visitors at the door.

'We do listen,' Wat explained. 'Some of the time.'

'But you haven't done any work on the post-Exodus prophets, have you?' Cwen asked nicely.

'Well, erm, that is, it needs a lot of research.'

'Which you can tell them all about.'

Hermitage was sure these men had not come about the post-Exodus prophets. If they had, they were going to be disappointed.

'We'll come with you,' Wat got up from his stool. 'If the nasty men have got a murder, we'll make sure they behave.'

Hermitage reluctantly stood and faced the door from the workshop towards the front of the building.

Wat dropped a hand on his shoulder. 'Unless they've come to murder you, of course.'

'Wat!' Cwen said.

'In which case, we'll get in the way,' Wat assured him with a smile.

With shaking steps, Hermitage got to the door at the front of the workshop and saw the two men standing on the threshold.

They were very well presented in neat and expensive-looking robes, the dress of clerics or officials. They were both young men, not much above twenty and were close-shaven and clean. Not locals, then.

They were standing in patient silence and had the look of men who spent a lot of their lives standing in patient silence.

Hermitage looked over their shoulders and saw a simple open cart with a horse standing on the track. These really were well-to-do fellows, and they must be important, or someone in town would have had that horse by now.

When they saw Hermitage, they both bowed solemnly. After this, the one to the left put a hand across his chest and rested it on his heart, as if displaying his honesty and devotion to his task, whatever it was.

'Do I have the honour of addressing Brother Hermitage?'

he asked in a very good voice, with the accent of a sophisticated and intelligent man. Definitely not locals.

'Erm, yes,' Hermitage replied cautiously.

He noticed that the fellow on the right had a leather satchel across his shoulder, and he now passed the strap over his head, obviously preparing to open it and retrieve what was within.

Hermitage had received written instruction from the king before, but that had turned out to be a horrible mistake. He hoped these men knew what they were doing.

'The King's Investigator of high repute,' the first man went on.

'Yes,' Cwen said. 'That's him.'

The fellow seemed undisturbed by the presence of Wat and Cwen.

'Might we attend upon you?' The man asked. The implication being that they would like to come in. 'Our business is best concluded in your private company.'

This was getting more and more confusing. If business was going to be concluded, it couldn't be a murder investigation, could it?

And in his private company? That sounded a bit worrying.

'Away from the street,' the man specified.

'Ah.'

'Yes, come in, come in,' Wat waved them to enter. Hermitage expected to hear the words, "Have you ever thought about a fine tapestry?", but they didn't come.

Entering the workshop, the two visitors continued to show impeccable manners and simply stood waiting to be directed as Cwen shut the door behind them.

'Perhaps the upstairs chamber?' Wat suggested. 'Away from the apprentices.'

The first man nodded a grateful acknowledgement and gestured that Wat could lead the way.

Once in the room, the two men stood like sentinels while the others took stools.

'Won't you sit?' Hermitage offered.

'Oh, no,' the first man replied as if he never sat.

He surveyed his audience and bowed once more. Hermitage thought he did a lot of bowing.

'I am Leudric and this is my companion Thodrum.'

Thodrum now bowed as well.

'If it is acceptable to Brother Hermitage, we can proceed?' Leudric was clearly making sure that Wat and Cwen being here was all right.

'Oh, yes, fine, do go ahead.' Hermitage had no idea what they were going to go ahead with, but he wanted Wat and Cwen with him. Bad news was always better shared. 'Wat and Cwen can hear anything you tell me.'

Leudric tipped his head to acknowledge the permission. He gestured to Thodrum, who reached into his satchel and produced a marvel.

Hermitage gaped and almost gasped. The most pristine, clean and perfectly trimmed roll of parchment sat in the man's hands. It had to be all of a foot long and was tied with an immaculate length of red ribban, the sort of material that would have graced the finest work in any scriptorium.

A large wax seal closed the roll and made the thing one of the most imposing pieces Hermitage had ever seen.

Wat and Cwen looked on like doting parents, happy that their child liked the wooden horse they had got him for Yule.

Hermitage watched unbreathing as Thodrum handed the parchment over to Leudric with yet more bows on either side.

Upon receipt of the work, Leudric turned it in his hands until the seal was the right way up and the ribban was straight, and stepped in front of Hermitage. With, of course, more bowing, he held the wonder out.

'For me?' Hermitage asked, wanting to make sure.

'For Brother Hermitage, the King's Investigator,' Leudric announced.

Hermitage managed to swallow and slowly reached out a hand he now knew was far too dirty for the task. He gently took the scroll between two fingers and lifted it away.

Putting his knees together, he rested the document in his lap and looked down upon it with kindness.

'Aren't you going to open it?' Cwen asked.

'Open it?' Hermitage didn't quite understand.

'Yes, open it. It looks like a scroll.'

'It is a scroll,' Hermitage confirmed. 'One of the finest. If not the finest.'

'It probably says something fine, then,' Cwen prompted.

Hermitage looked down and couldn't imagine ruining this masterpiece by actually opening it and reading the words. The ribban would get crushed. The wax would shatter. Far better to keep it as it was, surely?

He gritted his teeth and wondered if he could peek inside the tube and see some of the words without disturbing anything else.

'Shall I open it for you?' Cwen offered.

'No!' Hermitage almost shouted. He recovered himself.

Leudric and Thodrum did not seem at all put out, as if this sort of thing happened all the time.

'Do you, erm, know what it says?' Hermitage asked.

'I have been graced with the contents,' Leudric said. 'Necessary, you understand,' he apologised. 'In case there was any mishap on the journey and the work itself was lost or damaged.'

Hermitage felt a bit faint at that thought.

'Could you, erm, tell me what it says?'

That did cause Leudric's eyebrows to rise.

'It's just that I am a scribe myself and this work is a treasure. It has clearly come from the very finest hand and it seems a shame to disturb it.'

Leudric nodded that he understood. 'It is from the hand of the master scribe of Lord de Sauveloy.'

All of the joy in Hermitage's heart sank rapidly and escaped through his knees, which had started shaking.

'Lord de Sauveloy,' he croaked.

'Just so.'

'Oh, dear,' Wat spoke for them all.

Nothing from King William's scheming and manipulative confidante was going to be good news. Hermitage felt that most of the murders he had ever had to deal with had something to do with that man. It wasn't true, it just felt like it.

'I can assure you there is nothing of concern,' Leudric assured them, seeming to be puzzled by their response.

'Open it, Hermitage,' Cwen said with resignation. 'If it's from de Sauveloy, you're not going to want it festering on a shelf somewhere.'

Hermitage accepted that, and this masterpiece of the scribe's art had suddenly lost its allure.

It did seem an awful lot of trouble to go to to instruct him about a murder investigation, but the fine scroll was now sullied.

He immediately worried that de Sauveloy obviously knew they were back from Gernesey, an island he had forbidden them from leaving. Was this his instruction for their punishment? It seemed harsh that retribution should be delivered in so fine a package.

Feeling far less favourable towards the parchment, Hermitage took it in his hands and removed the ribban. He did carefully slide it off the end of the roll and laid it neatly on his knee as it might come in handy.

Taking a breath, he broke the seal, making sure the scroll was undamaged.

Opening the thing up with a heavy heart, he read the first words.

Then he frowned and read them again.

'Well?' Cwen prompted. 'What does it say?'

'Execution?' Wat enquired lightly.

'No,' Hermitage was still distracted. 'It says, fideli et honorabili fratri nostro Hermitagius...,'

'The English would be more helpful,' Cwen suggested.

'Oh, yes, erm, to our loyal and valued servant Brother Hermitage.'

'It says that?' Wat asked.

Hermitage checked again. 'Yes, that's it. And then it says, greetings.'

'Greetings?'

'Yes.'

'From Ranulph de Sauveloy? There aren't two Ranulph de Sauveloys, are there?'

'Not as far as I'm aware.'

'There is only one,' Leudric said with some pride.

'Why's he calling you a loyal and valued servant? What's he up to?'

'It must say more than that, Hermitage,' Cwen prompted.

Hermitage read on, scanning the excellent script quickly

before going over it more carefully.

'Oh, my,' he said when the full text had sunk in.

'What? What?' Cwen pestered.

Hermitage spoke to Leudric. 'This can't be right.'

'Perfectly correct, Brother,' Leudric said with another of his bows.

'But, but..,'

'Hermitage,' Cwen snapped at him.

'Well,' Hermitage still didn't believe this. 'It says that in recognition of my long and loyal service to His Majesty the King, Duke of Normandy, I am appointed to a seat on the Standing Conclave.'

'The what?'

'The Standing Conclave,' Hermitage almost whispered. 'Me. On the Standing Conclave. It must be a mistake.'

'Do we get to ask what the Standing Conclave is?' Wat said. 'And why, if it's standing, you get a seat?'

Hermitage swallowed and turned his eyes back to the parchment.

Seeing Hermitage's discomfort, Leudric explained. 'The Standing Conclave is a council that advises the king. Just as, in earlier years, the Witenagemot was council to the king, comprising the nobles and bishops, so King William is creating the curia regis, or royal council, which will advise him on a variety of matters.

'One of the sub-groups of the Witenagemot was the Standing Conclave, and the king has decided to maintain its function.'

'Which is?' Wat asked.

'Under the Witenagemot it advised the king on mainly ecclesiastical matters, but its exact remit going forward has yet to be confirmed.'

'And it's nobles and bishops and the like?' Cwen checked.

'Just so.'

'And now Brother Hermitage.'

'Indeed.'

'And this is from Ranulph de Sauveloy.'

'It is.'

'You're right,' Cwen said to Wat. 'He's up to something.'

Caput II: Here's A Plan

'This is a singular honour.' Leudric was puzzled by their response,

'It is,' Hermitage agreed, still in awe. 'The Standing Conclave.'

'And Ranulph de Sauveloy,' Cwen reminded him. 'If that man gave you a gold coin it would probably have poison on it.'

'Oh, come, come.' Leudric clearly thought this was now some sort of jest. 'You do Lord de Sauveloy a great disservice.'

'We can familiarise you with the disservices he's done us in the past if you like,' Wat said.

Leudric seemed to dismiss their nonsense. 'Whoever may have issued the parchment, this is the king's appointment. And believe me, the Standing Conclave is made up of the most honourable and upright individuals.'

Wat frowned at this. 'I thought you said it was nobles and bishops.'

'Just so.' Leudric clearly thought this was sufficient to trust their honour and uprightness, while Wat thought the opposite.

'What does it involve, then?' Cwen asked.

'Involve?'

'Yes. What does standing in this conclave actually mean? What does Hermitage have to do?'

'Well, he will attend meetings of the Conclave. There will be discussion of matters of import to the king, and he will contribute from his wide experience and expertise.'

Now Wat and Cwen frowned.

'You do know he investigates, murder,' Cwen said.

'Going to be discussing a lot of murder, are they, this conclave?' Wat enquired.

'I do investigate murder,' Hermitage had to speak up. 'But that is simply what I have to do. I am sure I can contribute in wider areas.'

'Of course,' Wat clicked snapped his fingers. 'The post-Exodus prophets?'

Hermitage scowled at him. 'We have visited many places in the course of the investigations. Met many people, and seen many things. Any of these could be of value. My knowledge of texts, scriptorium practice, monastic rule, these could all be useful.'

'Mainly ecclesiastical matters,' Cwen seemed to agree.

'As I said,' Leudric reminded them amicably. 'The exact remit has yet to be determined. It has clearly been concluded that Brother Hermitage would add to the wisdom of the Conclave and so he has been appointed.'

Hermitage was disappointed that the others weren't seeing this as the great honour it was. He had only been thinking about the punishment of having to investigate murders all the time, and here was the reward.

Yes, Ranulph de Sauveloy being involved was a worry, but there would be other people on the Conclave.

'Is Lord de Sauveloy a member of the Conclave himself?' he asked Leudric.

'Oh, no. This is an independent body to advise the king. Lord de Sauveloy merely provides the administration.'

'Hm.' Cwen was still not convinced. 'So, what happens now?'

Leudric appeared to relax as this unwarranted and unexpected challenge to the appointment appeared to recede. 'I confirm Brother Hermitage's acceptance of the position...,'

'What if he doesn't accept?' Cwen interrupted.

'Doesn't accept?'

'Yes. What if he says no thank you?'

Hermitage didn't mind Cwen asking questions, but she wasn't going to refuse this on his behalf. He suspected that Leudric wouldn't accept that, anyway.

'No one has ever refused the Standing Conclave.' Leudric seemed confused by the very idea. 'There are many who have great ambition to be a member. They strive for it, seek it, yet have no success. For it to be offered and refused is unthinkable.'

'It won't be refused,' Hermitage spoke up before Cwen could do the unthinkable.

'You have to think this through, Hermitage,' she cautioned.

'I have, and it is a great honour. Old Abbot Abbo used to speak very highly of the Standing Conclave. It did some marvellous work on the Wessex Gospels.'

'Before Ranulph de Sauveloy.'

'Even so. I cannot refuse this. What would Abbo say?'

Leudric looked to each face in the room to see if there was any more nonsense to be spoken. It seemed there was not.

'Assuming he does accept,' Cwen said, quite oblivious to the fact that he had accepted. 'What next?'

'Well, I make record of the acceptance.' Leudric nodded to Thodrum, who reached into his satchel once more and brought out a small portable inkwell and a leather roll, doubtless containing quills. There was also another small box, which he laid on a stool and opened. It contained a pot of wax and lamp and a selection of seals. This satchel alone was a marvel to Hermitage.

'Brother Hermitage and I will apply our seals to the

parchment, and the appointment is confirmed.'

'Ah,' Hermitage said apologetically. 'I don't actually have a seal.'

'Really?' Leudric seemed surprised by that.

'Not much call for them in murder investigations,' Cwen commented.

'I suppose not,' Leudric accepted. 'Well, we can sort one out for you. Members of the Conclave need their own seal.'

His own seal. This was getting better and better.

'A simple *accipio* under his name should be sufficient for now.'

Hermitage nodded, but Wat and Cwen looked blank.

'I accept,' Leudric translated for their benefit.

'Perhaps we had best find a better surface for writing,' Hermitage suggested. 'I have a small board in my chamber that I use.'

Leudric tipped his head in agreement.

'And when is the meeting?' Cwen asked before they could move. 'This conclave that meets and advises the king. Where does Hermitage have to go, London?'

'Not at all. The next gathering is in Nottingham, in around a week's time.'

'Well, isn't that convenient,' Cwen observed.

'I certainly hope so.' Leudric missed her accusation. 'The members come from many places, north and south, and Nottingham is a convenient spot.'

He seemed to lean closer to them, obviously to impart some confidence. 'There is even word that the king himself may visit the Conclave. To give it his blessing, you understand.'

'Oh, we understand all about William's blessing.' Cwen mused.

Leudric frowned at her. 'We are on our way there now, to prepare, you understand, and the journey most usefully passed Brother Hermitage's door.

'He is probably the closest of all the attendees. It will take no time at all on horseback, or even by cart.'

'Erm, I don't have a horse or a cart, either,' Hermitage said.

'Do you not?' If Leudric had accepted that you could investigate a murder without your own seal, he was having trouble understanding how it worked without a horse. 'How do you get around, then?'

'I walk.'

'You walk? Ah, such, erm, humility. Well, you shall have to get yourself a horse and cart. There may be travelling to do in the course of your duties.'

'Get himself a horse and cart?' Wat asked. 'And how, exactly, is he supposed to do that?'

Leudric didn't seem to understand the question. 'He goes to the horse trader or cartwright. I assume Derby has such people.'

'We have a cartright,' Wat confirmed. 'We're not that backwards. Not so many horses around, though. What with the Normans being the main users. But anyone who has a horse or a cart is going to want money for them.'

'Naturally,' Leudric agreed. 'But the honorarium should take care of that.'

'Oh, yes,' Wat said. 'And when do we meet the honorarium?'

'It's a payment, Wat,' Hermitage explained.

The word had its usual effect on Wat the Weaver and it was as if his normal suspicious and careful self had been thrown from his body. 'Payment?' The interest in his voice was almost sentient and came with its own greed.

'For the role on the Standing Conclave. There will be an honorarium. A payment for the office.'

'Well, why didn't you say so,' Wat was now full of enthusiasm for the position and clearly thought Hermitage couldn't take it up fast enough.

'And it's enough for a horse and cart, is it, this honorarium?'

'Oh, more than sufficient,' Leudric assured them.

'Ranulph de Sauveloy,' Cwen reminded them. 'And King William.'

'The honorarium,' Wat countered.

Leudric nodded once more, and this time, Thodrum's miraculous satchel produced a purse high in both quality and weight.

'I shouldn't really pass this over until the document is sealed,' Leudric said. 'But I think that is only a formality.'

He bowed yet again and handed the purse over to Hermitage, who took it reluctantly. It seemed a horribly tradesmanlike action in the greater process, sullying the Standing Conclave with money.

'Now, don't go giving that to the poor, Hermitage,' Wat warned. 'You've got a horse and cart to buy.'

'I really don't need a horse and cart to get to Nottingham.' Hermitage said.

'There will be other meetings in other places,' Leudric pointed out.

'And we don't have the facilities to look after a horse. I can simply pay for one as and when I need it. If I need it.'

Hermitage could see that owning a horse and cart would be a matter of considerable prestige, and would doubtless raise the reputation of Wat and the workshop significantly.

And, if Wat didn't have to pay for it himself, so much the

better.

'Let us go and attend to the parchment,' Hermitage invited Leudric to descend the stairs once more.

With Wat's face encouraging and Cwen's discouraging, Hermitage took the middle path and made his own mind up. It was an interesting sensation.

Down in his chamber, it was the matter of a moment for Leudric to put his seal on the parchment and for Hermitage to add his name and *accipio*, which he did with a rather shameful and indulgent flourish on the descending loop.

Leudric assured him that the parchment had been pounced, and he expected no less, really. The application of gomme sandarach, powdered tree resin, made his letters form wonderfully on the page, and they were soon dry.

'Thank you, Brother,' Leudric said as he and Thodrum stood by the door once more. 'We shall see you in Nottingham a week from today. You'll have a day to settle in, and then we can welcome you formally to the Conclave.

'Shall we bid farewell to Master Wat and Mistress Cwen?'

'Oh, no need,' Hermitage said. 'I can do that for you.' He didn't want Cwen raising any more questions about this role, nor Wat asking if there was another purse in the satchel.

With yet more bows, the two men left to get back on their cart, and Hermitage watched them plod off in the direction of Nottingham.

He turned and looked at the stairs, wondering whether to simply go to his chamber and consider his new-found position. Even though Leudric had taken the parchment with him, he could still picture it.

If he did that, he knew it would only be moments before Wat and Cwen found him, telling him what a good and bad idea this was at the same time.

Somewhat reluctantly, he trod the stairs once more, preparing himself as he went.

'I know what you're going to say,' he got in before they could begin.

'Cwen, you will remind me that Ranulph de Sauveloy is not to be trusted. He has led us astray before, and this could all be some horrible plot only enacted to advance his own deceitful designs. And if the king is to be there as well, I will only get embroiled in some hideous murder, which I could avoid by not going.

'Wat, you are going to say that there is good payment in this position and I should throw myself into it heart and soul.

'But, this is the Standing Conclave. It is real. I know that it is real. It has met for many years and is a body of good standing. Or was,' he got in before Cwen could interrupt.

'I shall simply go along and see what happens. If it is clear that this is some game of the Normans, I do not need to participate further.

'If its business is legitimate and worthy, I can remain.

'And don't forget, there will be other members present. It is not as if de Sauveloy is sending us off alone into some business of his own.

'The rest of the Conclave will be there and have their own views and opinions.'

'If they're not all Norman friends of de Sauveloy,' Cwen managed to get in.

'If they are, then I withdraw.'

'If they'll let you.'

'Who was on the Conclave before?' Wat asked. 'You know, when Abbot Abbo thought so well of it?'

'Ah, well,' Hermitage reminisced contentedly. 'There were several Archdeacons, the Bishops of Lindsey and Crediton, as well as some others, I believe. Two abbots from major monasteries, and representatives of the nobility, of course. Sixty years ago, even the Blessed Dunstan was a member.'

'Quite a big conclave, then.'

'It was. I imagine not everyone attended every gathering, so it was important to have numbers.'

'But important people.'

'Oh, yes,' Hermitage agreed. 'Which is why my membership is such an honour.'

'Hermitage,' Cwen said seriously. 'I know this is an honour, and it's exciting and it's a dream come true.'

Hermitage wasn't sure that was strictly true. He didn't recall ever dreaming of the Standing Conclave.

'And it could well be a real thing, meeting to consider serious matters and advise the king.

'But this is Ranulph de Sauveloy, who hates us. I don't want to put you down, but if the Conclave is full of important people, why on earth would he appoint you?

'We've been nothing but a thorn in his side. He even forbade us to leave Gernesey, but we did. And what's the first thing he does? Report us to the king? Have us taken to that Tower in London? Quietly removed from our beds in the night? No, he gives you an honour. Does that sound likely?'

'It may not be him,' Hermitage said. 'Leudric said that this was the king's appointment. He knows I've investigated murder, sometimes directly for him. It's possible that he instructed de Sauveloy.'

Cwen gave a grim smile. 'I don't think Ranulph de Sauveloy does anything he doesn't want to.'

Wat was nodding thoughtfully. 'So, if he has done this on purpose, it could be his way of keeping Hermitage under control,' he said. 'Get him on the Conclave, keep him busy and stop him interfering in any murders that de Sauveloy might want to get on with.

'He may have threatened us with all sorts, but perhaps he can't really make the King's Investigator disappear without risking the king's wrath.'

Cwen gave this a half-hearted smile. 'The same king who can never remember Hermitage's name? Still, get rid of the King's Investigator by giving him something else to do isn't as bad as killing him.'

Hermitage wasn't at all comfortable being the subject of this conversation.

'Exactly,' Wat went on. 'It's like when you have a rotten apprentice who ruins every tapestry he works on. You put him in charge of treadle maintenance. Anything to keep him away from the wool.'

'In which case, de Sauveloy might be in the middle of some scheme right now,' Cwen said.

'Right, Hermitage.' She clapped her hands as if some great decision had been made. 'You're off to the Conclave.'

He was glad that she had come round, but he was going anyway. Perhaps it was best to let her think it was her decision.

'And we're coming with you.'

'Oh, really?' Hermitage was rather hoping that this might be something he could do on his own. It was selfish of him, he knew, and he should be grateful for everything they had done for him, including letting him live in the workshop for free, but the Conclave was his. It had said so on the parchment.

'I'm not sure they'll let you in the Conclave,' he said carefully.

'Oh, we don't want to go to that. We need to find out

what's going on. De Sauveloy could be setting up something that will not go well for you.

'And it sounds like there will be lots of important people there,' Wat added with a glint in his eye.

'Who are not going to be sold tapestries,' Cwen said firmly.

'It's not my fault if they want to buy one, is it? We could do one of the Conclave itself, you know, sell copies to everyone who was there.'

'Erm,' Hermitage started.

'Yes?' Cwen asked.

'Are you sure that you ought to go?'

'Ought to go?' Cwen looked completely confused. 'What do you mean, ought to go?'

'Well.' He hesitated and glanced at Cwen's stomach, with what he hoped was an explanatory nod.

'What?' she asked, looking at herself as if there was something on her clothes.

'He means you are with child and shouldn't be going on carts at all, let alone into strange conclaves with suspicious motives,' Wat explained.

'Oh, don't be ridiculous,' Cwen dismissed the problem. 'It's only been a few weeks, and I'm not going to sit around here while you go. All that worry wouldn't do me any good at all.'

Hermitage hoped that he did not look convinced.

'And it is a conclave,' Cwen said. 'Lots of people sitting down in a room, talking. It's not as if we're going into battle.' She looked at them both in a very determined manner. 'We are all going to the Conclave, yes?' The question demanded only one answer.

'Yes, Cwen,' Hermitage gave the right one. 'But I wonder...,'

'Wonder what?'

'Might it be best to go incognito?'

'I thought we were going in a cart?' Wat sounded disappointed.

'No, I mean it might be best if people did not know you were there. You might discover more that way. If they knew that you were Wat the Weaver, and that Cwen was enquiring about what was going on, we might not discover anything. You could stay away from the actual conclave, but talk to people on the margins.

'And Ranulph de Sauveloy might even be there himself, despite what Leudric says. He'd be unlikely to give anything away if he saw the three of us.'

'Hm.' Cwen was giving this some thought. 'You could be right. You'll be in this conclave thing, which I assume happens in a room somewhere.'

'I would imagine so.'

'So, if we were in disguise..,' She seemed to think this was a much better idea.

Hermitage was thinking it was an awful lot worse.

Caput III: To Horse (And Cart)

Wat delegated himself to cart collection duties and set off into town first thing the next morning.

He asked for some coins from Hermitage's purse, and not knowing how much most things cost, Hermitage handed the whole thing over.

The weight of it in Wat's hands seemed to stop him moving. Hermitage was worried he had stopped breathing as well.

Cwen took the purse, opened it, selected a few coins and gave them to Wat. She handed the purse back to Hermitage.

Wat looked at what he had in his hands. 'What am I supposed to get with this, a dog and a basket?'

'You pay half for a serviceable animal and cart, the other half being payable when we get back. You don't get a stallion warhorse and a bishop's covered wagon.'

'Don't know where you'd get them in Derby anyway,' Wat grumbled as he left.

Cwen beckoned Hermitage to follow her back into the workshop proper. 'Now, Hermitage, I've been giving this some thought.'

He had worried that she probably would.

She sat on a stool and gestured him to sit opposite.

'It seems to me that you are now an important member of this Standing Conclave thing, so you are likely to have servants. Everyone else will have, and you don't want to stand out.'

'Don't I?' He had thought that he would be himself, a humble monk amongst the great and the good, only there to contribute what he could and ask for nothing in return. Even the honorarium was a bit of an embarrassment.

The other members would surely think likewise. They would attend to give their service to the king, not for their own advancement, or advantage.

'So, Wat and I can be your servants.'

'Oh, really?'

'No, not really,' Cwen said, seeing that he might have got the wrong end of the stick. 'Everyone will think we are your servants because we'll look like them.'

'I don't have any servants.'

'Pay attention.' Cwen looked him hard in the eyes. 'We will look like your servants would look if you had any.'

'Oh, yes, Cwen.'

'Wat can look after the horse and drive the cart, move the bags and carry things, and I'll attend to your food and clothing.'

'I've only got one habit.'

'Yes.' Cwen said this very slowly, making it clear that his only habit was a problem.

He knew that he should have another one. The Rule of Benedict made it clear that another garment was required for cleanliness. He'd just never got around to it. And it seemed such a luxury, somehow.

His current habit was the one Wat had bought him back in Lincoln, and it was of very high quality. Well, it had been of very high quality when he bought it, but that was quite a while and several murders ago. He glanced at himself and had to conclude that the garment was not looking its best.

'I'll get some cloth and make a new one.' She tutted to herself. 'I should have told Wat to pick some up from Frith, the cloth man. I imagine you have to make your own and don't buy them from a habit merchant?'

'Erm, no. No habit merchants.' Hermitage smiled at the

very idea.

'Right.' She looked him up and down, clearly measuring with her eye for the new habit.

A thought occurred to him. 'What bags do we have?'

'What?'

'What bags do we have? You said Wat would carry the bags, I just wondered what bags? If I've only got a spare habit.'

'There's all of our things. We'll need clothes. Might have to take our own chairs and tables, even.'

'Chairs and tables? I think the Conclave will provide them.'

'Really? Oh, all right, not them. But food.'

'And as we are important people, as you say, I am sure they will feed us.'

'All right,' Cwen said with some impatience. 'Just our things, then.'

Hermitage's thought was that Wat and Cwen were coming simply so that they could carry the things they'd brought with them. If they weren't there, there wouldn't be anything to carry.

'You can't go without servants,' Cwen clearly saw what he was thinking. 'You're an important person. You need servants to fetch you wine, send messages, prepare your bed, that sort of thing.'

He nodded silently.

'Bring some books,' she suggested.

'Which ones?'

'I don't know, do I? I don't know what books you've got.' She shook her head and mumbled to herself. 'Or why, come to that.

'You must need books for a conclave.'

'I suppose it's possible. But as we don't know what the

Conclave will be discussing, how will we know which ones to take?'

'Just pick some, Hermitage,' she instructed very clearly. 'Big ones.'

'Big ones?'

'Big books. They've got to be better, haven't they? Give Wat something to carry as well.'

'Big books are better,' Hermitage recited. 'Yes, Cwen.'

She had a thoughtful look on her face, which was another worry.

'Of course, we'll mix with the other servants while you're off with the important people. Which means we'll probably get to hear more. You know how servants gossip.'

Hermitage didn't know how servants gossiped as he'd never been one or had any. He knew it was said that servants gossiped, but he didn't have any evidence either way, so couldn't draw a reliable conclusion.

He thought this was just the sort of thinking that the Conclave would value, and the sort that would drive Cwen to distraction. He simply shrugged.

'Some of them might know what's going on,' she continued to speculate wildly. 'Some of de Sauveloy's servants may be there. That would be useful.'

Hermitage shivered at that. 'You had better keep away from de Sauveloy if you really want to be thought of as servants. He knows you and will see through a simple change of clothing.'

'Oh, I don't know. The rich never actually notice their servants, do they?'

'Does Wat know he's going to be disguised as a servant?'

'He will when he gets back.' Cwen was confident.

Hermitage took a breath. 'Why don't you simply come

with me as you are? You could be accompanying me on the road, which might be dangerous, after all. And you could have business in Nottingham.'

Cwen shook her head with a grimace. 'That wouldn't get us into the servants' halls, would it? We'd have to leave you to it and loiter in Nottingham.'

Hermitage thought that sounded quite good.

'How long is this conclave, anyway?'

'That's a good question. I don't know, Leudric didn't say. It may be a simple administrative meeting, without a substantive item for deliberation.'

Cwen looked at him and considered this. 'You mean you're all gathering in Nottingham not to discuss anything?'

'Oh, I'm sure there will be things for discussion, it's just that they could be quick. It might even need to meet simply to ratify me as a member.'

Cwen's look was now accompanied by an open mouth. 'You've joined the Conclave which now has to meet to confirm that you've joined the Conclave?'

'That's it.' Hermitage thought it was the proper way to go about things. 'Or, if there is something really important, a ticklish interpretive question, for example, it could take days, weeks, even.'

'Weeks?' Cwen sounded shocked and disheartened at the same time.

Hermitage was quite excited by the prospect.

'We can't stay there for weeks.'

'I suppose I could dismiss you.'

'Eh?'

'Send you about my business. If the Conclave is looking after everything, I won't need my servants.'

'If you're discussing some ticklish interpretive question for weeks, you won't need to dismiss us, we'll be long gone.

'All we need to do is find out what de Sauveloy is up to.'

'Won't it look a bit odd, though.' Hermitage thought about it. 'If my servants suddenly disappear because the Conclave is going on a bit? What else do you have to do, apart from serve me?'

'I don't know.' Cwen was clearly annoyed by the level of reason going into this. 'We've got to attend your estates, or something.'

'I don't think I would have estates, what with being a monk.'

Cwen frowned deeply. 'You're making this very difficult, Hermitage.'

He didn't think it was him making it difficult.

'And there's Leudric.' He suddenly remembered this. 'And Thodrum.'

'What about them?'

'They'll be there. Leudric said he would see me. And he knows who you are.'

Cwen tightened her lips as if convinced that everyone was conspiring against her. She took a deep breath.

'Right,' she said, having reached her conclusion. 'We'll come with you because the road is dangerous and you don't know how to drive a cart. And we can have some business in Nottingham. We'll just have to work out how to talk to the servants.'

'Good idea,' he said, congratulating her on repeating what he had said only a moment ago. 'I'm sure Wat would be happy with that. After all, servants of monks probably don't try to sell tapestries to conclave members.'

'Hm.' Cwen was clearly going to have some words about that as well.

'And,' Hermitage said, having thought of yet another problem, which it now seemed safe to raise.

'What now?'

'The Conclave is in Nottingham. It's likely to be at Lord Gilbert's castle. It's the only safe place, I imagine. And Gilbert knows us well from past, erm..,'

'Murders?'

'Well, yes. He would probably greet us fondly, which would be a bit odd, if you were my servants.'

'All right. We will not be your servants. But we still need to find out what de Sauveloy is up to. Whatever it is, it will not be good. And it will not be good for us.'

Hermitage grimaced.

'I've been thinking about this as well,' she went on.

'Oh, erm, good.'

'He told us not to leave Gernesey and we did.

'He can't move against us directly, because we know what he was up to down there, and that William wouldn't be happy about his scheming. (***No Murder Here*** will reveal all - or some.)

'So, he appoints you to the Conclave. He probably expects us to accompany you as we're usually together, and then he can deal with us all.'

'In the middle of the Conclave?'

'Not in the middle of the meeting, but it gets us away from the workshop and Derby.'

'Oh, dear.'

'Oh, dear indeed.'

Hermitage couldn't quite see this as a sensible course of action, not even for Ranulph de Sauveloy. 'The Standing Conclave is a serious institution, regardless of what de Sauveloy may be using it for.

'He has appointed me with a proper scroll and everything, and I will meet the other members. It could be a dangerous step to have anyone from the Conclave dealt with, as you put it.

'Surely it would be better to lure us away with some falsehood or other. A fake murder, for example.'

Cwen shook her head. 'He's not doing this for any reason but his own. And his reasons as far as we are concerned, are not good ones.'

They could not debate the matter further, as one of the apprentices called for Cwen's assistance.

Obviously, he didn't actually call for Cwen's assistance, rather he uttered an oath and kicked his loom.

'What have you done?' Cwen called as she stood.

The apprentice turned and the look on his face said that he knew immediately what he had done; not realised that Cwen was in the room, that's what he'd done.

Other heads around the room quickly bent to their work and Cwen went to deal with the problem.

Hermitage took the chance to return to his chamber and start thinking about which big books he had better take with him.

Scripture would obviously be essential. All the decisions of the Conclave would be based on that. But how was he to know which bit? He imagined reference material would be available if it was called for. He would take his Timothy. Letters from Paul provided so much guidance for all manner of situations.

Perhaps the snippet of Bede that he possessed might be useful as well. After all, knowledge of the past was the best means of avoiding its failures in the future.

Then he thought that this was now a Norman conclave,

and they would have their own ideas. He somewhat dreaded to think what they might be, but he would find out soon enough.

He busied himself for an enjoyable hour or so, reading most of the texts he picked, before putting them down again and deciding they wouldn't be much use.

He had found a scrap of text in old Greek which seemed to be all about triangles. He couldn't imagine what use that would be to anyone.

Before he had even made a single selection, Wat was back with the horse and cart.

The whole workshop turned out to see this marvel, and Wat stood proudly at the reins. 'What do you think of this, then?'

To Hermitage's eye, the beast appeared healthy and strong, and not a bit like the town headman's horse, which always looked as if it should be resting in the cart, not pulling it.

The cart itself was a solid piece of work as well. Four good wheels held up a simple deck of boards with a seat at the front.

Hartle, the old weaving master, was the first to examine it closely.

'Aye, not bad. Not bad at all.'

Hermitage had to admit that he was no judge of either horses or carts, so would have to rely upon the opinion of others.

Cwen came out and took Wat's arm.

'Well, well,' she said proudly. 'A horse and cart at the workshop, who'd have thought?'

Wat nodded. 'A shame it really belongs to Hermitage, and even he doesn't actually own it. Still, it's quite a thing.'

Hermitage thought that he shouldn't own a horse and cart

anyway. It didn't sit well with a vow of poverty. He wandered up to the vicinity of the horse, but didn't get too close, as he knew the animals didn't like him.

He didn't know what he had ever done to a horse, but the entire population seemed to hold a grudge against him. Throwing him from their backs, biting him, trampling him, they'd do anything to get their own back.

'Where did you get it?' Cwen asked.

'The tanner's.'

The tanner's?' Cwen didn't sound pleased about that. She leant forward and gave the horse a sniff, as if it would bear the unmistakable odour of that trade.

'It's all right. It's not the tanner's horse and cart, he just had it.'

'And how did he just have a horse and cart that wasn't his?'

'Some fellow from out of town had ordered a load of skins,' Wat explained. 'But when it came time to collect, the man didn't have the money. So, the tanner took his horse and cart in payment.'

Cwen frowned. 'The horse and cart the man had probably intended to use to take his skins away?'

'Could be.' Wat didn't seem concerned about the practicalities. 'When he's sold the skins, he comes back with the money and the tanner gives him his horse and cart back.'

'The horse and cart that we now have, and which will be in Nottingham.'

'True, but we won't have it for long. It's only got to get us there and back.'

'Hermitage says he could be there for weeks.'

'Weeks?' Wat was shocked at that idea. 'I haven't got the cart for weeks. I only agreed one week. If I keep it longer, I have to pay again.'

'If we're not done, you'll just have to bring it back and leave us there,' Cwen said.

Wat obviously didn't think much of that.

'And how much did it cost?'

'Oh it was only a few pence. And a few more when we bring it back.'

'I should think so as it isn't even the tanner's cart in the first place.'

'He did say there's a chance the fellow won't come back at all, in which case we can keep it.'

'Really?'

'Apparently, the skins he took could be worth more than the horse and cart anyway, and it might be cheaper for the fellow to simply buy another one.'

Cwen nodded. 'And so we get the horse and cart for a few pence?'

'Oh, no,' Wat shook his head that that would be a very strange trade. 'No, I've given the tanner the few pence and we have the cart for a week, but it still belongs to him. If we want to keep it longer we have to pay for each week, and then, if we want it for good, we give him another payment, as long as we haven't worn it out or broken the cart.'

'And if we have?'

'The payment is bigger.'

'How much bigger?' Cwen asked suspiciously.

'Four pounds.'

'Four pounds!'

'It's not bad for a good horse and cart.'

'But it's not for a good horse and cart, it's for one we've worn out and broken.'

'We won't break it,' Wat was confident. 'And if it's in good condition, it's only three pounds.'

Cwen was shaking her head slowly and frowning as she tried to understand.

'The tanner had a horse and cart that is promised to someone else, should he ever come back. We have given him money to borrow it, and have to give him more if we borrow it for longer. Then, when we bring it back, we have to pay him again and, should we decide to keep it, we have to give him the whole price. Even more if it's broken.'

'Good, isn't it,' Wat said. 'I was wondering it if would work for tapestry. You know, if people can't afford to buy one, they could have it by the week. If they keep it long enough, they'll end up paying more than they would have done in the first place.'

Cwen sighed heavily. 'And I thought Ranulf de Sauveloy was a schemer.'

'Oh, I've been having a think about him,' Wat said. 'As I was riding through town on my horse and cart.' He preened and stood proud by the animal.

'On Hermitage's horse and cart,' Cwen corrected. 'Which doesn't even belong to him, but to the tanner, or his customer, whichever comes first. And which you can now drive back into town.'

'What?' Wat sounded positively heartbroken at that. 'Give it back?'

'No, not give it back. I need to get some cloth for a new habit for Hermitage. You can drive me in the cart.'

'Oh, right.' Wat nodded as he could see that really, Cwen was as proud of the cart as he was.

'And make sure we drive past the tavern,' Cwen instructed as she climbed up. 'And wait outside until Mistress Angel sees us.'

'Good plan,' Wat smiled. 'You know, I think this conclave

thing really could be a reward.'

'Oh, yes, and how did you work that out?'

'De Sauveloy is actually pleased with us. He told us not to leave Gernesey but is impressed that we did. He sees that we've got courage and our own minds. That's just the sort of thing he needs on the Conclave.'

'Hm,' Cwen said. 'And I've been thinking about it as well, and I think he's setting us up for something really nasty.'

'Oh.' Wat was disappointed. He soon cheered as he snapped the reins and the horse plodded around the road to head back into town. 'Well, it'll probably be one or the other, won't it. Let's assume it'll be the good one.'

Caput IV: A Great Event

Departure for Nottingham the following day, which wasn't that far away, after all, seemed to have developed into some sort of festival. The apprentices were there, obviously, but a good gathering of townsfolk had turned up, perhaps expecting to see some great event or other.

When Hermitage politely enquired what Durselm the carpenter had come for, he confirmed that it was to see the great event.

There was obviously an interest in the cart as well, as the carpenter was wandering around it, checking the joints and tutting every now and again.

Suggesting that a horse and cart driving off might not be as great an event as he hoped for seemed harsh.

'Great event?' Hermitage asked.

'Your departure,' Durselm said brightly.

'My departure?' Hermitage didn't like to think that his leaving town was seen as cause for celebration.

He knew several of the townspeople worried about having the King's Investigator of murder close at hand, but no one had ever asked him to leave. Unlike Wat. A lot of people had asked him to leave at various times.

'Yes.' Durselm beamed. 'Of to the king's great conker.'

'His conker?'

'The one where all the nobles and bishops have one big conker. All they all have their own conkers.' He frowned. 'Something like that.'

'Conclave,' Hermitage explained. 'The Standing Conclave.'

'That's the one. Standing with the king and all them important people with their conkers.'

Hermitage wasn't going to bother trying to correct this. 'I

have met the king before,' he said modestly, although it didn't sound modest when he heard it.

'Yes, but that was about all them murders.' Durselm screwed his face up as if he had just trodden in something. 'This is the business of the land. And Derby in the middle of it. Who'd have thought someone from Derby would mix in such company? A horse and cart, as well.'

Word had obviously got out that Hermitage had been given a great and important position. Much more great, important and interesting than the one he already had.

How this had happened, Hermitage was not at all clear, as he certainly hadn't mentioned it to anyone outside the workshop.

He quickly concluded that Wat's journey back from town with the horse and cart, and Cwen's subsequent return, must have involved a considerable commentary on the fact that the workshop now had a horse and cart, and that Hermitage had been appointed to the Conclave.

'Is there going to be a procession?' Durselm asked.

'Only of the horse followed by the cart,' Hermitage explained.

'Oh. No king's guard or banners or anything?'

'I'm afraid not.'

The carpenter overcame his disappointment. 'Still, we can wave you off.'

'Yes, I suppose you can.'

Durselm seemed so happy at this exciting event, that Hermitage didn't want to belittle it.

He thought that something like a wedding resulted in a couple of people simply walking down the road, but still everyone cheered. The reason for the journey was the cause for celebration, not the physical act.

But the reason for his journey was tinged with the worry that Ranulph de Sauveloy would be at the end of it, his insidious scheme circling them like crows. Probably crows with their own horses and carts.

Durselm wouldn't know anything about de Sauveloy, and he shouldn't be told.

The carpenter now left Hermitage and got down on his hands and knees to consider the quality of the cart from below. The hissing of breath and the repeated "oh, dear, oh, dear, oh, dear, what have you got here?" indicated that the carpenter was not impressed.

'The Standing Conclave, eh?' said a voice so close to Hermitage that it made him jump.

He turned and saw the priest standing there, a worryingly interested look on his face.

The man was renowned for minding his own business to such an extent that his sacred duties came a very poor second. His service to the community was non-existent, his aid in times of trouble negligible, and his actual legitimacy as a priest at all extremely doubtful. That he had turned up here immediately set Hermitage's suspicions on alert; and that didn't even happen much in a murder investigation.

'Oh, erm, yes.'

'An important position.'

'I suppose so.' Hermitage knew that it was an important position and he was sinfully proud of his appointment, but he wasn't going to give the priest the satisfaction of being right.

'An honour, even,' the priest suggested. Although the way he suggested it made it sound extremely questionable.

'It is,' Hermitage admitted.

'Going to be discussing matters of great import, I imagine.'

'I'm afraid I don't know.' Hermitage had the distinct feeling that if he did know, he shouldn't tell the priest anyway. 'I've not been told what will be discussed, only that I have been appointed. Some sort of swearing-in will doubtless be required before business can be discussed.'

The priest nodded far too knowingly.

'Lots of important people on the Conclave,' the priest went on.

'Well, yes. Although I don't know the current make-up. A fellow called Leudric came and delivered the appointment. I shall meet the other members in Nottingham.'

'Nottingham, is it? Of course,' the priest said nonchalantly. 'I had some dealings with the Conclave myself, back before the Normans, obviously.'

'Is that right?' Knowing this priest as Hermitage did, he assumed the dealings were dishonest.

'I was of service in my small way.'

'Aha.' Hermitage wished that the man would get to the point.

'So, if you need any assistance in navigating the workings…' The priest said this so casually that he might have been offering to hold the ladder while you checked your thatch. His simultaneous glance at the cart made his request very clear.

'Oh, no,' Hermitage said rather too quickly. The last thing he wanted was the priest coming with them. 'I am sure all will be well. And Leudric is expecting only me.'

'And Wat and Cwen,' the priest pointed out, sounding a lot less casual now.

'They have business in Nottingham,' Hermitage said very plainly.

'Hm. I might have some business in Nottingham myself,

come to think of it.'

'Really?' Hermitage's natural urge to charity and to give assistance to his fellow man, was fighting with his distrust for and dislike of the priest.

He knew that he should distrust and dislike no one, and give the benefit of the doubt to all. But this priest had been so unhelpful on so many occasions, that Hermitage told himself he was only delivering the inevitable consequences of the man's behaviour, and that it was nothing personal.

'Well, we might see you there,' Hermitage said, ashamed of his own behaviour now.

He could tell that the priest was struggling to contain his irritation, but for once, Hermitage was the one with the authority. As well as having something that the priest wanted. Whatever it might be.

'Indeed,' the man said through gritted teeth. 'I shall make a point of it.' That almost sounded like a threat.

'I wonder if Aethelric is still engaged with the Conclave?' the priest seemed to ask the air.

Hermitage bit his lip to avoid provoking any further discussion.

'Bishop of Selsey, you know.'

'Ah.' Hermitage knew perfectly well that Aethelric was Bishop of Selsey, but wasn't going to let on.

'If you should see him, do give him my salutations.'

Hermitage raised enquiring eyebrows for more information. Such as the priest's name. He had never told anyone his name, saying that he could be called "Father" and that was sufficient.

The common suspicion was that if it became known who he was and where he was, trouble would descend like lightning. Whether it was Norman trouble, or old Saxon trouble was unclear, and didn't really matter.

'Just say the priest who went to Derby. He'll know who you mean. Only tell him, though. Make sure you only tell him. I, erm, wouldn't want to bother anyone else.'

Hermitage tried to look unhappy about this, and the part in some deceit that he was being asked to play. The priest who went to Derby, indeed! If salutations were to be sent, names must be exchanged. Hermitage felt under no obligation to follow these instructions.

And "the priest who went to Derby"? What sort of way was that to describe anyone? Not called to Derby, or appointed, or even sent. The one who went there. It was all disgraceful.

'If you are in Nottingham, you might be able to renew old acquaintances yourself.'

'Ah, would that I could, but I think the Conclave will be a closed affair. They always were in the past.'

'Ah, well, there we are, then,' Hermitage said conclusively.

'I am sure that the bishop would wish to hear that I am so close.'

'The priest who went to Derby,' Hermitage repeated with what he hoped was explicit criticism. 'I'll be sure to remember it.'

Before the priest had a chance to say any more, Wat and Cwen appeared from the workshop and, for some reason, got a cheer from the crowd.

Hermitage felt both nervous and slightly thrilled at the way he had dealt with the priest. He knew that Wat or Cwen would have been much more direct; something along the lines of "tell us your name, then". But, in his own way, he felt he had been the master of the conversation.

He immediately worried about what would happen when

he returned to Derby and either Bishop Aethelric hadn't been in Nottingham, or Hermitage hadn't mentioned the priest.

'What on earth is going on, Hermitage?' Cwen asked as she joined him. 'And why is the carpenter under the cart?'

'People have got the impression that this is some great event. In fact, Durselm, who's having a look at the cart's woodwork, I think, specifically said that he'd come for the great event.'

'Honestly,' she said. 'These people, eh?' she asked the air.

'It is a great event.' Wat held his arms out. 'Look. A horse and cart.'

'A horse and cart is going to Nottingham,' Hermitage pointed out the details. 'Hardly a great event.'

'It is around here,' Wat replied.

'And there's my appointment to the Conclave,' Hermitage added. 'They seem to know about that.'

Cwen nodded. 'Well, we had to tell people why we had a horse and cart.'

'People are interested in this sort of thing,' Wat added. 'And in the fact a large purse was involved.'

'They really didn't need to know that,' Hermitage said with some embarrassment.

'It's no bad thing,' Wat said. 'It's sad to say, but people are impressed by money.'

Hermitage knew one person who certainly was.

Cwen frowned. 'You've never worried about impressing the people of Derby before. In fact, you've gone out of your way to annoy most of them.'

Wat looked innocent as if he had only now come to the realisation that it was important to make a good impression on people.

'The Conclave.' Cwen nodded to herself. 'And all those tapestries. We could have the place awash with important folk wanting their tapestry made.'

'That's a good thing as well,' Wat pointed out.

'And it wouldn't do to have tapestry buying folk told that Wat the Weaver was a disgrace, his workshop was a blight on the town and he was the last person decent people should get a tapestry from.'

Wat tried to look as if he hadn't thought of that.

Cwen shook her head with a smile that this was just what she might have expected. 'Trust the people of Derby to follow a purse.'

Hermitage looked around at the crowd. 'And the priest was here.' There was now no sign of the priest.

'Really?' Wat asked. 'What did he want? Must have been something interesting to get him out of his church.'

'It was pretty clear that he wanted me to mention him at the Conclave.'

'Really? He didn't tell you his name, did he?'

'Oh, no. I was just to tell Bishop Aethelric that the priest who went to Derby sends his salutations.'

'And is this Bishop Aethelric going to be there?' Cwen asked. 'He sounds a bit Saxon for a Norman conclave.'

'I have no idea. As far as I know, he is still the Bishop of Selsey. But it seems that the priest had something to do with the old conclave. The one under Harold, or perhaps even Edward before him.'

'And now he sees a chance to restore his good fortunes, whatever they were.'

'Or avoid the ill fortunes that are currently looking for him,' Wat suggested.

'Either way, I don't think we're under any obligation to do

that man any favours,' Cwen said.

'He said he might have business in Nottingham, so he may be hard to avoid,' Hermitage half apologised.

'You didn't offer him a ride on the cart?' Cwen asked with obvious disappointment that it was just the sort of thing Hermitage would do.

'No, I did not,' Hermitage said. 'He obviously wanted one, but I offered nothing.'

'Well done, Hermitage,' Cwen said sincerely, although Hermitage felt it wasn't really well done at all.

'He can look after himself,' Wat said. 'It's all he's done since he came here anyway.'

'It is a bit of a taint on the Conclave though.' Hermitage was disappointed that this had been the start to the journey. 'After all, it should be a forum for discussion of weighty and important matters that reaches reasoned and sensible conclusions, not for some individual to seek their own benefit.'

'What?' he asked when he saw that Wat was looking at him in that way he did when he was about to impart some awkward truth.

'It may well be that weighty and important matters are discussed, Hermitage, but if this conclave is full of bishops and nobles, every one of them will be seeking their own benefit.'

Cwen nodded a sorry agreement.

'It's what they do.' Wat shrugged. 'Whatever the question, and whatever the answer, it will benefit one more than the other, so they will argue for themselves.'

'Not one of them can be seen to lose ground or face,' Cwen went on. 'So, as well as pushing themselves forward, they have to work hard to make sure the other members are disadvantaged or their reputations damaged.'

'Oh, I don't think..,' Hermitage began.

'After all, this conclave reports to the king,' Wat added. 'And everyone wants the king to think well of them.'

'Yes, but..,'

'And if he thinks well of me, it must mean he thinks less well of you. In which case, I need to help him think less well of you. A word here, a suggestion there should do the trick.'

'This is the Standing Conclave,' Hermitage insisted. 'It is not some marketplace of favour and advancement.'

Wat and Cwen looked to one another with expressions that said it was sweet that Hermitage thought like this, but he was going to be very disappointed before long.

Gunnlaug now emerged from the workshop, carrying the quite large box of books and parchments Hermitage had decided he could take after all, now that they had a horse and cart. Ink and quill were essential if he wanted to make any notes as the Conclave proceeded, of course. And naturally, a trimming knife and a ruler to make sure his lines were straight. At least he wasn't wasting space on any luxuries.

Wat and Cwen had brought their own packs, one of which included Hermitage's newly made habit, and everything was piled on the cart.

The three of them climbed up, Wat taking the reins, and the crowd gave another cheer as the horse woke to its task and stepped off along the track.

They all waved farewells to the apprentices and Hartle, and the whole assembly of weavers and townsfolk waved back. The townsfolk stayed to watch the horse and cart disappear down the track. The weavers went straight back indoors.

'Still,' Cwen said, as the workshop moved away behind

them. 'Look on the bright side, Hermitage. These conclave people may be manipulative, self-interested, deceitful and conniving, but at least they won't actually kill one another.'

'That's right,' Wat agreed cheerily. 'Far more satisfying for these people to destroy another's reputation and livelihood. We can be confident we won't have any murders to deal with this time.'

Caput V: Reunions, Good, Bad and Very Bad.

Hermitage rested with his back against the box of books, while Cwen and Wat sat on the cart seat behind him.

He enjoyed the pleasure of a journey at rest, and looked out at the countryside around them, comfortable that their direction and progress were being taken care of by Wat and the horse - which was far enough away from Hermitage not to worry him.

Wat and Cwen chatted away, and it wasn't clear whether they were talking to one another, or including Hermitage. There seemed no call for any contribution and so he enjoyed this period of enforced idleness, and drifted into a half-sleep, jolting awake every now and then with the bumps of the road.

'Of course,' Cwen was saying when he woke one time. 'It could still all be a trick. It wouldn't be beyond de Sauveloy to come up with two fine servants, a bit of parchment and a large purse. We could find there is no conclave and we've been lured to Nottingham.'

'Don't forget the seal,' Hermitage said.

'Ah, awake again, are we? What about the seal?'

'I looked at it more closely, and it was the seal of the Standing Conclave.'

'Which I imagine Ranulph de Sauveloy looks after.'

'True. But if the administration of the Conclave is running to order, a record will have been made of what document the seal was applied to, to whom it was sent and when.'

'Really?' Cwen sounded both surprised and somehow disappointed that anyone would go to that level of trouble.

'Oh, yes. And so that would create a trail of de Sauveloy's actions. Not very helpful if he really is trying to trick us.'

'I think there's another reason to believe this conclave is real,' Wat said.

'There is?'

'Absolutely.' Wat half turned around and dropped his voice to a whisper. 'Don't look, but the priest has been following us ever since we left the workshop behind.'

'He hasn't?' Cwen sounded quite excited. 'How do you know?'

'Erm, because I've seen him.'

Cwen nodded. 'You being used to having people follow you.'

'It's happened once or twice,' Wat admitted.

'Does he know you know?'

'Does it matter? He clearly thinks it's worth his while, so he must believe we really are going to the Conclave.'

'Or he's been tricked along with the rest of us.'

'At least he believes there is a conclave. And it has his bishop on it, or might have.'

'Aethelric,' Hermitage said.

'He must be desperate for something,' Cwen said. 'He never comes out of his church, let alone the town. What could this bishop have that he wants so much?'

'Reward or relief,' Wat said. 'It's all anyone ever wants. Reward to improve their lot, or relief to stop it getting worse.'

'There are other motivations in life.' Hermitage was disappointed at this cynical attitude. Disappointed but not really surprised. 'There is service. That brings no reward or relief. There is aiding the sick, relieving their suffering. There is granting succour to the poor.

'Those whose lot, as you put it, is already comfortable, have a duty to apply themselves to the improvement of others.

'Not every action we perform must be for our own personal betterment.'

'All right, if I grant you that,' Wat replied. 'Apply it to our priest.'

Hermitage saw the problem.

Wat continued. 'A man who has never applied himself to anyone but himself. Which means his attempt to see this bishop is not for succour to the poor.'

It was a sad fact of the world, perhaps the saddest fact, that people like the priest only ever acted in their own interest. Or, if they appeared to be doing someone else a favour, it would be a ruse of some sort.

Worse than that, they never had a qualm about their actions. When confronted with the effects of their behaviour, they looked puzzled and thought the person criticising them was some sort of loon.

Quite a few well-to-do people had thought Hermitage a loon over the years.

'Got to be relief,' Cwen said. 'We all know he's hiding from something. He never goes out, hasn't told anyone his name and twitches whenever the Normans and the battle are mentioned.

'He did something horrible, ran away, and Bishop Aethelric is the one who can get him out of it. Where did you say he was bishop of, Hermitage?'

'Selsey.'

'That's south, isn't it?'

'Long way south,' Wat confirmed.

'Which would be a bit far for our priest to get to unharmed,' Cwen speculated. 'Lo and behold, Aethelric is coming to him. Nottingham. Just around the corner, and Hermitage is going there. He's not going to get a chance like this again.'

'We don't even know that Bishop Aethelric is going to be there,' Hermitage said. 'Apart from Leudric and Thodrum, we don't know any names.'

'Still worth a chance. If you're a priest in hiding.'

'Well, it's all very interesting, but I'm not sure there's anything we can do about it. Or even should do about it.'

'It's good to know, though.' Wat said. 'In case the bishop is there and we start getting bothered by the priest.'

As the cart trundled on, Hermitage now looked back down the track, instead of dozing against his books. There was someone coming along, but whoever it was was far behind them. It could be the priest, it could be anyone.

He would just have to wait for any events to unfold themselves and hope that none did.

The journey wore on and the relaxing pace of the horse, the warmth of the sun and Wat and Cwen's gentle chatter settled Hermitage, and his thoughts wandered.

They must have wandered quite far as he woke with a start when the movement of the cart stopped and they were greeted with a shout.

He quickly became alert and turned to face forward, where three horsemen were approaching. Three Norman horsemen.

They were at walking pace, so he assumed this wasn't an attack of some sort, although an attack at walking pace would have been just as effective as a running one.

Doubtless, this was some Norman patrol who would want to know what the three of them were doing. It was a shame he didn't have the Conclave parchment anymore, as he was sure this would have given them safe passage.

Two of the horses drew up to the cart, one on either side,

and the Norman soldiers glared down at them from their saddles.

At least weapons weren't drawn, and a hasty surrender should avoid any unpleasantness.

The third rider, who appeared to be the leader, as he was better dressed and equipped than the others, brought his animal to the front of the cart.

He released his reins and reached up to his helmet, which he unbuckled and lifted from this head. With the large nose-piece out of the way, the man's face was revealed.

'Lord Gilbert.' Hermitage said with great relief as the Norman smiled at them all. Although he thought there was something forced about that smile.

'Well met,' Gilbert replied nodding his head to them all.

'What brings you to the Derby road? We are coming to the Conclave in Nottingham, we thought it would be at your castle.'

'Aye,' Gilbert agreed wearily. 'It is.' He clearly wasn't very happy about it. 'Fellow called Leudric arrived days ago.'

'Yes, he saw us too, and appointed me to the Conclave.'

Gilbert nodded and sighed. 'And he's taken over everything. I can't move in my home for arrangements.'

'Arrangements?'

'Rooms taken over, supplies organised, furniture brought in, mine taken out. Instructions for the stables and the cooks and the servants, most of which weren't good enough, apparently, and got replaced with new people. Even bits of the castle had to be repaired.'

Knowing Lord Gilbert as he did, Hermitage sympathised. The man was a warrior at heart, but an honest one, which made a change. He was never happier than when facing an enemy or organising a defence, but he always treated his opponents with respect, as worthy equals.

Thus, he didn't really fit in with the rule of England, now that most of the conquest was done. Nor did he suit William's way of doing things, which was to treat your defeated foes as a possible future threat, and kill them, just to be on the safe side.

'Ever since he arrived, I've spent most of the days surveying my lands. Anything to get me out of there.' He took a very deep breath and revealed even worse news.

'And because of this conclave, Aveline's come back.'

'Oh, no,' Wat said with genuine anxiety.

'Your daughter.' Hermitage thought Gilbert would be pleased about that. He worried a lot about his daughter and had even made Hermitage find her when she went missing once. (***The Tapestry of Death*** - missing daughters too.)

If Lord Gilbert was happiest in the throes of battle, Aveline considered them disorganised, troublesome and above all, dirty. All things that made her profoundly unhappy.

She found the castle of her father to be a dreary and dull place; she had no friends, nothing to do and was wasting her life.

The last they had heard, she had had to go to Paris as one of William's hostages to the King of France.

The fact that no one but Aveline seemed to know about the King of France wanting hostages from William in Paris was by the by. Gilbert reported she was very happy there, and if she was happy, he was happy.

'She's come back,' Wat almost whispered the words.

'Aye. Apparently, this conclave is important and full of people who need to meet her.'

'They need to meet her?' Hermitage didn't understand.

'That's what she said. Now, she's thrown herself in with Leudric and is turning the place upside down.'

'Still,' Wat tried to sound encouraging. 'I expect it will be over in a day or two.'

'Please God,' Gilbert said with desperate sincerity.

'And you just happened to be coming this way today,' Hermitage observed brightly, trying to bring some cheer to the meeting.

Gilbert shook his head. 'Leudric got me this morning before I could get away. Said he needed to go over the list of attendees. As if I care who's coming?

'Sheriff this, and Baron that, Bishop so and so, Archdeacons all over the place. And worst of all, Robert of Mortain, the king's own brother. As if the rest of them weren't trouble enough. Apparently, I have to greet them all, being the host.'

'With Aveline,' Cwen suggested.

Gilbert appeared to shiver. 'Oh, yes. Definitely with Aveline. And who should I see on the list but Brother Hermitage.' His mood did lighten at this. It soon darkened again. 'What did you do to deserve this?'

'Well,' Hermitage said. 'Although the Standing Conclave is clearly an inconvenience to you, it is a body of considerable import. It has been meeting for very many years, long before King William's time. It is a bit of an honour.'

'An honour?' Gilbert clearly doubted that. 'You don't have the thing in your house.'

'Did you notice a Bishop Aethelric on the list?' Wat asked. 'From Selsey?'

Gilbert looked into the air. 'There were quite a few bishops.'

'With Saxon names?' Cwen queried.

Gilbert nodded slowly and carefully. 'I think there was one with that sort of name. Don't swear me to it, though. I tried to stop listening. And all Saxon names sound the same to me.

'Why? Do you want him?'

'No, but someone we know does,' Wat explained. He tapped his nose to indicate that he couldn't say more at the moment. 'We're being followed,' he whispered.

Gilbert raised himself in his saddle and looked back down the track. 'Anyone who comes to this thing voluntarily has my sympathy.'

'To be honest,' Cwen said. 'We're a bit worried about why Hermitage was picked for the Conclave at all.'

'You're a bit worried,' Wat corrected. 'Hermitage had a fine parchment appointing him as reward for his loyal service to the king.'

Gilbert considered this. 'Doing the murders, you mean? It's possible, I suppose. If I was appointed, I'd think it a punishment.'

'And we thought de Sauveloy might be behind it.'

'Aye,' Gilbert seemed to sag in his saddle. 'He's behind a lot of things no one really wants to do. Including conclaves.'

'It wasn't long ago that de Sauveloy forbade us from, erm, doing something,' Cwen said. 'Which we went ahead and did anyway. It seems odd to be rewarded.'

Gilbert grunted. 'Nothing that man does can be judged by normal standards. Sometimes, he seems to like people standing up to him, other times, not. If not, things do not go at all well.

'Most likely is that you're going to be of use to him. He never deals with anyone unless they're going to be of use to him. This past misdemeanour of yours may be a pale, wispy thing compared to what he's got in mind now.'

'Or it was a genuine appointment by William?' Hermitage suggested hopefully.

Gilbert did not dismiss this immediately. 'Again, possible, but less likely. The king tends not to know who he's dealing with unless they're standing in front of him.

'And even if he did issue the instruction, de Sauveloy would find a way not to do it if he didn't want to. And this conclave is his, believe me.'

Hermitage found all this rather disheartening. He had held such high hopes for the Conclave. Still, perhaps the subjects for debate would be rewarding, never mind his reason for being there.

'Shall we travel on together, then?' he suggested.

'Gods, no,' Gilbert replied quickly. 'Sorry, Brother, but I've got hours I can stay away yet. You carry on, I'm sure Leudric will make you comfortable.' He gave them a rather horrible grin. 'And Aveline.'

He nodded to his men. 'Would you like us to dissuade your follower?' he asked Wat.

'No, let him come. It might add a layer of interest even de Sauveloy hasn't anticipated.'

Gilbert nodded. 'Oh, and there's one other name I didn't mention.'

'Oh, yes, who's that?'

'What with all these high and mighty people gathering in one place, they've got to be kept safe.'

'Yes,' Wat said slowly. 'Isn't that the host's job?'

'Oh, I'm not be trusted with something as important as this on my own. Someone has to assure himself that everything is being done properly. And with the king supposedly coming, who better to be a strong arm around the place? Le Pedvin.'

'Oh, God,' Hermitage cried out sincerely, just before he whimpered and crossed himself. The cadaverous Le Pedvin, whose main preoccupation seemed to be making other people into cadavers for the king, was a man of few words, but hideous intent. A lot of people talked about the fear of God being put into someone, but Le Pedvin could deliver it in person.

'Ah.' Wat said.

'He's coming here?' Cwen asked quietly.

'He already has. Another good reason to be somewhere else.'

'Le Pedvin and de Sauveloy,' Wat sighed. 'What have we got ourselves into? All we need is William and we'll have the three, erm..,'

'Woes?' Hermitage suggested. 'From the book of Revelation. Grief, anguish and affliction.'

'Sounds about right,' Wat agreed. 'Hard to decide which of them is which.'

'Oh, de Sauveloy's not coming,' Gilbert said.

'He's not?' Hermitage asked. At least that was some good news.

'No. He likes delegating things to other people and then blaming them when they go wrong. Not that this had better go wrong. Too many important people. But, for his own reasons. He's set the Conclave going, now he's keeping away.'

'He's sent Hermitage, instead,' Cwen observed.

Hermitage fervently wished that he still had the parchment now. He could look at it and tell himself that everything was all right, really.

Caput VI: On the List

Entry into the grounds of Nottingham Castle was not at all straightforward. If the master of the place and the organiser of the Conclave knew that they were coming, no one had told the men at the gate.

The horse plodded up to two very well-presented Norman guards, looking alert and ready for anything. They lowered their spears at the approaching threat.

Hermitage thought it would require a leap of imagination to see a monk and two Saxon weavers as much of a threat to anyone.

And these did not look like men of imagination. They even had a glint of fear in their eyes, suggesting to Hermitage that Le Pedvin had already issued his instructions. Quickly followed by the consequences of not following his instructions.

'What do you want?' One of the men at least spoke reasonable English.

'We are here for the Conclave,' Hermitage said, peering between Wat and Cwen.

'No, you're not. Clear off.'

'I assure you we are. Well, I am. Brother Hermitage.'

'What?'

'I am Brother Hermitage.'

'Brother Hermitage?'

'Yes. Funny name for a monk, I know.'

The Norman did not look as if he found it at all funny. He looked as if he wasn't finding anything funny just at the moment.

'I assure you that I am expected,' Hermitage pressed. 'Master Leudric saw me only last week and gave me my appointment.'

The first Norman frowned at this and stepped over to consult with his colleague. They exchanged a few low mutterings before the second one went over to the side of the gate and retrieved a large square of leather from a hook on the wall.

To Hermitage's eye, this looked like a simple parchment case; a piece of leather folded over and stitched so as to protect a single sheet or even a small collection.

Sure enough, the first Norman pulled out a parchment with writing on one side.

Hermitage looked on eagerly. He hoped this wasn't his parchment that had been handed on. It was being treated quite roughly.

The Norman handed the leather back to his fellow and held the parchment out in front of him. He scanned it up and down.

'You're not on the list,' he said.

'I beg your pardon?'

'You're not on the list.' The Norman waved the parchment about. 'This is the list, and you're not on it.'

'Ah.' Hermitage understood. 'The list of people to be admitted to the Conclave. I see. Well, I don't know what to tell you. I am most certainly supposed to be here and so I ought to be on your, erm, list.'

'Well, you're not.'

'Perhaps under H for Hermitage or B for Brother?'

The Norman's eyes narrowed at the monk who was giving trouble by trying to get in when he wasn't on the list.

'Could one of you go and ask Leudric? He will vouch for me.'

'We are not going anywhere.' That sounded very much like

adherence to a Le Pedvin instruction.

Hermitage was at a loss. He wouldn't be able to contribute much to the Conclave if he wasn't allowed in. He supposed that they would have to wait for Gilbert to return and order their admittance. But that could be hours.

'Excuse me,' Cwen asked very politely.

'What?' the Norman countered brusquely.

'The list.' Cwen nodded to the list.

'What about it?' The Norman clutched it to his chest as if she might be about to attack it.

'Can you actually read it?'

The Norman seemed annoyed by the question, which was quite rude.

'What do you mean, can I read it?'

'Can you read it?' Cwen repeated. 'It looks like a lot of names, even from here.' Bit of a task to be able to read all that, I'd have thought.' She smiled sympathetically. 'Especially if it's in Saxon English.'

'Listen.' The Norman took a step forward and pointed a finger. 'I don't have to read it to know you're not on it.'

Cwen sounded apologetic for bringing it up. 'I rather think you do. You know, what with it being a list and all. Otherwise, you'd have to remember it. And no one could be expected to do that.'

Wat picked up on the theme. 'I imagine Leudric, or one of the people organising this read it out, expecting you all to remember it. Every name. I ask you, is that fair?

'You're a fine-looking soldier, by the look of you, not a list rememberer, let alone a reader.'

'Did he rush the names?' Cwen asked. 'I'll warrant he did.'

'And Le Pedvin,' Wat added with a grimace. 'I suppose he said you're not to let anyone in who isn't on the list.'

The look on the Norman's face, and the way he scratched his neck, as if someone was reaching out to strangle him, said that this version of events was mostly accurate.

'And we'd have to admit that we don't look like the other members,' Wat said. 'What with all those bishops and barons and the like.'

'Let Brother Hermitage have a look,' Cwen said. 'He can read all the letters.'

The two Normans exchanged worried looks and appeared to be working out whether letting someone who wasn't on the list, read the list, was either very stupid or very clever.

The first man narrowed his eyes as if he were being extremely cunning.

'Only him,' he said.

'Of course,' Cwen agreed. 'We know we're not on the list. We're just with him.'

The Norman considered them all suspiciously and beckoned that Hermitage could climb down from the cart.

Doing so, the Norman took him to one side to make sure that no one else had a chance to read the list. He didn't even let go of the thing but held it for Hermitage to examine.

He had to bend to do so, and the first thing he did was reach out to gently turn the list the right way up.

'Ah, Latin,' he said as he saw the words. 'Now, let's see.' He tried to sound as if he was doing the Norman a favour. 'Bishop, bishop, bishop,' he muttered as he went down the list. 'Very good, and no more than I would expect of Leudric.' He nodded to the Norman. 'Alphabetical order,' he said, pointing at the list.

'Not that I've been told,' the Norman responded defensively.

'No, it means, oh, never mind. Here I am.' Hermitage

tapped the list at his name.

The Norman turned the thing around and peered intently at it.

'You see,' Hermitage said, helpfully putting his finger on the right spot. 'F for frater and H for Hermitagius.' As he said this, he knew it would not go well.

'Eh?'

'It's Latin,' Hermitage explained. 'Frater means Brother.'

The Norman looked anxiously to his fellow to see if this sounded at all reasonable. All he got was a shrug in return.

'Frater Hermitagius. It means Brother Hermitage. Just as the bishops aren't written as bishop, that's more of an English word. Well, from the Greek, originally. It says Episcopus, you see?' He pointed again to the right spot.

The Norman considered the letter carefully and started to nod slowly as if the Latin was as familiar to him as the dagger at his belt, and he had known this all along. He was only testing Hermitage to see if he was genuine.

'I know that,' he snapped as he pulled the parchment back. The man was obviously not going to let his ignorance be completely exposed.

'All right,' he said. 'You may enter. But no weapons.'

'Weapons?' Hermitage asked, wondering if he really looked like the sort of monk who went around armed.

'Le Pedvin's orders,' the guard confirmed. 'No weapons.'

'Except his own, probably, Wat muttered.

'We haven't got any weapons,' Hermitage said.

'Saxons aren't allowed to carry weapons,' Cwen pointed out.

'I shall check.' The guard said.

He looked Hermitage up and down and seemed content that there were no swords or daggers hidden in his habit.

Turning his attention to Wat and Cwen, they both stood on the cart and held their arms wide to confirm they weren't concealing anything. Seeing no daggers at belts, he gestured that they could sit.

He then looked over the cart, even underneath it to check that nothing was concealed below.

'What's in here, then?' he asked of Hermitage's box.

'Books.'

'Books?'

'Yes, that's right.'

The guard was carefully considering whether books constituted a weapon. 'And you need books, do you?'

'Oh, yes.'

'How many people are in the castle?' Wat asked as the inspection continued.

'Dozens,' the guard complained. He had obviously had to let every one of them in, confirming that they were on the list had didn't have any weapons.

'I don't think the three of us would be much of a threat, then. Even if we had a bag of arrows.'

'No weapons,' the guard simply repeated. 'Le Pedvin's..,'

'Orders. Yes, I understand. Can we go in now?'

Begrudgingly satisfied that the monk and two Saxons weren't planning to storm the castle, the guard waved them on. 'But Henry will take you up to the keep.'

'What?' The guard called Henry did not sound happy about this.

'Make sure Leudric knows they're here and there hasn't been some sort of mistake,' the first Norman said pointedly.

'Oh, right.' Henry quickly realised that any mistake might be theirs, and the consequences would be horrible.

'And if there has,' the Norman added to Hermitage. 'He

will bring you back and we will both throw you out.'

'No mistake, I assure you,' Hermitage nodded his gratitude. 'Thank you for your help.'

Still considering them through narrowed eyes, the Norman put the parchment back and lifted the bar across the gate, pulling it wide.

Wat flicked the reins and made the sort of noise people make to get a horse moving.

The animal stirred itself and stepped through the gate, Henry the Norman jumping up onto the cart as it moved.

'This way,' he said, helpfully pointing to the large castle keep that glowered from the hill in front of them.

'Good job you're here,' Cwen said. 'Wouldn't want to get lost.'

Henry scowled at them, looking reasonably confident that they were being difficult, but not knowing quite why.

The track wound its way backwards and forwards up the steep slope to the castle. At least this was a natural feature of the land and not some monstrous pile of earth that the conquered Saxons had been forced to construct.

No one said anything as the slow journey progressed, which Hermitage found increasingly awkward.

'I see Bishop Aethelric is on the list,' he said by way of conversation.

'Is he now?' Wat asked. 'That's interesting. Be nice to see him again,' he said for Henry's benefit.

'Of course, just because someone is on the list doesn't mean they will be here.'

'I suppose not,' Cwen said as the conversation died a quiet death.

Up at the gate to the keep, more soldiers guarded and patrolled as what looked like servants bustled to and fro with supplies.

'What do you want?' One of the guards asked the cart of Saxons.

'Oh, not again,' Cwen muttered.

'Visitors for the Conclave,' Henry reported.

'This lot?'

'The monk says he's a friar.'

'So?'

'Frater,' Hermitage corrected. 'Master Leudric is expecting us,' he said to the new man.

This fellow frowned but did turn to one of the other guards nearby. 'Fetch Leudric', he instructed. 'This doesn't look right at all.'

He stood and said nothing to them, simply staring as if the truth of their deceit would suddenly occur to him.

'I expect Le Pedvin will be pleased to see us as well,' Wat said with a smile.

This only caused the Norman's frown to deepen.

There was a disturbance at the door and Leudric appeared.

'Ah, Brother Hermitage,' he said with obvious relief. 'This fellow said we were being attacked by a cartload of Saxon friars.'

The fellow shrugged that he could have been right.

'It's all right,' Leudric assured the men. 'Brother Hermitage is a member of the Conclave.'

The Norman soldiers didn't look at all happy about this.

'He is an important servant of the king.'

The men still looked suspicious, but most of it now seemed directed at Wat and Cwen.

'Do excuse the men,' Leudric said quietly, but loud enough for the men to hear. 'The Conclave is a somewhat beyond their normal business.'

'Do I go back to the gate, then?' Henry asked as he got off the cart.

'I don't know,' Leudric replied with some impatience. 'Is that where you came from?'

'Yes.'

'Then you'd better go back there.'

Henry nodded as if it took a man of Leudric's importance and intelligence to work out that he should go back to the gate. He set off down the hill.

Leudric released a sigh. A conclave of important people, gathering to discuss matters of significance to the king, clearly did not sit well with a band of ordinary Norman soldiers. It looked as if Leudric was having a hard time of it.

'I must say, I was not expecting all of you. Although I see you got the horse and cart.'

'We have business in Nottingham,' Wat explained. 'And the roads are not always safe. It was a good opportunity to share the journey.'

'Ah, excellent.' Leudric sounded relieved that he did not have the problem of Wat and Cwen to deal with.

'Perhaps we can attend to the animal in the stables and then be on our way?' Wat asked.

'Of course, of course,' Leudric said.

'I've, erm, brought some books with me,' Hermitage said.

'Really?' Leudric's one word actually said: "what on earth did you do that for?"

'Yes. In case reference needs to be made.'

'Oh, well, if you like, I suppose.' Leudric waved two of the guards to come and take the box from the back of the cart. 'That's a lot of books,' he observed as the men struggled with the weight.

'I'll get it taken to your chamber. Come and find me when

you're ready.' Leudric nodded to Wat and Cwen and hurried back inside.

The guards still looked at them with suspicion.

'Right, let's get the animal sorted.' Wat moved the cart off around the corner of the keep, towards the rear, where they knew the stables were.

'What am I going to do?' Hermitage hissed urgently when they were out of sight.

'Go and find your chamber, I think,' Wat replied. 'Make yourself comfortable, and we'll probably see you in the morning.'

'I mean about the Conclave and my appointment and de Sauveloy.' Hermitage couldn't believe they'd forgotten why they were here. 'If you go, how am I supposed to find out what's happening.'

'We're not going,' Cwen said as if he was being stupid.

'But, you told Leudric you'd sort out the horse and then be on your way.'

'Yes,' Wat said with mock patience as he explained the plainly obvious. 'That is, indeed, what we said. But we're not going to do it. Now we're in, we stay. If we left, we'd never get back in again, would we? Not past those two idiots at the gate.'

'But what if Leudric sees you?'

'I think he's got far too much to worry about to spot us. And we'll keep out of the way. Make sure we aren't conspicuous.'

'Le Pedvin?' Hermitage asked the horrible question about the horrible man.

'We'll avoid him if we see him. And for all he knows, we're supposed to be here.'

'I think he'll work it out. For all his faults, he is not stupid.

He's probably seen the list.'

'But he tends not to care about anything unless it's a fight he can get involved in. At least de Sauveloy isn't going to be here, he would be difficult.'

'We'll tell him we're here to look after you. He'll believe that,' Cwen said.

'He does think I'm an idiot,' Hermitage acknowledged.

'Don't take it personally, he probably thinks everyone is an idiot.'

'Talking of idiots,' Wat said. 'I can't see our priest making it through that gate, what with not being on the list.'

Hermitage nodded. 'I might be able to have a word with Bishop Aethelric. Simply mentioning that I have come from Derby might prompt some comment.'

'There is another possibility I've just thought of,' Cwen said.

'Oh, yes. What's that?'

'That our priest doesn't want to meet Aethelric because he can help, he wants him because he caused the man's trouble in the first place.' She let the thought sit in the air.

'Revenge, you mean?' Wat said with interest. 'Could be.'

Hermitage, upon hearing this, felt his stomach churn.

'Don't worry, Hermitage,' Wat said. 'He won't be able to get in. After all, this is your conclave. I'm sure we won't have a murder or anything.'

Caput VII: Well Met?

'Well, well, well, Brother Hermitage.' The very well-dressed, mature man approached Hermitage across the hall, his hand outstretched in welcome, a broad smile on his face.

Hermitage had had a very restless night, worrying that the whole conclave was going to be ruined by the arrival of the priest, bent on the murder of Bishop Aethelric.

He told himself that such a fancy was ridiculous, and priests murdering bishops was the sort of thing that only happened in tales from history. These were modern times.

As soon as dawn arrived, he had ventured from his chamber, which he had to admit was very comfortable, and had thought that there would be no one about.

Wat and Cwen must have stayed at the stable, around the back of the keep, where the storage caves for the castle were.

He still shivered at the thought of those caves, and what had been found in them. (***A Murder of Convenience*** - the clue is the murder bit.)

Walking around the keep in the first light of dawn, he was surprised by the greeting.

'It's Haimo, Haimo Vicecomes.' The man was anxious to prompt Hermitage's memory.

'Ah, yes, Master Haimo, of course.' Hermitage could not forget him. He just hadn't expected him to pop up in a castle in Nottingham at first light. He had glanced at that list the soldier at the gate had but only got as far as F for Frater. Haimo Vicecomes, Sheriff, would have been a lot farther down.

'Sheriff of Kent, isn't it? Lord Odo's man.' Hermitage thought it might be worth asking, in case the situation had changed.

'That's it,' Haimo said brightly.

Hermitage's heart sank. He had met Haimo and Lord Odo when he had all that business with the tapestry for Bayeux to sort out. Well, embroidery, as Wat pointed out several times.

He had sincerely hoped never to meet either of them again. Another hope dashed. Mind you, Haimo himself had not been a problem, rather he seemed to be chief sycophant to Odo, William's half-brother, who was a monster, plain and simple.

'What, erm, brings the Sheriff of Kent all the way to Nottingham?' Hermitage asked by way of conversation.

'Why, the Conclave, of course. What else?'

'I, erm, didn't know you were a member.' Hermitage thought that sounded rather rude. 'I had a very brief look at the list of attendees, but obviously know no one.'

'Ah, well, I attend on behalf of Bishop Odo.'

And Hermitage definitely hadn't seen Odo's name on the list. That, he would have noticed.

'I see,' he said. He didn't but hoped he might do later.

'And I perused the list and saw Brother Hermitage.' Haimo was full of enthusiasm, as if they were the oldest of friends, when, in fact, they'd only met once. And then the Sheriff had taken him before Odo, which wasn't the sort of thing friends did to one another.

'Appointed for service to the king, Leudric tells me.'

'Ah, well, yes, that's what the parchment said.'

'Very well deserved,' Haimo congratulated him. He reached out and touched Hermitage gently by the arm. 'I may have, erm, put in a word myself.' He gave a series of tiny nods that were obviously supposed to imply some knowing scheme.

'Is that right?' Hermitage couldn't believe it was.

'After all that business with the nuns and the tapestry for Bayeux turned out so well.'

Hermitage didn't reply, thinking that the business with the nuns and the tapestry for Bayeux had turned out very badly.

'And this is your first conclave,' Haimo said. 'You must allow me to be your guide, as it were. Help you through the twists and turns.'

'Oh, really?' Hermitage didn't like to say "No, thank you".

'It's a strange world.' Haimo gestured that they might take benches either side of the large fireplace, which only glowed gently at this time of the morning.

Hermitage took the one on the left and Haimo to the right. After sitting for the merest moment, the Sheriff stood and came to sit a bit too close to Hermitage.

'Much of it discusses nothing at all,' Haimo confided.

'Really?' Hermitage had attended a few church conclaves, including that dread one at the monastery in De'Ath's Dingle, but they discussed a fascinating range of topics.

He had to admit that frequently it was only him and the Conclave participants who found the topic fascinating, and sometimes not even them, but they were all worthy events.

'Oh, yes. Rambling on for hours about tiny issues that matter not to man nor beast.' Haimo leaned ever closer. 'And most of the Conclave members are so old and useless, they spend half the time asleep.'

That was a common problem in long debates, but not one the church suffered. The duty brother with the large stick who patrolled each conclave looking for the merest sign of relaxation ensured full attention from all.

'Now, our leader this time is going to be Walter de Arsic, but he is a very fine fellow. Just the sort we need to keep things on track. Organising this lot is like asking sheep to gather a herd of cats.'

'Ah.' Hermitage felt he had to say something every now and again. 'And, erm, what is to be the topic of debate? Or topics, perhaps?'

'Very good question.' Haimo looked impressed at Hermitage's insight. 'Obviously, there is your appointment to be approved.'

'Approved?' Hermitage now worried that he might be turned down.

'A mere formality, what with Leudric reporting the king's wishes. And it's not as if you are a controversial figure.'

'Erm, well, no. I don't think so.'

'Absolutely not. Sorting out all those murders? Wonderful work.'

'Hm.' Hermitage didn't think it was wonderful work.

'Do you have anyone else who is speaking on your behalf?'

'Oh, well, I don't know,' Hermitage said. 'I didn't know I was supposed to have anyone.'

'I expect Leudric will have sorted it all out. Not to worry.'

'Could you?' Hermitage asked.

'Me?' Haimo seemed highly amused by the suggestion. 'Oh, no, no, no.'

'But you said that you had put in word for me before.'

'I did, but that was different. I am not at the Conclave in my own right, I am here for Bishop Odo. I can't say what he would not say, no matter how much I would like to, obviously. Sorry.'

'Hm.' Even to Hermitage's ear, unfamiliar as it was with machinations like this, it sounded a bit like an excuse.

'Is anyone likely to speak against?' he asked this with some horror. Not only might the promise of the Standing

Conclave be taken from him, but someone might not like him. And he didn't know any of them, so how could that be fair?

'Oh, I very much doubt it. Do you know any of the other members?'

'I don't think so. I didn't get a chance to see the whole list. I did see Bishop Aethelric is on it.'

'Ha.' Haimo seemed to think this was funny, for some reason. 'Sorry, do you know him?'

'Well, no. It's just that I have heard the name.'

Haimo nodded. 'Just as well. He's an old fool. Take my advice, Brother Hermitage, I should not concern myself with him.'

'A great knowledge of old Saxon law, I understand,' Hermitage said, it being the only thing he did understand about Aethelric, apart from some connection to the priest of Derby, which he was not going to mention.

'Quite.' Haimo said this as if it was a bad thing. 'A great knowledge that he interjects at length into every debate, whether it is required or not.

'He is not taken seriously by the Conclave. Accommodated, really. He has given years of service and will probably die in his seat.'

'Poor fellow.'

'And then there's Richard de Tunbridge,' Haimo continued as if Aethelric dying in his seat was a bit of a distraction. 'An untrustworthy fellow, be careful of him.'

'Really?'

'Oh, yes. Comes across as a holy one, but don't believe it. He came over with William but has since done his best to build his own kingdom in the east. All hidden from the crown, of course.'

'Oh, dear.'

'Then there are the other bishops, but they seldom contribute anything at all. Use the thing as an excuse for eating and drinking and getting away from the problems at home.'

This conclave was not fulfilling any of Hermitage's expectations. It was not sounding at all like a forum for the discussion of great and important ideas.

Haimo was continuing. 'Then you've got a few Barons, minor ones, mainly from Saxon times.'

'Saxons?'

'Oh, no. Normans who are now the Barons the Saxons used to be. Taken over the land, you see, and the place on the Conclave has gone with it.

'Most of them don't know what's going on, but an honour is an honour, and if there's a title going begging, there's nothing like a minor Baron to snap it up.'

Hermitage's disappointment was growing. 'I thought the Standing Conclave discussed mainly ecclesiastical matters.' It was sounding as if there wasn't anyone capable of discussing an ecclesiastical matter if it fell on them. Never mind bringing his books, he was starting to worry how many of the Conclave members would be able to read them.

'That's right,' Haimo confirmed.

Well, that was a bit of a relief.

'Ecclesiastical land, mainly.'

'Land? You mean holy sites and the like?'

'No, no.' Haimo leaned back on the bench now, which was also a bit of a relief.

'Brother Hermitage, the country is in a mess.'

There was no disagreeing with that.

'King William has a plan to make a record of some sort,

but what has gone on in the past is simply deplorable.

'Land has been granted here, taken there, reallocated left and right. Awarded, confiscated, re-awarded and declared for the crown. No one knows who owns what anymore.'

Hermitage thought this was a bit mundane for a conclave on ecclesiastical matters.

'Take Kent, for example.'

Hermitage tried to look interested.

'It's clear that the land is that of Odo. He is the king's half-brother and appointed Earl of Kent. It only stands to reason.

'And Archbishop Stigand supports this. So where is the argument?'

'I don't know,' Hermitage said, who didn't know there was one.

'Some in Canterbury are suggesting that ancient disputes between the old Archbishop, Robert, and the Saxon Earl Godwine have a bearing. How ridiculous is that? It was all fifteen years ago.'

'Was it?'

'And this is just the sort of thing the Conclave can sort out. Get clear once and for all.'

Hermitage thought this all sounded extraordinarily dull. He'd much rather debate whether the shrine at Walsingham was superior to that of Saint Winefride, which was in the far reaches of Wales. He imagined the Conclave didn't have jurisdiction over Wales, so that might be a problem.

'But I'm sure we can count on your support,' Haimo said casually.

'Oh, well.' Hermitage had started drifting off. 'I don't really know anything about it.'

'You do now,' Haimo pointed out.

'Yes, I suppose so.'

'Excellent.' Haimo gave Hermitage's knee a hearty pat as he stood. 'I look forward to your support in the Conclave.'

Hermitage frowned as he wasn't following this at all well. 'I thought you were not at the Conclave in your own right.'

'I am here as Bishop Odo,' Haimo said quite firmly. 'And this is his view.'

'I see.'

'I hope you do.'

Hermitage's frown didn't lift. He thought there was something going on here but he couldn't quite work out what it was. Perhaps a talk with Wat and Cwen would provide some illumination.

In fact, after listening to Haimo for so long, it would be a relief to see friends again. He had a strong suspicion that despite appearances, the Sheriff of Kent was not a friend.

'What are you up to, Haimo?' A voice called across the hall.

All prospect of comfortable conversation with Wat and Cwen fled up the chimney as that voice rang in Hermitage's ear like the toll of a funeral bell.

'My Lord Le Pedvin,' Haimo said brightly, although there was a crack in his voice. 'How nice to see you.'

'I doubt that,' Le Pedvin said as he drew near.

The singular eye that seemed to peer from the face of a skeleton, considered Hermitage, who wilted under its gaze.

He also wilted under the gaze of the patch that covered the other eye, even though it wasn't looking at him.

'Good God, it's the monk,' Le Pedvin said.

'Brother Hermitage,' Haimo sounded as if he were making the introductions at a court function.

'That's the one,' Le Pedvin agreed. 'What the devil are you

doing here?' His eye narrowed. Hermitage didn't know it could do that and shivered. 'Not another murder?' Le Pedvin seemed to ask this quite hopefully.

'Brother Hermitage is a member of the Conclave,' Haimo reported.

Le Pedvin considered this for the briefest moment. 'No, he isn't.'

Hermitage was prepared to believe that and leave straight away.

'Appointed by the king,' Haimo added.

'The king? Why would the king appoint him?'

'For all his service.'

Le Pedvin put his hand on the back of the bench. Hermitage was sure he could feel the woodworm leaving.

'The king appointed you?'

'He did,' Haimo confirmed.

'Haimo,' Le Pedvin said. 'Shut up.'

Haimo shut up.

'Well?'

'Oh, well, erm,' Hermitage began. He knew he had to say something, he just didn't want to. 'A parchment, you see, and Leudric, who bought one. To me. That is. Saying. About the Conclave. You know.'

Le Pedvin shook his head from side to side. 'When did this happen?'

'Oh, erm, only last week, really.'

'Last week really?'

'Yes. Last week. A week ago. Today that is. Only today as it was last week.' Hermitage told himself very firmly to stop talking.

'You're not on the list I was given,' Le Pedvin peered hard at Hermitage as if his real identity would be revealed.

'Ah. I was on the list the guard at the gate had.'

'Were you? I shall check, you know.'

'Excellent.' Hermitage was starting to hope that Le Pedvin would decide to have him thrown from the castle. The Conclave wasn't all that important or interesting, after all.

'I don't know what the place is coming to.' Le Pedvin's singular gaze continued to pierce those who fell under it.

'I know one thing, though.' These words seemed mainly for Haimo. 'The king doesn't appoint anyone, or if he does, he gets de Sauveloy to do it for him. Which means that weasel of a man is up to something.'

It was seldom that Hermitage agreed with Le Pedvin. Perhaps he was going to find out what it was de Sauveloy was up to.

'Though what he intends to do with one idiot monk is beyond me.'

No revelation, then. Hermitage was at least relieved to hear that Le Pedvin was treating him with contempt. It was much more comfortable than the alternatives.

'And you, Sheriff,' Le Pedvin added. 'Stop bothering people. You know you're not a member of this conclave, and if you keep whispering in peoples' ears about your various bits of land, I shall send you back to Odo in enough pieces for one bit each.'

'I am Bishop Odo's formal representative.' Haimo seemed to find some courage. 'And I trust the security of the Conclave will be such that no one ends up in pieces.' With that, he turned on his heels and walked stiffly away.

Le Pedvin watched for a moment, before slapping the back of the bench and laughing. It wasn't a nice laugh or the sort of noise that anyone, upon hearing it, would assume came from someone who was happy. Nevertheless, it forced

Hermitage to conclude that this was what the man sounded like when he laughed.

He sincerely hoped never to hear it again.

'Watch that one, monk,' Le Pedvin warned. 'If there's going to be a murder here, he'll be the one.'

'He would commit murder?' Hermitage had to ask.

'Or be murdered,' Le Pedvin said nonchalantly. 'One or the other.'

Caput VIII: How It All Works

'Oh, this is awful,' Hermitage bleated to Wat and Cwen. 'I want to go home.'

'Hermitage.' Cwen spoke soothingly. 'This is the Standing Conclave, the great honour, the thing you thought most highly of. What would Abbo say?'

Hermitage slumped even further into the chair of the victualler, who looked increasingly concerned at the number of strangers in his storeroom. Thankfully, he was also keeping his distance, as he had said he remembered exactly who they were, and he wasn't going to have that sort of trouble in his store again.

'Anyway,' Wat added far less sympathetically. 'I don't think you can leave. Not now you're on the list. The guards probably have orders. It was hard enough getting in, they definitely won't let you get out.'

'You are not helping,' Cwen told him. She turned back to Hermitage. 'We knew Le Pedvin was going to be here, Gilbert told us.'

'Yes,' Hermitage accepted. 'But I thought he'd be out patrolling the grounds, or seeing to defences and the like. Not creeping about indoors, frightening people.'

'And Haimo,' Cwen said. 'We've met him before.'

'We have. But that was only briefly, and it didn't give us the opportunity to discover what an awful man he is.'

'He was lining you up for the Conclave. I should think it's perfectly normal,' Wat said.

'Normal?' If this was normal, it was another reason to leave.

'Whenever a large number of people gather to make a decision, the chances are the decision's already been made by the same people in private discussions.

'It's the same for the weavers. A bit of persuasion here, a bribe there, the odd threat to bring people in line. Quiet words in corridors, promises made to garner support. That's all this is.'

'But this is the Standing Conclave on ecclesiastical matters,' Hermitage protested. 'It's not some land market.'

'It is as far as Haimo's concerned. He's probably working his way around all the other members, sounding them out, seeing where they stand, and then applying the levers.'

'Levers?' Hermitage wondered if that parchment on triangles might have been some use after all.

Wat wearily listed the levers. 'Persuasion, bribery, threat.'

'But he now expects me to support him when he argues about this land.'

'Don't worry about it.' Wat was sounding very relaxed. 'It sounds as if he isn't well thought of anyway, so the question might not even come up.'

'And if it does?'

'He can expect what he likes, and you do what you like. Support him or not.'

Hermitage thought that sounded terribly dishonest.

'Did you actually say you would support him?'

Hermitage recalled the conversation. 'Well, no. But he said he was sure he could count on my support.'

'Well, that's his problem, isn't it? You reply that you never promised him anything. He's made rash assumptions. You've had more recent information. The situation has changed since you spoke.'

'I think we're listening to a master,' Cwen observed.

'Selling tapestry to the court of King Harold was lucrative,' Wat said. 'But never straightforward. There was always some noble trying to stick his nose in.'

'But Haimo might not be pleased.'

'Ah, Hermitage, there's the problem,' Wat said with great satisfaction. 'In fact, I suspect, there are a lot of problems. Stop caring whether other people are happy or not.'

That sounded like the most appalling way to approach anything.

'Not the people you love and care for, obviously,' Wat added hurriedly, with a sideways glance at Cwen. 'Just everyone else. This Haimo in particular.

'You've only met the man once, and then he took you to Bishop Odo. Now, he's slithering around the Conclave trying to persuade people about his land. Why do you care if he's happy or not?'

'I care that everyone should live good lives of righteous contentment.'

'That rules Haimo out, then. At best, the man is a weasel doing his master's bidding, right or wrong. At worst, he's a robber in his own right.'

'A bad man,' Cwen spelt it out.

'Even better,' Wat went on. 'He does seem ill thought of.'

'Ill thought of by Le Pedvin,' Hermitage said. 'But then, we're all ill-thought of by Le Pedvin.'

'True. But if others think the same, you could well be best advised to distance yourself from Haimo. Opposing him in the Conclave could see you in the majority.

'If Haimo is on the way down and then out, you don't want to be caught up.'

'And you said he's not even a member of the Conclave at all,' Cwen said. 'How's he going to argue anything?'

Hermitage was feeling slightly better now. He'd known Wat and Cwen would help.

'In any case,' Cwen said. 'I don't think you can leave.'

'Excuse me,' Wat put in. 'I think that's what I said in the first place.'

'Yes, but you didn't say it nicely.'

Wat wiped a hand across his face. 'But, more interesting than Haimo, Le Pedvin thinks de Sauveloy is up to something.'

'Well, that's what he said,' Hermitage reported.

'And we know how well those two get on,' Cwen said. 'We could have an ally in Le Pedvin.'

Hermitage didn't like the sound of that at all.

'We're suspicious about what the man is up to appointing you here, now, so is Le Pedvin,' Cwen explained. 'And he has a bit more authority than any of us. He can probably dig into the Conclave. Find out what other little schemes are going on.'

Wat nodded. 'Haimo won't be the only one. He might be the worst and the most blatant, but the others will be up to the same. Have you met any of them yet?'

'No, not yet, but Haimo told me about them.'

'And I think we now know not to believe anything he says.'

Hermitage hadn't made the leap from dishonesty in one matter to dishonesty in all. He supposed that he probably should.

'He said that the leader of the Conclave is going to be Walter de Arsic.'

Cwen splurted a cough 'Arsic?' she giggled.

'Yes,' Hermitage replied.' Walter de Arsic. Do you know him?'

'Do I know him? Hermitage, his name is Arsic.'

'Yes?'

'It's funny.'

Hermitage thought about it. 'Oh, I see. Arsic. Yes, very good.' He gave Cwen a frown for such childishness. 'Anyway, Haimo reported that this, erm, Walter is a fine fellow.'

'Another robber, then,' Wat concluded.

Hermitage took a mental note.

'He said that the bishops were mainly old fellows of little value who fell asleep a lot.'

'Young men with their eyes on Haimo,' Wat translated.

'And that someone called Richard de Tunbridge was an untrustworthy fellow.'

'Right. Richard de Tunbridge is the one to talk to. I must say, Haimo is very bad at this.'

'It is a poor way to behave.'

'No, I mean bad at what he's doing. He's very bad at trying to be bad. You don't walk up to the first member of the meeting you see and come out with a blatant request for support. You sound them out, you test the ground, you see where their inclinations lie and try to point them in the right direction.

'Then, you have three or four more goes at them over the days to come.

To Hermitage's ear, that sounded even worse.

'And I don't think there's any need to worry about Haimo being murdered,' Wat added.

'Why so?'

'He's not worth the bother. He seems so inept. And for him to murder anyone, he'd have to apply at least some intelligence.'

'Le Pedvin's just teasing you,' Cwen said.

That did not make Hermitage feel any better.

'Doesn't this conclave start today?' Cwen prompted him. 'Aren't you supposed to be in it?'

Hermitage nodded. 'No one else was about when I came down and I wanted to escape Le Pedvin. Perhaps people are waking now.'

'We've got an in to the servants' hall through our friend the victualler, here,' Cwen said. 'So we can follow that trail and see what they're gossiping about.'

The victualler looked over and grumbled.

'You find Bishop Aethelric,' Wat said. 'At least you know his name. And this Richard de Tunbridge, if you can.'

'I shall want to meet all the members.'

'Quite right,' Wat agreed. 'And now you know what to do.'

Hermitage raised an eyebrow.

'Sound them out, test the ground, see where their inclinations lie.'

Hermitage stood and left them to their own plan, with determination that he was going to do no such thing.

Back in the main hall of the castle, more people were moving about. They mainly seemed to be servants carrying things to and fro, and they mainly ignored Hermitage.

One of them did tut as he walked by, as he was in her way, but he assumed she didn't know he was a member of the Conclave. He was just some monk in the hall.

He took himself back to the bench by the fire and waited patiently for someone to come by. He assumed he would be called when the Conclave was to begin, but that must be some time away, yet.

After the flurry of servants had subsided, doubtless attending to the needs of those waking, Leudric did appear at the far end of the room.

He was stepping quickly along, with Thodrum at his back. They were engaged in a low and quite urgent discussion, by the look of it, but did pause and divert their path when Hermitage was spotted.

'Ah, Brother Hermitage, good day to you.'

'And to you Master Leudric,' Hermitage replied, standing at the bench.

'The day of the Conclave has arrived,' Leudric went on. 'And all manner of last-minute arrangements and changes to be managed.'

'I can imagine.'

'Have you met any of the other members yet?'

'I don't believe so. I did see Haimo, the Sheriff of Kent, you know.'

'Oh, he is no member of the Conclave,' Leudric dismissed the name. 'He attends on behalf of Bishop Odo, who is not even a member himself. However, he is the king's half-brother and says he has an interest in the deliberations, so he can hardly be refused, eh?'

'I would think not. Haimo said that Walter de Arsic was leading the Conclave.'

'Oh, my, did he indeed?' Leudric laughed and shook his head. 'Master de Arsic is the attendant to the Conclave, not its leader. Granted, he takes the ceremonial staff once the Conclave has sat, but after that, he sits and waits to see if anyone wants bread or wine. Leader of the Conclave. Ho, ho. How amusing.'

'So, when does the Conclave itself start?'

'It will be at noon. In fact, I had just come to start getting the room set out.'

'Oh, it's here?' Hermitage looked about the hall and it was a big room. Perhaps there was nowhere else suitable in the castle.

'Yes. We'll get the servants working on the tables and

chairs. You are welcome to retire to your chamber until the bell.'

'Bell?'

'Another of Walter de Arsic's important responsibilities. He rings the bell.'

'Rings the bell and carries the staff.'

'And that's about it.'

Hermitage's opinion of Haimo was sinking fast, which might help when it came time to dealing with the man again.

'Is there one of the Conclave I should talk to before the meeting?' he asked. 'So that I can get some idea of what's required and what will happen?'

'A good idea, Brother. It's been so long since we had a new member that it's assumed everyone knows. The Normans are all new, but they have no knowledge of the Conclave at all. It will be good to have fresh eyes. There might be all sorts of strange things we get up to that appear completely pointless.'

Hermitage couldn't imagine that the Standing Conclave did anything pointless.

'I could take you to Bishop Aethelric, perhaps. He is a very learned fellow on the workings of the Conclave.'

'Oh, erm, yes, that would be most useful.' Hermitage thought it would, but immediately worried what he would say. He could hardly start the conversation with "Hello bishop, I think the priest of Derby is coming to kill you."

'Excellent.' Leudric nodded to Thodrum as if he was supposed to take a note of this. Which he did.

'For the Conclave record, you understand,' he explained. 'Even meetings outside of the main conclave have to be recorded as taking place. In case there is any dispute later on.'

'How, erm, organised.' Hermitage saw that this would be useful to stop the sort of scheming and frankly underhand business that Wat had suggested.

However, it was also an indication that the Conclave might be ripe with scheming and underhand business.

'We had best give it a while though,' Leudric said. 'Aethelric is an elderly fellow and takes time to get going in the morning.'

'Of course.'

'If you are content to wait here while we work around you?'

This comment clearly said that Leudric would rather he went away while they did their work.

'No, no,' Hermitage said. 'I shall take a walk and return later.'

'An hour should do it.' Leudric nodded that Hermitage could go straight away if he liked.

With a brief nod of the head, Hermitage wandered down the hall to the main door, not really having any idea where he was going.

Once he had got to the door, he had to go through it. He would appear most foolish if he turned around and went in some other direction. It would look as if he didn't know what he was doing.

And, as he was wearing a habit, he felt that he couldn't even pretend that he had forgotten something, pat his sides looking for it, and then wander off.

Trying to look as if he had intended to leave the room all along, he opened the small door that was set in the main body of the gate and went outside.

It was still chill in the morning air, and he wondered how long was reasonable to stand out here before he could turn around and go back in, it being assumed that he had been for his walk.

Surely, the easiest thing was to really go for a walk. A

rather pointless exercise, but it would pass the time, and perhaps help order his thoughts about Haimo, and prepare them for Aethelric.

He turned to the right, for no other reason than the wind would be behind him, and wandered along.

The guards outside considered him with suspicion, but as he had come out of the castle gate, he was probably all right.

They obviously still couldn't understand why a monk was going for an aimless walk at this time of the day, but it was none of their business. Only if he turned and attacked the castle would it become their business. Which they judged to be unlikely.

Hermitage wandered on and came to the corner of the building and now, being under the gaze of the guards, he felt obliged to walk around, as if this had been his specific intent.

Once around the corner, he sighed as he saw yet more guards and so would have to keep walking.

At this rate, he would end up going right around the castle, when he hadn't meant to go outside at all.

Leudric had said he could go back to his chamber. Why hadn't he done so? He shivered in the wind that had now come around the back of the castle and was bothering his thin habit.

One more corner, he told himself, and then the rest. He might as well get on with it, then he could legitimately go back to his chamber because he would be freezing.

At the back of the building, only one guard disconsolately meandered up and down, and he only started doing that when Hermitage appeared. He looked very surprised that anyone had come round here at all. Guarding the back of a castle was probably a lonely outpost.

Hermitage gave him a nod and the sort of look that tried to

say he had a perfectly good reason to be walking around the back of a castle on a cold morning.

He looked up and considered the walls of the building as they stretched above him, making a play of showing interest in the construction.

Apparently content with the jointing of the timbers, he moved on.

He noticed a window opening, cut into the wall some eight feet up, well above his head. And stood back to consider the way the carpenter had achieved this.

He had no idea, or interest, in how the carpenter had achieved this, but at least it was something to look at.

It was also something to hear, as voices drifted out of the window. If it had been a quiet conversation, he doubted he would have heard it at all, but it wasn't. It was two men talking with some anger.

He didn't recognise the voices, but then he hadn't spoken to many people yet.

'Of course, it can be done,' one of the voices snapped.

It didn't sound like a master berating a servant. It wasn't a voice of impatience or dissatisfaction. It had much more serious intent and gave Hermitage cause to worry.

A barely audible reply responded, and this seemed to be a third person.

'And during the Conclave,' the second voice now instructed.

It seemed clear that there were at least three people in this room, two of them instructing the other.

A further mumbled reply was followed by a door being closed.

Hermitage thought the third person had now left, as the two other voices continued to talk in a much lower tone.

So, something could be done, and it could be done during the Conclave. The question remained, what was it?

Hermitage had a horrible feeling that it wasn't carrying a staff or ringing a bell.

He felt another talk with Wat and Cwen coming on.

Caput IX: A Chat With The Bishop

Re-entering the castle, Hermitage now had somewhere to go. He could have headed for the store caves from outside, but the guard of the castle's rear was looking at him in a funny way, so he had to move on.

'Ah, Brother,' Leudric called as he entered.

The hall was busy with servants now, clearly preparing the place for the Conclave.

'Now that I have this underway, I can take you to Bishop Aethelric. I am sure he will have risen by now.'

'Ah, right, yes.' Hermitage couldn't really think of an excuse not to go. He certainly couldn't tell Leudric that he'd been listening at castle windows.

'His chamber is towards the back of the building.'

'Is it?' Well, that was interesting. When he got there, Hermitage would have to have a look out of the window.

Leudric led the way and they went through a myriad of corridors, twisting left and right. From the outside, the castle didn't look big enough to accommodate all of this.

Eventually, they arrived at one door, where Leudric made sure his clothes were neat before knocking.

After a moment, a voice called, 'Enter', but it sounded as if it had had to think about this quite carefully.

Leudric nodded at Hermitage and pushed the door open.

Inside, the first thing that struck him was the warmth. The place was as hot and stifling as a summer's day. His immediate expectation was that this would be a place of luxury. Fine drapes and soft, feather-stuffed cushions would be scattered about.

In fact, it looked a bit like a cell. A cell with no window, he noticed.

A simple cot sat close to one side of the fireplace, which burned brightly and had a stack of logs standing ready. In front of this was a single hard wooden bench, and upon that sat Bishop Aethelric, who turned as they entered. At least, Hermitage assumed it must be him as there was no one else in the room.

He didn't really know what he'd expected the bishop to look like. He'd only seen bishops in their official capacities and had certainly never met one when he'd only just got up in the morning.

Aethelric was plainly an old man. Not ancient, or bent, but perhaps over sixty, and, even though he had a thick robe around him, was as thin as a sparrow's leg.

Wisps of grey hair emerged from a simple cap on top of his head, and he was drawn so close to the fire, Hermitage was surprised to see he wasn't steaming.

'Ah, Leudric,' the bishop said in a voice stronger than his frame justified. He tapped a parchment he was holding. 'I have been considering the application of King Alfred's code to the legitimacy of the Conclave, and indeed, referring to Cunwulf of Mercia's missive to the bishop of Worcester, which was many years ago. But, of course, that refers to the handling of wrong-doers, which we hardly are.' He gave a light chuckle at this.

'Indeed,' Leudric responded. It sounded as if he was used to conversations starting like this. 'I have brought Brother Hermitage.'

Aethelric turned his eyes to Hermitage and he considered him with nothing but interest and curiosity.

Hermitage had never been looked at like that by a bishop. Most of the time, he hadn't been looked at at all, as his abbots tended to send him on some lowly errand whenever a bishop was visiting. When the episcopal gaze had fallen on him, it generally moved quickly on, not seeming to spot him at all.

And the tales Hermitage had heard of bishops made him grateful for his anonymity. The demands and expectations he heard about were always high and, to his mind, some of them were positively sinful.

He had to be frequently reminded that bishops did not sin. How could they? They were bishops.

But Bishop Aethelric was not fulfilling his expectations.

'Brother Hermitage, eh?' Aethelric said the name as if it was his most earnest desire to hear more. 'The King's Investigator, no less.'

'Erm, yes, my Lord,' Hermitage bowed.

'Oh, no need for all that. Come, sit.' Aethelric patted the side of his bench. 'Thank you, Leudric,' he said. 'I'm sure Alfred and Cunwulf will keep for later.'

Leudric left, looking quite grateful.

Hermitage took his seat, despite the blazing fire being a little too close for comfort.

'Ha,' the bishop called cheerily. 'My old bones need the heat straight on 'em. Take the stool to the side, young man.'

Hermitage quickly moved away from the force of the fire.

'So,' Bishop Aethelric continued to show great interest in Hermitage, which was a little unnerving in itself. 'Rewarded by the king for your service in all those murders, eh?'

Hermitage gave an awkward shrug. 'Not a calling of my choice.' He didn't need to ask how the bishop knew so much. He simply came across as someone who was very well-informed.

'We seldom get to choose our callings,' Aethelric said amicably. 'But even then, there are those who do not carry them out to the best of their ability. You have performed some marvels, I hear.'

'Oh, well,' Hermitage felt himself blushing.

'The business with Umair, the Monasterium Tenebrarii, even the dread De'Ath's Dingle of infamy.'

He was very well-informed.

'There might even be an argument for codifying your findings into some sort of what, Chronicle? For the benefit of those investigating after you?'

Hermitage thought that him stumbling about in a state of confusion and just hanging on until something occurred to him, could hardly be codified into anything.

'Give it some thought.' Aethelric did not press the matter. 'So, you join the Conclave, eh?'

'So it seems,' Hermitage replied apologetically.

Aethelric nodded knowingly. He seemed to do most things knowingly, but not in the annoying way of a know-all.

'You have some doubts.' Aethelric simply stated a fact.

Hermitage felt that he could tell this man anything. There was no question about trusting him, not like Haimo. That man was after something and made it plain. What could Bishop Aethelric want? He had his simple chamber, his fire and his texts. He had no need to take anything from anyone.

'I have seen who is on the Conclave,' Hermitage said. 'Yourself, obviously, a number of other bishops, barons, nobles. And me.' He didn't want to sound ungrateful.

'Of course, it is a great honour. And I have long been an admirer of the Conclave. My old Abbot, Abbo, spoke of the wonderful work on the Wessex Gospels.'

'Ah, dear Abbo, how is he? Still alive?'

'As far as I know. He went through a difficult period when everyone insisted he was dead, but I managed to show that he wasn't. (*The Case of The Cantankerous Carcass.*)

'Ah.' Aethelric frowned at that but didn't ask more. 'And you wonder why you have been appointed.'

'I do.'

Aethelric paused for a moment. 'Frankly, my boy, so do I.'

'Oh.'

The bishop held his hands up, indicating that he meant no offence. 'I cast no doubt on your abilities. It seems clear to me that you are an honest, devout and decent fellow. The sort we need more of on the Conclave. You will make a great contribution to its work, I am sure.'

'But?'

'But. But indeed. Appointment to the Conclave is through the king. Now, as we agree, you have done great service to the king, and it might be reasonable that you have some reward.

'But that could be a piece of land or a position of importance in a monastery. Charge of a scriptorium, perhaps?'

Hermitage beamed at the thought of that.

'The king's appointments to the Conclave have all been men of, how can we put it?'

'Import,' Hermitage suggested.

'Import?'

'I know that I am not a man of import, and I have no wish to be. I have no views on the rule of the country, I have no advice I can give the king on how he should distribute his lands, or deal with his subjects.

'I might have some comments on the finer points of scripture, but even those would be open to debate. And, from my meetings with him, I know that these are not matters that interest the king.'

Aethelric nodded. 'I know what you mean, Brother, but I

think you do yourself a disservice. Import comes in many guises. Just because a man has no land or power over others, does not rob him of import.'

'I think it does in the context of the Standing Conclave,' Hermitage said.

Aethelric did not contradict this. 'Which leaves us the question of why. Why have you been appointed to this body?'

'And appointed by Ranulph de Sauveloy.'

'Ah, that man.' Despite the intense heat, the bishop seemed to shiver. 'Yes, I suspect he is behind a lot of the king's actions. Some of which, even the king doesn't know about.'

'And he has, erm, reason to dislike us.'

'Wat and Cwen. I take it they are here, somewhere?'

'Oh, erm, yes.' Hermitage was surprised by the bishop's knowledge once again and felt he had to apologise.

'Oh, don't worry. Wat the Weaver. Who'd have thought, eh? It just goes to show that even an old and wily man like me can still be surprised. But you say de Sauveloy has reason to dislike you.'

'I'm not sure I should go into details. I wouldn't want his dislike to spread.'

'As you please. Although I think dislike oozes in and out of that man with the tide.'

Hermitage tried to phrase it carefully. 'Suffice to say that in the course of some business, information was obtained that cast Lord de Sauveloy in a poor light.'

'I suspect he lives in a poor light. But he might want to make sure this particular information never emerges?'

'Just so.'

'In which case, why reward you?'

'Exactly.'

'Unless it was to put you in harm's way?'

'Really?' Hermitage was disappointed that they hadn't thought of anything quite so direct. 'We wondered if he was trying to get me out of the way for some reason. Put me on the Conclave, which would keep me busy.'

'Another possibility,' Aethelric acknowledged.

'Even Lord Le Pedvin was surprised to see me,' Hermitage added.

'There is a man of a simple nature. Crude and nasty, but simple. And we know that he and de Sauveloy are at daggers drawn. Although, in Le Pedvin's case it is drawn, de Sauveloy has it behind his back, hidden in a scroll.

'But, if Le Pedvin didn't know, it means de Sauveloy has a scheme of his own.'

Aethelric beckoned that Hermitage should lean close.

'No mention of this, Brother,' he said.

Hermitage nodded.

'Wat and Cwen will be fine, but no one else. Leudric is in de Sauveloy's pay, you know.'

'He did speak highly of his master.'

'Aye. He is a trustworthy fellow and a good organiser. Not one of de Sauveloy's confidantes, but he should not hear that we have doubts. Certainly not that I have any.'

'He will not hear it from me.'

'Good.'

Hermitage had to ask the question. 'Do you really think harm could befall us here?'

'I honestly don't know.' Aethelric nodded slowly to himself as he was now considering the problem. 'On balance, I think not.'

Well, that was a relief.

'It is a significant forum, and you have been appointed to it.

For you to be murdered in the middle of it would be more trouble than de Sauveloy generally wants around him.'

Hermitage had only thought of harm, thus far. Surely murder was a bit much? He tried to think of some harm that wasn't deadly. Or didn't even hurt that much.

'And Wat and Cwen are with you, as, no doubt, de Sauveloy would expect.'

'Would he?'

'You do go everywhere together.'

'Oh, yes, I suppose we do.'

'It would be another great step to see all three of you dealt with in the middle of the Conclave, though.'

'What can he be up to?' Hermitage scratched his chin. 'I was bothered by Haimo as soon as I was up this morning.'

'Oh, Haimo. Yes, he bothers most people most of the time.'

'Could he be part of it? He said he wanted my support over some business with land. Is that why de Sauveloy sent me?'

'No, no.' Aethelric dismissed this quickly. 'Haimo and his land are irrelevant. And he is Odo's man through and through.'

'Yes, I met them both when dealing with a matter in Kent.'

'Bad luck. Odo is well named, from *odium*, eh?'

'Hatred?'

'Quite. He is an ambitious and self-important man with designs on pretty much everything anyone else has. Even his half-brother, the king.

'Naturally, he and de Sauveloy smile and simper with one another, but their ambitions are in conflict. They would throw the other off a cliff if they got near enough.

'De Sauveloy is happy to be the power behind the throne. I suspect his ultimate ambition is to make the throne do exactly as he wants.

'Odo wants to be the throne, and he doesn't want anyone behind it.'

'Odo would rebel against William?' Hermitage whispered the awful idea.

'No. William is too strong, and there is some loyalty between them. I suspect Odo is helping himself to bits of the kingdom under William's nose, though. Which may come back to bite him.'

'Hence Haimo and the land,' Hermitage nodded.

'You have it. Although what he thinks the Conclave is going to do about it, I have no idea.'

Both men sat in silence for a moment and pondered the flames. Aethelric drew his robe about him.

'Would you like another log on the fire?'

'Ah, yes, Brother, thank you.'

Hermitage stood, braved the furnace blast of the fire, and put a new log on top, retreating quickly before his habit started to char. As he did so, he knew that he could confide fully in Aethelric. The conversation they had shared gave him confidence that this was a man to be trusted.

'I heard something,' he said as he sat again.

'Oh, yes?' Aethelric asked as if this was going to be an interesting comment on the code of Alfred.

'While I was outside.'

The bishop raised his eyebrows.

'I got out of Leudric's way while he was preparing the chamber and took a brief stroll around the castle.'

Aethelric's face said he thought this a most peculiar thing to do but said nothing.

'And around the back of the building, there is a window, rather high in the wall.

'Well, I just happened to be passing it by when I overheard voices.' Hermitage didn't want the bishop to think he was in the habit of listening at windows.

'Voices, eh?'

'Loud voices. Two of them. One issued an instruction of sorts. "Of course, it can be done," it said. Another then added "And during the Conclave." It seemed clear they were talking to a third person, who I could not hear.'

'How very interesting,' Aethelric said with a thoughtful look. 'Men, yes?'

'Yes, two men. Although I don't know who the third might have been. Of course, they could have been discussing something entirely innocent.'

'And this was recently?'

'Just before I came to see you.'

'An early hour for loud discussion.'

'It might have been about some arrangement?' Hermitage suggested hopefully. 'You know, more tables and chairs, that sort of thing.'

'It might. It might indeed. Then again, it might not. A room with a window is unlikely to be allocated to a servant or some functionary.' He looked around his own room. 'I despise windows,' he explained mischievously. 'They let in the draught.'

'What shall I do?' Hermitage suddenly felt in league with Aethelric. It was wonderful to have someone else to talk with about this sort of thing. Wat and Cwen were marvellous, obviously, but Cwen's reaction was usually to ask him to do something bold and dangerous, and Wat's was to do whatever was easiest.

Aethelric pursed his lips. 'I think we need to find out whose room it is.'

'Ah,' Hermitage saw that would be a great step forward. 'I could ask.'

Aethelric shook his head quickly. 'Don't ask Leudric. We know he is de Sauveloy's man and this must be kept from him.'

'Lord Gilbert? He is a helpful and honest man.'

Aethelric shook his head once more. 'He is, as you say, honest and helpful. I would rather not drag him into this if there is no need.'

'Then?'

Aethelric said nothing but raised his eyebrows in an encouraging manner.

Hermitage breathed out heavily. 'I have to go through the castle until I find the right room, and by some means discover who it belongs to. All without them knowing I am trying to find out who it belongs to.'

Bishop Aethelric smiled and nodded.

He might as well have asked Cwen.

Caput X: Use Your Loaf

The victualler very quickly realised that the only way he was going to get rid of these two was to help them get into the servants' hall.

He remembered them from the last time they had been here, and that had been a very unpleasant experience. If he didn't want another one, he needed them out of here.

The woman nagged and pestered him, while the man kept suggesting Lord Gilbert needed a tapestry, and perhaps he could put in a word.

Why they wanted to get into the servants' hall, he did not know, and he did not want to know. He was sure that they were up to no good, but better that they were up to no good somewhere else.

A fresh delivery of loaves from the baker had to be taken up, and at least it would save him the bother.

For some reason, they wanted to wear smocks on top of their clothes, sprinkle themselves with flour and put on floppy hats.

As long as they left soon, they could sprinkle themselves with whatever they wanted.

Laden with sacks of loaves he pushed the two of them out of the door and closed it behind them. If they came back, he wouldn't be in.

Working their way up to the main castle, Wat and Cwen were confident of their disguises.

'Nothing like a baker for a bit of gossip,' Cwen said as they approached the front door.

'Put the sack on your shoulder,' Wat instructed. 'In case we bump into anyone we know.'

Cwen did so. 'And asks why Wat the Weaver has taken up

bakery?'

They grunted at the guards they passed, who gave them some odd looks but did nothing to halt their progress.

Once at the main entrance, Wat pushed at the door, which helpfully opened for him, as someone was coming out.

He couldn't see who it was as the sack on his shoulder was obstructing his view, but the awkward so-and-so didn't get out of the way. Wat was about to give him a stern word, and probably a rude one.

'What's this?' Le Pedvin asked as he unhelpfully closed the door behind him.

Hopefully, he couldn't hear them swallowing behind a sack of bread.

'Loaves, sir, for the castle, sir,' Wat said in a rather poor impression of the baker of Derby, who had a deep, gravelly voice.

'I'm sure they are,' Le Pedvin agreed. 'But they don't come in the front door, do they?'

The "do they?" was not a polite enquiry.

'Ar, no sir,' Wat said.

'We're new,' Cwen explained in a high-pitched tone that wasn't really an impression of anyone.

'New bakers?' Le Pedvin didn't seem to understand that.

'Oh, not new bakers sir, been baking for years, haven't we, erm, Theklun?'

'Oh, that's right sir,' Wat agreed. 'Years and years of baking. Very experienced bakers, me and erm, Eowyn.'

'Eowyn and Theklun the bakers, they call us,' Cwen helpfully explained.

'I imagine they would,' Le Pedvin observed. 'So, why are you new?'

'Erm, new to the castle, sir,' Cwen explained. 'We usually

bake for the town sir, but we got word of a big gathering.' She sounded very impressed by a big gathering.

'That's right, sir,' Wat confirmed. 'Very big gathering.'

'That needed extra loaves,' Cwen continued. 'Well, what with us being such experienced bakers, having done it for years and years, we thought we'd see if there was need for our bread. And what would you know, there was.'

Le Pedvin took an alarming step forward and pulled open the sack on Wat's shoulder. He took out a loaf and considered it.

'Compliments of Eowyn and Theklun the bakers,' Wat said.

'I don't want a loaf of bread. I'm simply checking that two idiots like you really are bakers. I certainly wouldn't trust you with a hot oven.'

'Very kind, sir, I'm sure.'

Le Pedvin checked the loaf and seemed satisfied. 'Now take them through the kitchen door on the side.'

'Oh, kitchen door,' Cwen confirmed. 'Yes, that'd be best.' she turned to the left.

'It's that way,' Le Pedvin pointed to the right. 'If you're such well-known local bakers, how come you don't know where the kitchen door to the castle is?'

Even through the sack of loaves, they could feel his stare upon them.

'Oh, we've never been lucky enough to have business with the castle, sir,' Cwen said.

'A bit of a dream, it was,' Wat went on. 'Business with the castle and all the important people. And now there's the gathering. Well, we want to make a good impression.'

'You're not doing a very good job.'

Wat hoped that his sack of loaves wasn't shaking as Le

Pedvin came close once more. He wondered whether they should run if he identified them, but thought there was no point.

He imagined that people who ran away from Le Pedvin stopped running quite quickly anyway, precisely because they got his point in the middle of their back.

Perhaps a simple confession would do. After all, they were trying to find out what de Sauveloy was up to, which should be of interest.

Just as the possible fatal moment arrived, the door to the castle opened again and Le Pedvin turned away.

'Lord Gilbert,' he said. 'Going out again?'

'Ah, yes,' Gilbert replied. 'Some, erm, business has come up in one of the villages.'

'Business seems to come up every day,' Le Pedvin observed.

'Ah, well, the trials of lordship, eh?'

'Today the Conclave starts. Do you have no one else you can send? Anyone would think you were trying to avoid the whole thing.'

'Oh, heavens no. Great disappointment and all that.'

'Well, perhaps you can help with these Saxons, who say they are bakers.'

'Eowyn and Theklum,' Wat said.

'I thought you were Eowyn and Theklun?' Le Pedvin asked.

'It's all the same sir,' Wat said quickly. 'You know Saxon, eh?' And he tutted that the language couldn't make up its mind between m and n.

'Can you vouch for them?'

'Me?' Gilbert asked with some surprise. 'I don't really have much to do with bakers. The victualler deals with all that.'

'Have you seen them about the place? They say they don't

deliver to the castle, but with all the time you spend away from it, you might have come across them.'

'Why do you think they aren't bakers?'

'I don't know exactly. They're just odd.'

Gilbert must have thought this was a peculiar request but was probably willing to do anything to keep Le Pedvin happy.

He stepped from the gate and came down to Wat. He bent forward and looked under the hat. And barely stopped himself jumping backwards.

'Oh,' he said.

'They are bakers?' Le Pedvin asked.

Wat couldn't see Le Pedvin's face, but there was something very worrying about his tone.

'Bakers, erm,' Gilbert hesitated and turned back to Le Pedvin.

'They would have to be bakers, wouldn't they?' The way Le Pedvin said this made Wat consider taking up the trade if it would get them out of here. 'Coming into the castle like this.'

'Oh, erm, yes. Have to be, I suppose,' Gilbert agreed, although he didn't sound at all sure. There was a horrible pause that Wat didn't really want to think about. 'Just wasn't expecting to see Thek, erm...'

'Lun,' Wat prompted.

'Yes. Not expecting to see Theklun up here. What with him baking mainly in the er...'

'Town,' Wat hissed

'Town,' Gilbert said.

'So, they are definitely bakers?'

'Oh, yes. They've got the bread, see?'

'Hm. Very well. You can carry on. This time.'

'Thank you, sir,' Cwen piped, and the two of them quickly

headed off in the direction of the kitchen door.

'Do you know,' Gilbert said as they went. 'I think you may be right. I am neglecting my duties as host of the Conclave. Perhaps I had better stay here and let the village sort itself out. It's more important that I attend my duties and make everyone welcome.'

'Good idea,' Le Pedvin said, congratulating Gilbert on getting the answer to this one right.

'Great Gods that was close,' Wat said when they got inside the castle and dropped the sacks.

'If he'd looked, he'd have got us for sure,' Cwen agreed, bending double and breathing deeply.

'Man like him probably doesn't look at bakers. Lucky for us.'

'Oy,' a voice shouted. 'What do you think you're doing?'

'Oh, Lord, what now?' Cwen sighed.

'Important people got to eat that bread you dung buckets. It's no good if you throw it all over the floor, is it?'

A very angry-looking woman strode over to them and stopped a couple of feet away with her hands on her hips.

The kitchen door was well-named as it had opened straight into the large room that doubtless fed the whole castle.

A huge fire blazed in a hearth big enough for a small crowd to walk into and not get burnt. Pots and pans hung all around the place, some on griddles close by the heat, others on hooks waiting to be used. A whole pig turned on a roasting iron, operated by a boy who was half the size of the pig.

The woman who confronted them was dressed as a cook, so they assumed she was a cook. From her demeanour, it was safe to assume that she was *the* cook. An apron covered her from neck to ankle, below which, sturdy wooden clogs clipped the floor.

She was of no great age, perhaps thirty or so, but her face had been contorted for so long, by so much anger, that it was hard to judge.

She had the red complexion of someone who spent most of their time in front of a fire, and the apron was painted with so many stains of various hues, that it would probably make a good meal on its own.

Her hair was tied back on her head so tight that it was probably being punished for something.

If this was like any other great kitchen, she would have to spend a lot of her time shouting very loudly at people to get them to do what they already knew they had to do.

Then she would shout at them for not doing it the way she would have done it, having not told them what that was in the first place.

She clearly had to spend a lot of her time angry, but was the sort of person who naturally spent all her time very angry. And now, she couldn't get any more angry because she had reached capacity.

Everyone around her had got used to the constant level of anger, so didn't take it as seriously as they should. Which only made her angry.

Wat smiling at her did not help her mood.

'Bread from the victualler,' Wat said.

'I know what it is,' the woman shouted. 'I have not been a cook all these years not to recognise a loaf of bread when I see one. What I do not want to see is a loaf of bread on the floor.

'Now, pick them up, wipe them off and take them to the hall.'

'Erm, right you are,' Cwen tried to sound helpful.

'What?' the woman screamed to the roof.

'She means, yes, cook,' Wat said. 'You have to say "yes, cook", to them,' he hissed at Cwen.

'Why?'

'Don't know,' Wat said quietly as he picked up the fallen loaves. 'I think it's like an importance thing. Once you get to be in charge of the kitchen, people have to say "Yes, cook."'

'Hm.' Cwen did not look as if she would be saying, "Yes, cook", very often.

The cook released a roar of fury, threw her hands in the air, turned on her heels and left, muttering obscenities about bakers.

'I don't think we'll ask her to find out what's going on,' Wat suggested as they put the loaves back in the sacks and looked around to see which way the hall might be.

'Oh, I don't know,' Cwen replied. 'If anything odd was going on, she'd probably get very angry about it.'

'Which she wouldn't notice from the rest of the time she was very angry.'

With the sacks now secured, they moved across the room towards a door that they'd spotted on the far side. On the way, they passed a young man with a mop and leather bucket, who was clearing up something or other. Whatever had been spilled didn't look very appetising.

'You've met the cook, then?' he observed.

'Nice woman,' Cwen replied.

'You should see her when she's angry.'

'There seems to be a lot going on,' Wat said. 'Enough to annoy anyone, I suppose.'

'Not having anything to be annoyed about annoys her,' the fellow, who was not much more than a boy replied. 'That the bread, then?' he asked.

'Erm,' Wat looked at the sack full of bread that he held.

'Yes, this would be the bread.'

'Thought so,' the lad nodded as if he had imparted great knowledge to the conversation.

'Would you like a bit?' Cwen asked quietly.

'Love some,' he replied longingly. 'But it'd be more than my life's worth.'

'Oh, I'm sure we can slip you a bit.' Cwen fiddled about and broke off a piece of one of the loaves. Holding it close, she looked around and held it out low for the boy, who took it and quickly hid it away.

'What's going on, then?' Wat asked. 'We were only visiting the victualler, and he's got us delivering bread.'

'Oh, it's a great gathering.'

'Is that right?'

'It is. Lots of important people, we've been told. Got to be doing our best for everyone or there'll be hell to pay.'

'Ah.'

'Mind you, when Lord Gilbert's here on his own and he just wants a bit of cold meat, there's hell to pay. You get used to it.'

'Been strangers about, then, erm?' Cwen said asking the lad's name.

'Bladdon,' he replied. 'Place is full of 'em.'

'I'm erm,'

'Eowyn,' Wat reminded her.

'That's right. I'm Eowyn and this is Theklun. We bumped into some horrible Norman outside, and had to tell him we were bakers from town.'

'And it's full of horrible Normans,' Bladdon complained. 'Seems to have been for weeks.'

'Weeks, eh?' Wat asked with interest. 'The victualler said this gathering isn't going on for long, and some fellow, oh, what did he say his name was? Leudric, that's it, Leudric had only been here for a few days?'

Bladdon frowned a little at this question.

'Causing trouble, of course,' Wat scoffed. 'Like they all do. And him a Saxon, as well.'

'He's the head complainer, as far as I can tell. "Not this way round, not over here, not that colour," drives you to distraction, he does.'

'But you've had to put up with some even before him?' Cwen sounded sympathetic.

'Oh, Gods yes. There was an even worse one here a while back. Nasty piece of work he was.'

'What did he do?'

'Nothing.'

'Nothing? Doesn't sound too nasty.'

'Didn't say much, didn't order anyone around, just drifted through the place like some evil spirit. Even put the fear of God up Lord Gilbert, and that man's scared of nothing.'

'Except Ranulph de Sauveloy,' Wat muttered very quietly. 'So, he's been here already.'

'Was this a very well-dressed Norman, tall, and looked at everyone as if whatever they were doing, they were doing it wrong?' Cwen asked.

'That's the one.' Bladdon recognised the description immediately. 'I've never been more ashamed of my own mop. You don't know him, do you?'

'Come across him,' Wat said. 'He's called Ranulph de Sauveloy.'

Bladdon nodded. 'Aye, I heard that name.'

'What was he doing here so long before the gathering?'

'How should I know? As far as I could tell it was like some inspection. Is this de Sauveloy more important than Gilbert?'

'Friend of the king,' Wat confided.

'Close friend,' Cwen added.

Bladdon shook his head, appalled that anyone could be a close friend of the king.

'So, you just get him out of your hair and Leudric turns up.' Cwen sympathised with the burden that had been put upon Bladdon.

'Oh, he was just the start. We had that Haimo arrive soon after. And he's one I wouldn't trust with the slops from my bucket.'

'Really?'

'Always looking at things as if he's deciding what to do with them, you know the type?'

'Even if they don't belong to him, yes, I've met a few,' Wat agreed.

'And the rest been coming ever since. I just hope they go quickly when all this is over.' Bladdon frowned for a moment. 'What do you want to know all this for, anyway?'

'You can never know too much, can you?' Wat said.

Bladdon didn't look at all sure about that.

'When it comes to Normans and who's who. Which ones are going to be trouble and which not.'

'We wouldn't want to get on the wrong side of the wrong one,' Cwen explained. She broke off and handed him another piece of bread.

'As you like.' Bladdon whipped the bread out of sight. 'But, if anyone asks, you heard nothing from me.'

'Absolutely not,' Wat confirmed with a serious nod. 'And if anyone asks who was asking, it wasn't us.'

Bladdon winked and returned to his mop.

'What are you still doing here?' The voice of the cook ripped through the air and assailed them. Even from a distance, it felt as if she was standing right next to them.

'Just cleaning the loaves with this mop and bucket,' Cwen called back, before pushing Wat quickly across the floor and out of the door.

Wat briefly wondered if the scream that followed them might have its uses in a kitchen. It probably frightened the rats away.

Caput XI: Search For The Room

Hermitage was trying to orientate himself inside the castle in order to understand where the chamber he had stood outside might be. It was not going well.

Several times, he had faced the front gate, or at least where he thought the front gate would be, and mentally paced through the building. As soon as he got to the back of the main hall, he was lost.

He decided that he would have to physically walk the place, keeping the location of his target in mind.

At least the servants, who busied themselves about the preparations for the Conclave, were happy to ignore the strange monk who kept walking up and down, muttering to himself.

Unfortunately, the location of the target kept moving or got dislodged by a sudden thought about something more interesting. Or less interesting.

Perhaps he should start from the back.

For heaven's sake, the place wasn't that big. He had found his way around the monastery of De'Ath's Dingle, eventually, after several weeks of regularly getting lost. And that place had been designed to sow confusion and disorientation in any who tried to tread its paths. If it had been designed at all and was not simply the result of a hideous catalogue of mistakes.

This was one room in one castle. It couldn't be that difficult.

He thought he was making quite good progress on one of his attempts when he came across something he was not prepared for; a stair. It hadn't occurred to him that the room he sought might be on a different level from the front gate.

Now he thought about it, the land outside did slope and perhaps that window had been up one level. Or was it down?

He recalled long discussions with his father, who had tried to explain how felled trees were built into the structure of a house. He got so far in understanding, but then the whole thing seemed to merge into one large mess of tree trunks going in every direction.

He'd concluded that his mind simply didn't work like that. If he had been given a written description, it would have been fine, but he could not do pictures in his head.

His father had muttered something about his mind not working at all but had been happy to come to his son when some missive arrived from the lord that he couldn't read.

That was it. Hermitage needed a quill and parchment and then he would write down his progress. Turn left, turn right, up, down. They all made sense as words, just not as pictures.

Of course, he might have made up some reason and simply asked a servant where the chambers were, but that seemed too open. He needed to know without anyone else knowing.

Now, all he had to do was find parchment and quill. And ink, and a desk.

The quill and ink in his chamber would have to do, and so he hurried off to get them; only briefly forgetting the way to his own room.

Once equipped, he returned to the main gate and set off afresh. This time, he wrote each change of direction on his hand, S for sinister and D for dexter. The Latin made it more accurate, somehow.

After only a short while, the back of his left hand was crowded with S's and D's, one after the other. He had started writing large letters but soon realised they needed to be a lot smaller.

He glanced at the wash of ink and letters crammed together and was relieved to see that it made perfect sense. It was obvious where he was. He just hoped no one would look at his hand and spot what he was up to.

He had now made it to the back of the castle, and the chambers that faced him must be the ones that looked out over the land to the rear.

The chamber with the window had been about halfway along the back wall, and so he paced until he thought he was in about the right spot.

There was still the question of up or down, and he had ignored two wooden staircases on his way here.

It was a shame that the Latin for up and down was sursum, deorsum, as more S's and D's on the back of his hand would only confuse the picture. Perhaps he should have used his right hand for elevation and his left for direction. But he had never been able to write well with his left hand.

'Can I help you, Brother?' A voice startled him from his reverie on the system of navigation he might just have invented.

'Oh, erm, no, thank you.' Hermitage saw that there was a servant in the corridor with him, and he had no idea where he had come from or how long he had been there. Had he been watching him for some time?

He was a neat and upright man, perhaps over forty years of age, who looked well-settled to his position, which must be of some reasonable significance, judging by the frank appraisal he was giving Hermitage.

'I used to get lost in my own monastery,' Hermitage joked, except, of course, it was true. 'And now that I am here for the Conclave, I am trying to find my way around. I seem to have confused myself already.' He hid his hands behind his back.

The servant didn't look convinced that anyone could get lost in a castle this small, but he wasn't about to contradict a member of the Conclave.

'The main hall is that way.' The servant pointed back the way Hermitage had come.

'Is it? Ah. Excellent. I believe my own chamber is in that direction as well.' He gave the doors nearby obvious scrutiny. 'These do not look familiar.'

The servant stood slightly straighter and had a look of pride about him. 'These are the chambers of Lord Gilbert himself, Lord Le Pedvin and Robert, Count of Mortain. I am their attendant, Rablan.'

'You attend three great men, Rablan.' Hermitage managed to comment without his voice breaking.

Lord Gilbert was fine, Le Pedvin gave him the shivers, but Robert was another pot of worms.

King William's own half-brother was almost as bad as having King William himself here.

Hermitage had never met the man, but he had met Odo and William, and a third along the same lines did not bear thinking about.

And Robert's reputation didn't bode well. A great leader, well-favoured by the king and strong in arms, was how the Normans described him.

A bad-tempered and particularly stupid Norman best avoided, was the Saxon version.

'Oh, er.' Rablan sagged a little. 'I, erm, attend the chambers, not the men.'

'Still a great responsibility.' Hermitage tried to drag his thoughts away from Robert.

'I am a simple Saxon monk, brought into the Conclave for reasons that even I am not sure about,' he confided. 'I am not used to mixing in such exalted company.'

He was grateful that he had met this man. The last thing he had wanted to do was enter some chamber surreptitiously, only to find Le Pedvin in there. He now knew that finding the Count of Mortain would be even worse.

The voices he had heard had not belonged to Gilbert or Le Pedvin though, so perhaps Robert of Mortain was the one he was looking for. Which was not something he wanted to think about.

Of course, he still wasn't sure he was even in the right place. He needed to see into the rooms to check that they had windows, and which was the precise one. He could hardly do that with this servant watching him.

'I imagine their rooms have to be of the highest standard.' Hermitage complimented the man on his duties.

'Indeed,' Rablan agreed. 'Most of the castle servants were found wanting by Master Leudric, but I kept my place.'

'Most commendable.' Hermitage was feeling distinctly nervous as he led the man on. 'Although, I have met Lord Le Pedvin before, and he is a man of Spartan tastes.'

'He's a what?'

'Oh, sorry, they were Greeks., Well, they were Spartans, which was a sort of Greek. But they led a simple and perhaps harsh life. No comforts or indulgences, if you see what I mean.'

Rablan did not look convinced.

'So, I imagine Lord Le Pedvin's chamber is a simple one. No luxuries, like, say windows, or anything?'

'He has a window,' Rablan said very slowly, looking as if he would rather not be in a corridor at the back of the castle, alone with a monk who talked about Greeks and windows.

'All the chambers here have windows.' Rablan smiled and

relaxed as he seemed to realise what was going on here.

'Does your chamber not have a window?' he asked.

'Erm, well, no, as a matter of fact.'

'And you want to move to a better one.'

'Oh, no, I wouldn't dream...,'

'I quite understand, but don't know what I can do,' Rablan apologised.

'I assure you...,' Hermitage did not want this fellow to think he was some prideful monk who thought his chamber was not good enough for him. Or who sought to use his position to better his conditions. Still, if it could get him into one of these chambers, the deceit might be worth it.

He inwardly castigated himself for such appalling behaviour.

'We're full, you see,' Rablan explained. 'It's the Conclave. 'Even the important servants have had to give up their rooms and start sharing.' It was clear that Rablan was one of them.

'We've had stores turned into chambers, would you believe? We haven't got a single thing with a window left. Where's your chamber at the moment?'

'Oh, erm, over to the east, I think. Above the kitchen.'

'Hm. They are a bit small over there. Still, at least you get the warmth from the fire below.'

'Oh, it is quite comfortable, I assure you.'

'If you can sleep through the cook shouting, of course,' the man winked.

'Aha,' Hermitage smiled, not having a clue what he was talking about.

Rablan now looked surreptitiously up and down the corridor, in the way people do when they are about to make an offer they shouldn't be making. 'Do you want to have a look?'

'Have a look?'

'At one of the chambers? They're the best in the castle.'

'Oh, I'm not sure I should,' Hermitage managed to say, instead of "Yes please". 'After all, the occupants might not be happy.'

'Oh, they're all out. Le Pedvin's off walking about the place, as he does. Lord Gilbert's gone for the day and Count Mortain is in private conference somewhere or other.'

'Oh, well.' Hermitage tried to sound as if he was secretly keen to engage in this little act of misbehaviour. Never having been keen to engage in misbehaviour at all before, he wasn't sure what he was supposed to sound like.

'Come on, then.' Rablan tipped his head knowingly.

He led over to a door on his right.

'Chamber servant,' he called as he pushed the door open.

He turned to Hermitage. 'You have to call that out before you go in, in case they don't want to be disturbed.'

Hermitage thought about this. 'Wouldn't it be better to knock, call it out and then wait to be invited in?'

Rablan frowned at this as if it was a most peculiar suggestion. 'They're all out anyway.'

'Do they not have personal servants?' Hermitage asked as they entered the room.

'If they're wanted, they're with their masters. If not, they're off lazing somewhere near the victuallers ale or the cook's food. Not that anyone lazes near the cook out of choice.'

Hermitage was in the room now and it was a fine chamber of great comfort. Clearly, this one wasn't Le Pedvin's.

A large cot stood against the wall to the left, covered with heavy cloth and looking as if a feather mattress lay underneath. Despite his devotion to the simple life, Hermitage wondered what it would be like to sleep on.

At the end of the bed, three comfortable chairs sat with a table between them. The occupant of this room would be able to carry on all their business without leaving.

And opposite the door was a window. It was hung with a heavy drape, which had been pulled to one side to let the light in, and was not a large opening, but it was there.

'It is most impressive,' Hermitage said, wandering into the space. 'And you look after all of this?'

'Oh, yes. It's one of the better duties in the castle.'

'And whose room is this one?' Hermitage made a point of wandering nonchalantly over towards the window.

'Count Mortain. Lord Gilbert's is down the way, and, as you say, Lord Le Pedvin's is a bit different.'

'In what way?'

'He had the feather mattress taken away.'

'Aha.' Hermitage had now made it to the window and, as if fascinated by the fact that windows could be looked out of, leant out.

Considering the ground below, he quickly realised that this was not the right window. The one he had been under was next along to his right.

He thought that he had done so well thus far, but now he was going to have to get Rablan to reveal who was in which room.

Treating the fellow in this manner really was not the way to behave. Deceit about his reason for being in the corridor in the first place, feigning interest in getting a better room. It was all disgraceful.

Did the ends justify the means, though? He would only find out when he reached the ends, by which time it would be too late to apologise.

'Being next door to one another must be a convenience. All

three important people able to meet easily.'

Rablan seemed to scoff at that idea. 'Between you and I, Lord Gilbert is doing his best to avoid everything and everyone. I don't think he wanted the Conclave here in the first place and will be glad when it's gone.

'He's out first thing in the morning and doesn't come back until night.

'Lord Le Pedvin isn't interested in anyone. He just prowls about and looks disappointed that he hasn't got someone to do battle with.'

'And Count Mortain?'

'Too important for any of them, what with being the king's own blood.'

And he was the man in prime position to be involved in whatever it was was going on. He would know de Sauveloy well and was an important figure to even be at the Conclave.

But it had not been his window from which Hermitage had heard the voices, there was no doubt of that.

And, being Robert of Mortain, Hermitage imagined he did not go to other peoples' chambers. They came to him.

'We had better leave,' Hermitage said. 'I wouldn't want the count to return and find us in his chamber.'

Rablan nodded at this. 'I'd be all right, but I suppose he might ask what a monk was doing. Blessing the room, perhaps?'

That seemed an odd thing for anyone to do, so Hermitage quickly got back to the door and Rablan shut it behind them.

'Le Pedvin that way?' Hermitage asked idly. 'Robert of Mortain in the middle and Gilbert next door. What a corridor.'

'Aye,' Rablan agreed with pride.

'And who has the next room? Another worthy personage, I

imagine?' Hermitage nodded to the door which would lead to the window he wanted.

'We're not going in there,' Rablan was suddenly serious, even a little scared.

'No, no, of course not. We have already seen one chamber. And I thank you for that.'

'You don't want to go in that one,' Rablan cautioned. 'Even I don't want to go in that one, but I have to.' The man swallowed and looked suddenly quite pale.

That was interesting. If the occupant of the chamber that most interested Hermitage, was a worrisome individual, identifying them and the nature of their business, might be reasonably straightforward. Awkward, but straightforward.

'Whose is it?' Hermitage dropped his voice to a whisper.

'It's,' Rablan almost sobbed. 'The Lady Aveline.'

Caput XII: Bakers On the Prowl

'Well, well,' Wat said when they were safe in the main hall. 'De Sauveloy has been here already, eh? The question is, what did he come to do?'

'Not make sure that the castle was still here,' Cwen answered. 'He was setting something up.'

'And only after he's done that, do we get a message that Hermitage is appointed to the Conclave.'

'Oop, hats down,' Wat said quickly. 'Leudric on the march.'

Leudric was plainly distracted as he fussed about the tables and chairs that were now set up in the main hall.

This was obviously going to be a great council. A rectangle of tables filled the space, with at least twenty identical chairs set all around. A small gap down near the main gate to the hall allowed access to the centre space.

Where anyone had managed to get so many identical chairs was a good question, but kings probably had that sort of thing.

In the centre of the rectangle, a single table was set with seating for two people, who would look down the hall. Probably the officials, attending to the needs of the Conclave and taking any record. This would be Leudric's spot, no doubt, but his main attention was currently on the seating for the Conclave members.

He was going to each chair in turn, after it had been put carefully in place by a servant. He then moved it half an inch one way or another, in or out, before looking at it, and then moving it again, back to where it had been in the first place.

The rolling eyes of servants were almost a tide in the room, as he followed them around, undoing their work, and then doing it again.

At each place around the table a fine goblet was placed, doubtless to be filled by servants who would loiter in the room, waiting to be called. Leudric moved each of these by a tiny amount.

'I think he'd only notice us if we moved a chair out of place,' Cwen said, but she did keep her head low.

To prove her right, Leudric glanced up at that moment.

'Is that the bread? Where has it been? Well, don't loiter there, put it out, put it out.'

Wat and Cwen looked around to try and see where this bread was supposed to be put.

'On the table.' Leudric pointed to a table set against the back wall and issued his instruction as if they knew this perfectly well, and were simply being lazy and difficult.

'Right you are, sir,' Wat said in his Derby baker voice.

They moved over to the table and started taking the loaves out of the sacks and putting them out.

'Not like that,' Leudric now called in despair that anyone could put loaves on a table so badly. 'A neat row of loaves across the front. For heaven's sake. What sort of bakers are you?'

Wat was sorely tempted to tell him, but he put a hand up in acknowledgement of his instructions.

'Then leave the sacks under the table. The Conclave staff will put more out as and when they are needed.' He watched them from across the room for a moment to make sure that they had got the measure of this tricky task.

'Then you can be gone,' he instructed. 'And quick about it.'

Cwen took her time arranging the loaves on the table, tipping her head over at each one and moving it so that it lined up with its neighbour. If she had one whose shape didn't quite suit the overall design, she exchanged it for one from the sack.

By the time she had done this and got six loaves in a pleasing pattern, Leudric had turned his attention to a slovenly servant who had put three of the goblets on the wrong side of the seating position.

He seemed to find it staggering that anyone could be so stupid and still be able to walk and talk.

His worries elsewhere, Wat and Cwen looked around the room.

'We need a castle servant,' Cwen said. 'I think a lot of these have been brought in just for the Conclave.'

'I know,' Wat agreed. 'Don't even know how to arrange bread,' he tutted.

Cwen ignored him. 'Someone who would have been here when de Sauveloy came visiting and might know what he was up to.'

'Why did Gilbert not mention that de Sauveloy had already been?' Wat asked.

'To be fair, we didn't ask him, so it may well be worth finding him now. But, if de Sauveloy was up to no good, he'd hardly have given himself away to Gilbert. A servant would be much more use.'

'De Sauveloy considering them worthless and invisible,' Wat said.

'Quite. But who?'

'We've already ruled out the cook.'

'God, yes.'

'The mop boy?'

Wat shook his head. 'I don't think Ranulph de Sauveloy would need mopping up after.'

'You know,' Cwen said thoughtfully. 'If I were a castle

servant and someone had moved in to organise everything while telling me I was doing it wrong, I'd keep out of the way.'

'Hide, you mean?'

'Exactly. It looks like Leudric's brought in more than enough servants to sort out the Conclave. And we know that the master of the castle is doing his best to avoid the whole thing.'

'So, his staff follow his lead.'

Cwen nodded. 'We just need to find where they've gone.'

Two young women approached at that moment and stood at either end of the bread table.

'Problem?' Wat asked.

'Of course,' one of the women replied with an obvious irritation, which at least didn't seem directed at them. 'This table's half a foot too far to the left, isn't it?'

'Is it?'

'Should be obvious to anyone.' The woman did quite a good impression of the person who had issued the instruction.

'Leudric,' Wat said.

'Who else? Sooner this thing's over, the better. Next, he'll be wanting the castle turned around because it faces in slightly the wrong direction.'

'You work here?' Cwen asked.

'Me? No. I was minding my own business in town when the Normans turned up and told me I was a castle servant for the week.'

'Still, I expect the pay's good,' Cwen said.

The woman's look said that she did not find that at all funny.

'Where have all the castle's own servants gone?' Wat asked.

'Cleared off, most of them. Or hiding somewhere,' the woman snorted. 'Knew what was coming and left us to it. Of course, Leudric didn't help turning up with us lot and telling them they were useless.'

'Is there no one left?' Wat asked. 'No one to check Leudric isn't taking the place apart?'

'Oh, God, don't put ideas in his head. I think Lord Gilbert's own man is loitering around the place, but no one else comes near.'

'What does he look like?'

'What do you want to know for?' The woman now considered them with some suspicion.

'Want to make sure we get paid for the bread. The victualler's being difficult.'

'Why does that not surprise me? Alan, he's called. He's an old boy. Grey hair, but not much of it. Thin as a slice of sky.'

'Thank you. We could put in a word for you, erm?' Wat enquired for her name.

'God, no thank you. I never want to come here again. In fact, I'm thinking of moving to Derby. I've heard they don't have a Norman lord looking down on them.'

'They've got Wat the Weaver,' Wat said brightly.

'Oh, yes, that's a point. Perhaps not Derby, then. Oh, look out. He's on the prowl again. Probably noticed that the ceiling's too high.' The woman and her companion departed quickly.

'We better get out of sight,' Cwen said as she pulled Wat away.

They were only just in time as Leudric passed by the bread table, noticed the arrangement, tutted and started moving the loaves into their proper positions.

Once out of sight of the hall, in a small corridor to the

right. They stopped and took stock.

'How do we find a grey-haired man who is probably doing his best not to be spotted?' Cwen asked.

'But a grey-haired man who needs to keep an eye on what's being done to his castle.' Wat stepped back to the end of the corridor and scanned the room from the safety of his hiding place, Leudric having turned back to defects with the layout of the tables now.

'Up there,' Wat said, pointing to a corner of the chamber, where the roof timbers joined the wall. Built into the structure, there appeared to be a small gallery of some sort. Perhaps only big enough for one or two people, it looked inaccessible.

'What is it?' Cwen asked.

'Somewhere to defend the keep floor from, I suppose. If your enemy gets through the door, you can go up there and throw things at them.'

Cwen turned and spotted another one on the opposite corner.

'Typical Normans,' she said as if this was a despicable sort of thing to build into your castle.

'Nice spot to watch from,' Wat observed. 'All we've got to do is find our way up there.'

The corridor they were in seemed the best place to start, and so they moved back. Looking to see if there was a stair or ladder.

'There is an upper level,' Cwen said. 'Perhaps you go down into the gallery, rather than up.'

'That would make sense,' Wat agreed. 'Stop the enemy climbing the ladder and throwing things at you.'

The staircase that led to the upper chambers was in the back left corner of the hall, which meant they would have to cross it to get there. Which meant risking Leudric's gaze once more.

They came back to the edge of the corridor and looked out again.

'Do you know,' Cwen said. 'There is someone up there.' She nodded to the gallery opposite. 'I can see something moving.'

'That'd be him, then. Now, how do we get across the hall?'

'Dress as carpenters come to move the staircase?'

'Very helpful.' Wat thought about it for a moment. 'We just walk over looking confident.'

'Really?' Cwen was not convinced.

'Always works. If you behave like you know what you're doing, people will believe you know what you're doing.'

'Even Leudric?'

Wat hesitated. 'Well, maybe not him. He doesn't seem to think anyone knows what they're doing.'

'And why are bakers going upstairs? It's not usually where you keep the bread.'

Helpfully, one of the servants moving things around for about the tenth time, chose that moment to drop one of the goblets.

Leudric's flight across the room seemed almost magical as he descended on the site of the disaster.

'Quick,' Cwen urged.

They stepped across the hall and onto the stairs. They both thought that running would be too risky, as Leudric seemed able to see anything unusual out of the back of his head.

Once on the upper floor, it didn't take a moment to locate the entrance to the gallery.

A small opening in the corridor, through which Wat had

to duck, went down two steps onto a wooden platform, enclosed by rails and planks.

Cwen squeezed in behind him, and with the grey-haired fellow who was already there sitting on a stool, there wasn't much room at all.

'Hello,' the man said, as if delighted to have company.

'Alan?' Wat asked.

'I am,' Alan confirmed happily.

'Lord Gilbert's man.'

'The very same.'

'And taking care of several flagons of Lord Gilbert's wine, by the look of it.' Wat raised his eyebrows at Cwen and she leant forward.

'Phew,' she said. 'It smells like a tavern in here. How much have you had?'

'As much as I please,' Alan replied, the slur in his voice now being obvious, along with its cause. He pointed down towards the floor of the hall. 'And he can't tell me otherwise.' His gaze followed his pointing and he suddenly looked confused about what his finger was doing out there. He drew it back.

'Leudric,' Cwen noted.

'Bloody Leudric.' Alan tried to spit, but couldn't manage it. He took a swig of wine from the goblet he clutched instead.

'Seems like you and Lord Gilbert have been displaced.'

'Coming in here, telling me how to run my own household. And all because the king wants a con cave.'

'Conclave,' Wat corrected.

'Pardon?'

'It's a conclave. The Standing Conclave.'

'Is it?' Alan said with interest, nodding his head as he considered this. 'So my suggestion that they should use one of the caves for it wasn't right, after all.' He sniggered at the memory.

'And Lord Gilbert is simply keeping away.'

'It's all right for him. I can't take a horse and ride out all day, can I?'

'I suppose not.'

'And I can't bring one in here,' Alan giggled again. 'Wouldn't fit.'

'Erm, yes. We were actually wondering about someone else who came earlier.' Cwen was obviously keen to get on.

Alan looked as if he was struggling to focus his eyes on them.'What? Other bakers?'

'No, not other bakers. De Sauveloy. Ranulph de Sauveloy.'

Alan almost choked. 'What did you bring him up for? That's not nice, is it?'

'He was here?'

'Oh, he was here, all right.' Alan looked at his goblet with a haunted gaze, as if all the wine in the world couldn't eradicate that memory.

'What did he want?'

'What did he want? What did Ranulph de Sauveloy want? Who knows what that man wants. If man he is, and not some crawling thing from the depths.'

'All right,' Cwen sighed. 'What did he do? When he was here?'

'Crept about.'

'Crept about?'

'All over the place. Here, there, everywhere. In my kitchen, my hall, my chambers. Stuck his nose everywhere.'

'Did you get any idea why?'

'He said the mighty con cave was coming. That was it, wasn't it?'

'Yes, that's right. Con cave,' Cwen indulged him.

'And he said everything had to be just right.'

'Isn't that Leudric's job?' Wat asked.

'I didn't know that at the time, did I? I didn't know worse was to come.'

'Leudric worse than de Sauveloy?'

'Well, not worse, exactly,' Alan admitted. 'Just not quite so bad, but in a different way.'

'And de Sauveloy checked every room?' Cwen confirmed.

'He did. He had me show him everything, then he tells me to get back to my duties while he goes round on his own.'

'Not even with Lord Gilbert?'

'Lord Gilbert's a fine man,' Alan slurred on. 'As brave as some lions. Face anything, he would.'

'Well, that's good.'

'But he was hiding from de Sauveloy.'

'Hiding?'

'Well, just had a lot on, you know. Busy with this and that.'

'I can understand,' Cwen said. 'We've met de Sauveloy ourselves.'

Alan considered them and shook his head slowly and sadly. 'Have a drink,' he offered.

'No, thanks. I think we need to find Lord Gilbert and have a word.'

Wat nodded. 'Try to find out what a great man like Ranulph de Sauveloy is doing checking that the rooms are in order.'

'It's a good question,' Alan said, although he didn't seem to know why it was a good question.

Wat nodded at Cwen that they could leave Alan to his lonely watch.

'You know,' Alan said as seriously as he could manage.

'What?'

'If I keep drinking wine, I'm going to be sick.'

'I wouldn't be at all surprised,' Cwen said.

Alan pointed downward with a crooked smile on his face. 'All over his nice clean floor.'

Caput XIII: The Conclave Begins

Rablan's mood had waned considerably at the mention of Aveline's name, and he escorted Hermitage away from the fine chambers.

'It'll be time for the Conclave procession, soon,' he said quite abruptly. 'I must have everything ready.'

'Ah, of course,' Hermitage agreed, this being the first he had heard of a conclave procession.

He would return to Aethelric with news of the chamber, and find out what was going on.

None of the voices he had heard by that window had been Aveline's, he was sure of that. Of course, there was no telling whether she was in the chamber at the time or not, but even the low, indistinguishable individual had been a man.

But the connection to Aveline might provide an alternative explanation for the words he had heard. It was quite possible that she wanted something done and had instructed others accordingly. She frequently wanted something done and almost always instructed others.

The "it" that could be done during the Conclave might be something harmless. Well, not harmless exactly, but more to do with Aveline's desires than some plot of de Sauveloy's.

From Gilbert's words, it was clear that the important folk at the Conclave had drawn her back to the castle and the life she hated, a hatred she had made clear on several occasions. Knowing her as he did, from the energetic criticism and complaint that she had directed towards him personally, he thought it would have to do with her station in life.

Being born the daughter of a fighting man had obviously been a great disappointment, but when Gilbert was made up to a lord, albeit a minor one, her status had lifted. Not far enough, obviously. Her self-organised departure to Paris was evidence of that.

The Conclave would give her the chance to move amongst more elevated people and might see her one step closer to her ambition, whatever that might be. A place in court, perhaps. Although Hermitage thought, unkindly, that Queen of the World wouldn't be enough for Aveline.

Had she simply been trying to organise introductions to the right people? A role in the Conclave itself? Her room was next to that of Robert, he would be a good connection to make.

It was interesting speculation, but there was still Ranulph de Sauveloy to worry about, and he was one who schemed and plotted in his sleep.

These musings were all very well, but he felt frustrated that nothing was certain.

He was quite pleased that he managed to find his way back to Bishop Aethelric's chamber, only getting lost twice.

He knocked on the door and was invited to enter.

Inside, Aethelric was standing in the middle of the room, while two attendants fussed about him, fiddling with the most magnificent robes. The bishop looked as if he was putting up with this with decreasing grace.

'All right, all right,' he said, waving his arms to swat the servants away as if they were flies buzzing around his head. 'That will do.'

'But the amice has shifted under the alb,' one man said with obvious irritation.

'I dare say it has, but that will not affect my deliberations, will it. Ah, Brother Hermitage.' The arrival was obviously a relief from being dressed.

The servant with the amice problem, tutted, sighed, shook

his head, and continued to fiddle with the clothing, despite the bishop's instructions.

'What wonderful robes,' Hermitage said.

'Oh, this old thing.' Aethelric held his arms out as if bored of the heavy robe, embroidered with gold, and edged with fine fur that hung from his neck to the floor.

The most delicate shoes peeped out from below, and Hermitage saw the bishop's mitre was on a chair, waiting for installation on the episcopal head.

'Stand still or the cope won't hang properly,' the one who seemed to be the chief dresser instructed.

'I don't want the cope,' Aethelric replied.

'You're not going out without your cope.'

Aethelric sighed, and Hermitage could see that the two men actually had quite a good relationship.

'Byrht here has been attending to me as long as I can remember.'

Byrht gave Hermitage a peremptory nod. 'And he's been trying to dress you properly for as long as he can remember.'

'What do I need a cope for, I'm not going outside?'

Byrht sighed and explained as if telling a pestering child why rain was wet. 'The Conclave is a formal occasion. You are processing into the formal occasion. When you process, you wear your cope. That's why you're wearing your cope.

'You are the Bishop of Selsey, you know, not some ignorant village priest.'

Aethelric rolled his eyes.

'And what's Brother Hermitage's business?' Byrht asked. 'We are in a bit of a rush here.'

'The Brother is a member of the Conclave.'

Byrht was behind Aethelric, adjusting the cope on his shoulder, and now leant around and looked Hermitage up and down.

The appraisal was not a comfortable one, and Hermitage felt horribly exposed for some reason.

'Is he going like that?' Byrht asked. The answer to this was in the man's question; he could not possibly go like that. No one could go like that.

'Well...,' Hermitage held his arms out slightly to consider his dress. 'I do have another habit,' he said. 'But it's just the same as this one.'

'Brother Hermitage is a monk,' Aethelric explained. 'He does not have to dress up like a peacock simply to walk into a room.'

'I know, but really.' Byrht was not at all happy and stood with his hand on his chin considering Hermitage. 'Tell you, what, I've got a spare maniple in the box, he can have that.'

'A spare maniple?' Aethelric asked. 'What have you got a spare maniple for?'

'I've got spare most things,' Byrht replied. 'And I don't know where we'd be if I didn't.' He went to a box by the bed, opened it and withdrew a length of material of the richest quality, finely embroidered and immaculately clean.

'I couldn't possibly,' Hermitage said.

'You wear it over your arm,' Byrht instructed brusquely.

'Yes, I know,' Hermitage replied, feeling a little irritation. 'And it should be worn for Mass, and by a priest. There is no Mass and I am not a priest.'

Aethelric sighed. 'I give my dispensation, Brother.' Aethelric's look said they had better do as Byrht suggested, or he'd never hear the end of it.

Reluctantly, Hermitage held out a hand for the garment.

Byrht ignored this, stepped over to Hermitage, pulled his right arm out in front of him and arranged the maniple over the forearm, moving it two or three times until it was in a satisfactory position.

'It'll have to do, I suppose.' Byrht stood back and considered Hermitage with a look that said he was ashamed of himself, but more ashamed of Hermitage.

'Let us go, Brother,' Aethelric said with enthusiasm to get out of this place.

'The mitre, the mitre,' Byrht fussed. 'Honestly, you'd forget your crook if you didn't need it to walk with. And we haven't heard the bell, anyway. You don't want to be early.'

Aethelric gave Byrht a mischievous look. 'I am the Bishop of Selsey. I can do what I like.' He gestured that Hermitage could lead the way, and they left the room, Byrht still fussing around the hem of the robe.

Once out in the corridor. Hermitage glanced back and saw that Byrht had stayed at the door. He was still considering them with disappointment and the obvious thought that he could have done a much better job if he'd only had a few more hours.

'What's discovered, Brother?' Aethelric asked quietly.

Hermitage fiddled with the maniple over his arm, which was a most uncomfortable thing as it kept slipping off.

'You have to keep your arm up,' Aethelric said.

'The chamber in question is that of Aveline,' Hermitage said as he held his arm across his chest.

'Aveline?'

'Lord Gilbert's daughter.'

'Oh, I have encountered Aveline.' Aethelric said with some feeling. 'Lord Gilbert's confident and ambitious daughter.'

'Yes. Although the voices I heard were men, I did wonder if they might be carrying out some instruction of hers.'

'It is possible. I had a visit from her myself.'

'Did you?'

'I think I was a disappointment.' Aethelric smiled at the recollection.

'Really?'

'When she saw that I was an elderly Saxon, and turned out to be Bishop of Selsey, which even I admit is miles from anywhere, she couldn't wait to get away.'

'She does seem intent on her own advancement. Or at least securing a place amongst the finer folk.'

'She asked me if I knew Stigand.'

'The Archbishop of Canterbury?'

'And if he'd like to meet her.'

'He'd like to meet her?' Hermitage was horrified at such presumption.

Aethelric chuckled. 'She is a remarkable woman. She'll either go far, or someone will send her far. Time will tell.'

'I have met Aveline before as well,' Hermitage said. 'And she could not wait to get away from her father and his, erm, military life. It would take something of great interest to bring her back here.'

'I gather she was working her way around the members of the Conclave,' Aethelric reported.

'So, the words I heard could have been to do with her needing something done. Something to her own personal benefit.'

'It is possible,' Aethelric accepted.

'But we still have Ranulph de Sauveloy and my place here to consider.'

Aethelric nodded. 'Whose were the chambers near to Aveline? Did you discover that?'

'I did. Le Pedvin and Robert of Mortain, as well as Gilbert's own.'

'Well done, Brother. I can see why Aveline put herself there.'

They had reached the end of the corridor now, and the next steps would lead into the main hall, which was abuzz with servants running to and fro, with Leudric in the middle, directing them like some queen bee.

'We had better wait for the bell,' Aethelric said. 'Don't want to discomfort these people in the midst of their work.'

Hermitage considered Aethelric and thought that he had never met a bishop like him. True, he had never really *met* a bishop in any formal sense, but he had seen them pass by and had been told all about them.

He had met Stigand, of course, and he had turned out to be quite a normal man. Conniving and perfectly capable of manipulating those around him, which probably was normal for Archbishops of Canterbury, but he was perfectly approachable.

Aethelric seemed almost like an elder brother. Hermitage had completely relaxed in his company, and if he wasn't wearing all that regalia, he would have forgotten he was a bishop at all.

'Of course,' Aethelric said thoughtfully. 'De Sauveloy himself is a man of exalted position, none more so, except perhaps for the king's own family, or Le Pedvin. Aveline might well see benefit from cooperating with him in some way.'

Briefly, Hermitage thought that the simple answer would be to ask Aveline. It was only briefly.

'If that is the case, it still leaves the question of what de Sauveloy is up to.'

'Which, knowing the man, he won't even have told her. He would have sent word asking for some favour or other, without ever revealing its true purpose.

'She, receiving some missive from one so close to the king, would have been only too pleased to help.'

Hermitage breathed deeply. 'This is all speculation. The only evidence we have of anything is two voices overheard saying that something could be done during the Conclave. That could be anything.

'It could have been Byrht talking about cleaning your robe.'

Aethelric seemed distracted and was gazing into the distance.

'It wasn't Byrht,' Hermitage confirmed. 'I know his voice now.'

'Pardon, Brother? Oh, I'm sorry, I was just having the most unworthy thoughts. About Aveline.'

'Really?' Hermitage didn't like the sound of that at all.

'Her ambition could be her weakness,' Aethelric explained.

'Could it?' Hermitage asked very carefully.

Aethelric seemed to have ordered his thoughts now.

'The young woman's main preoccupation is her own advancement, yes?'

'Her only preoccupation,' Hermitage confirmed. 'Although she does spend some time denigrating others.'

'Do you think she would be loyal? You know, honest and capable of keeping a confidence that she has promised?'

Hermitage knew the answer to that one. 'Absolutely not,' he said. 'She wouldn't hesitate to break her word to a saint if a better saint turned up.' He couldn't think how one saint would be better than another, but it was the principle of the thing.

'Excellent.' Aethelric smiled quite horribly for a bishop. 'So, if she were to see some advantage from revealing what, if anything, she has done for de Sauveloy, she would do so.'

'It would have to be a significant advantage,' Hermitage said. 'We've already agreed that de Sauveloy is close to the king. What could be more tempting than that?'

'From what you have said, it sounds as if your encounters with Aveline have not been, what can we say, amicable?'

'They have not. I helped Lord Gilbert recover her when she had gone missing, but it turned out that she did not want to be recovered.'

'And so blamed you.'

'Oh, yes. And when we met her again, some considerable time had passed, but she still wasn't happy.'

Aethelric nodded as if this was exactly what he wanted to hear. 'You haven't seen her since you arrived?'

'No, we only had word from Lord Gilbert that she was back at all.'

'Which means she is going to be very surprised to see you at the Conclave.'

'I suppose so,' Hermitage agreed. It was one of the things he had not been looking forward to.

'The monk who has made such a poor impression on her, and who probably thinks very little of her in return.'

'Oh, well, charity in all things,' Hermitage said.

'No, no,' Aethelric corrected. 'You think very little of her,' he prompted. 'She will be watching the Conclave meet, I have no doubt, and this first session will be mainly administrative matters, including your welcome.'

'I see.' There was something going on, but Hermitage couldn't see it at all.

'If I make great play of welcoming the highly important Brother Hermitage. King William's own personal investigator of high renown, appointed here by the king himself, I suspect Aveline will have a fit of some sort.

'Here is the very monk she has been despicable towards in a position of power.'

'I hardly think...,'

'You are in a position of power,' Aethelric confirmed. 'Which means Aveline will need to establish good relations.'

'Will she?' Hermitage wasn't sure he wanted good relations with Aveline.

'After all, you could be talking to all the other members of the Conclave, telling them what an awful person she is. Including Robert of Mortain, for example.'

'Could I?'

'Probably inevitable. She'll need you on her side. Which means she could be persuaded to tell you what was going on in her chamber.'

'Persuaded?'

'Not so explicitly, of course. You would need to make some idle gossip about her being back in the castle, and did she have a nice chamber. Work your way around to it.'

'Around to it,' Hermitage repeated numbly.

'Yes. I'm sure this is the sort of thing you do all the time in your investigations.'

'Oh, erm, are you?'

Before Hermitage could explain that it wasn't at all the sort of thing he did and that they'd need Wat or Cwen for anything like this, a bell rang.

The servants in the hall scattered to the walls and Leudric was in position in the middle of the room, looking important and very official.

'The Standing Conclave is called,' he announced and rang the bell that he was holding once more.

'Off we go, then,' Aethelric said brightly as he took Hermitage's arm and encouraged him to step forward.

He did so, and only then noticed that all around the room, people were waiting in corridors to come forward.

Leudric put down his bell and took up a staff of some sort, which he held high, until it banged into the timbers of the roof, after which he lowered it a bit.

He stepped out of the rectangle of tables and started to walk solemnly around the room.

Each waiting group in turn followed him out until he had quite a train of people walking behind him.

When their turn came, Aethelric and Hermitage joined the back of the queue and followed all around the tables.

Leudric led on, and Hermitage noticed that each person was stopping at a chair and standing behind it. The last two were his and Aethelric's.

Hermitage paused to take in the enormity of this moment. Him, taking a seat at the Standing Conclave. Next to Bishop Aethelric and with the great and good of the country around him. Whatever chain of events had led him to this point, however convoluted Ranulph de Sauveloy's schemes, he was actually here.

Only as he looked around the gathering, mainly to note whether people were sitting, or still standing, perhaps for an opening prayer, did he realise that every single pair of eyes was staring at him, and many of them did not look friendly.

Caput XIV: Look Who It Is

'Where are we going to find Gilbert if he's hiding?' Cwen asked. 'We know he was only out visiting his villages to avoid the Conclave.'

'He did tell Le Pedvin that he was going to attend to his duties as host.'

'Yes, but telling Le Pedvin to his face is one thing. When his face isn't there anymore, it must be tempting to disappear.'

'His chamber?'

'And where's that?'

'We find out. Investigate.'

'Don't you start. One investigator in a weavers' workshop is more than enough.'

Wat frowned and looked at her.

'What?' She enquired, looking at herself as if something must be wrong.

'We're all investigators,' he said. 'Have been for ages. You don't think Hermitage could manage any of this on his own?'

Cwen considered this for a moment. 'I suppose not,' she said with some resignation. 'I still think of myself as a weaver, though.'

'Me too.'

'You?' Cwen sounded surprised.

'I am,' Wat insisted. 'I've even got a workshop to prove it. And Hermitage is a monk. There you are, three not-very-good investigators make one good one.

'You shout at people and threaten them. I wheedle and lie a bit, when necessary, and Hermitage takes it all in, spends most of the time confused and disappointed, and then works out what it all means.'

Cwen shook her head. 'Is that how it's supposed to work, do you think?'

'I shouldn't think anyone knows how it's supposed to work. At least we've learned that if we want to find something out, we ask someone.'

'I think I knew how to do that before,' Cwen said. 'It's what do you call it?' She looked to the ceiling and then clicked her fingers. 'Common sense, that's it.'

'Oh, you don't want to let common sense get in the way of an investigation. But in this case, we go and ask Alan.'

'If he's still awake.'

Wat held a hand up, indicating that Cwen should wait, while he nipped back to Alan's hidey-hole.

He returned in a few moments. 'Towards the back of the castle. There's a whole corridor of fine chambers. His is the last one.'

'He told you all that? In his condition?'

'It helps if you can speak drunk.'

'Must be this way, then.' Cwen indicated the right direction and they set off.

'What are two bakers doing up here?' she asked after they'd gone a little way and all signs of activity had faded until they were completely alone.

Wat shrugged. 'Lost? Taking Lord Gilbert's personal order for bread?'

'I just hope we don't bump into Le Pedvin again. I don't think we'd get away with that twice.'

They explored the distant reaches of the castle, surprised that it seemed to be bigger on the inside than it was on the outside.

'Devious Norman builders,' Cwen commented. 'Put up a castle and then give it more rooms than will fit.'

'How would that work?' Wat asked. 'Oh, here we are.'

They had rounded one corner, and a wide corridor opened in front of them. It had fine doors down one side, each spaced apart, indicating large chambers within.

It was clear that this was an important part of the castle, intended for the finer inhabitants. The straw was fresh, the muck had been cleared quite recently, and there was even an attendant with a birch-twig broom, arranging it neatly.

The man didn't notice them, and they ducked back quickly.

Cwen whispered to Wat. 'Do you think he's a local or one of the brought-in servants?'

'A straw sweeper?' Wat snorted. 'Skilled job like that needs years of practise.'

'He still might be a straw sweeper who doesn't let bakers into his master's chamber.'

'Leave this one to me,' Wat said. 'Wheedling and lying a bit, remember. You stay out of sight back here. If he needs shouting at, I'll call for you.'

'Ho, there,' Wat said as he stepped confidently along.

The straw sweeper turned and faced him.

'What are you doing here?' they said simultaneously.

'I asked first,' the priest of Derby said.

'No, you didn't,' Wat replied. 'And anyway, I'm supposed to be here.'

'Oh, yes? I don't think so.'

'What's he doing here?' Cwen asked as she joined them.

'That's what I asked,' Wat replied.

'I might have known you'd be here,' the priest sniffed at her.

'We're supposed to be here,' Cwen replied.

'That's what I said as well,' Wat put in.

'I think Lord Gilbert will have something to say when he's told that the priest of Derby is creeping around his corridors pretending to be a straw sweeper,' Cwen folded her arms.

'No less than he'll have to say when he finds Wat the Weaver and Cwen pretending to be.., What is it you're supposed to be? Bakers?'

'Lord Gilbert knows we are here. He's seen us,' Cwen pointed out.

'And he said it was fine for you to dress up as bakers and creep around his chambers?'

'We're not creeping, It's you that's creeping.'

'Did you see me creeping? It's you two who are hiding in corners whispering to one another. I'm sweeping. Nothing wrong with sweeping. '

'There is when you're the priest of Derby who should be in Derby, erm, priesting.'

'What are you doing here?' Wat got back to the main question. 'We know you followed us from Derby. Lord Gilbert offered to see you off, but we said no, let you come.'

'How kind,' the priest sneered.

'And we know from Hermitage that you have a great interest in Bishop Aethelric.'

'And how did you get in?' Cwen asked. 'Told the guards that you were the straw sweeper who'd been sent for? Bribed them with some of the church's money that you keep for yourself. Or simply climbed over the wall?'

The priest gave no answer.

'You want something from Aethelric and have deceived your way into the castle to get to him. One word from us and you'll be outside the walls again.'

The priest did not seem cowed. 'And if Lord Gilbert knows you are here, why are you prowling the corridors dressed up as bakers? I'll warrant a word to Lord Le Pedvin and we'll all be looking in from the outside.'

The two sides stood glaring at one another for a silent moment.

'Look,' the priest said. 'Hermitage has been appointed to the Conclave, although heaven knows why, and you seem to know that I would like a word with Aethelric. He's near to Derby, so I've come over to see him.

'You came with Hermitage, I understand that, and if you want to dress up as bakers, that's up to you, I suppose. What you two get up to is of no interest to me. Just don't get in my way.'

'Don't get in your way?' Cwen snorted. 'If you want to see Aethelric, why not simply go to Selsey? Is it because you'd probably be spotted by one of your many enemies and wouldn't make it as far as Repton?'

Wat was looking hard at the priest. 'We don't know why Hermitage was appointed to the Conclave,' he said seriously. 'And neither does he. Something is going on and you turn up in the middle of it. Not behaving like a decent visitor who knocks on the door and asks if the bishop is in.'

'We'll just have to agree that we're all creeping about a bit, won't we?' the priest said. 'I have my business and all I will say is that it is nothing to do with Hermitage being on the Conclave. That has simply turned out to be useful.'

Somewhere off in the castle, a bell rang out.

'Sounds like the Conclave is about to begin,' the priest said.

'Not going to get to Aethelric now, are you?' Wat pointed out.

The priest looked down the corridor and bit his lip. 'They won't be too long. I actually do know how the Conclave works, you know. They'll all agree that they're here, confirm

Hermitage's appointment and then disperse until tomorrow.'

'I thought they were supposed to discuss important matters,' Cwen said.

'Depends what you call important,' the priest replied. 'And they never rush at anything. Too old, most of them. They always allow a day in case there are any latecomers. It's also suspected that they wait a day to see if anyone is going to die from the journey to get here. It gets very confusing if someone drops in the middle of the discussions.'

'Charming. So, you're going to stay here sweeping straw until the bishop comes back, are you,' Cwen asked.

'How do you know his chamber is even here?' Wat asked.

'Bound to be. These are the best in the castle.'

'For a priest, you know a lot about creeping around castles and finding out where people are. Never mind sweeping straw,' Cwen observed.

The priest said nothing.

'Or,' she said thoughtfully. 'You're someone who creeps around castles finding people and is only pretending to be a priest.'

'What are you two doing up here, anyway?' The priest ignored the accusation.

'We're going to speak to Lord Gilbert,' Cwen said. 'The lord of the castle who knows we are here. At least we're not hiding from everyone.'

'Please yourself,' the priest said. 'I've no business with him. And when I've spoken to Aethelric I shall probably be gone, so you won't have to worry about me, will you?'

'It's still too much of a coincidence,' Wat said carefully. 'And we've learnt never to trust a coincidence. You being here just when Hermitage is appointed to the Conclave. It's suspicious.'

'You two being here when I want to talk to Aethelric is suspicious,' the priest retorted. 'And you don't need to go telling Lord Gilbert that I'm here. This is nothing to do with him.'

'We've only got your word for that,' Cwen said. 'And I don't trust your word.'

'But I'd be a distraction, wouldn't I?' The priest sounded horribly confident. 'Whatever this business with the Conclave is that you're trying to discover, you don't want Gilbert chasing some priest all over the place. Particularly one who will be gone as soon as he can.'

'We'll make no promises,' Wat said.

'I wouldn't trust them if you did.' The priest aimed this comment at Cwen.

'All right,' Wat agreed carefully. 'But if the need arises, your name arises with it. If we knew what your name was, of course.'

The priest shrugged that this was acceptable and that he still wasn't going to tell them his name.

Leaving him to his straw sweeping, they approached the door at the end of the corridor. Before Wat could knock, it opened and Lord Gilbert stood there.

'I heard the bell,' he said without looking at his callers. Then he looked. 'What the devil do you two think you are doing here?' the lord's voice rose in volume.

'Oh, yes,' they heard the priest mutter behind them. 'Lord Gilbert knows we're here, everything is fine.'

'And what are you doing dressed as bakers? You were nearly caught by Le Pedvin.'

'Yes, we're sorry about that,' Wat said.

Gilbert noticed the priest. 'What are you doing here? Clear off and sweep straw somewhere else.'

'Yes,' Cwen repeated. 'Clear off.'

'Le Pedvin,' Gilbert repeated when they were alone. 'You do know him? The man it does not pay to get caught by. And somehow, I ended up lying to him.'

'Yes, but we're trying..,'

'I don't care what you're trying. I want to know why you're trying it my castle. And dressed up like that?'

There was a lull in the tirade, which allowed the start of an explanation.

'We're trying to find out what de Sauveloy is up to.' Wat said, sounding annoyed that Gilbert wasn't giving them his support.

'Brother Hermitage is the one on the Conclave, remember? He was invited. You were not.'

'Yes, but he can't do this on his own.'

'And you have to dress as bakers, do you? And in front of Le Pedvin, of all people?'

'We wanted to get into the servants' hall and find out what the gossip was about the Conclave. After all, even de Sauveloy might give something away in front of a servant.'

'Him not thinking them important enough to listen,' Cwen said.

'Ridiculous,' Gilbert snapped.

'And we did find something out,' Wat said.

Gilbert looked at them with the clear demand that this had better be good.

'De Sauveloy came here weeks ago.'

'What?' Gilbert looked confused.

'De Sauveloy. He was here weeks before the Conclave.'

Gilbert's mouth was open. Eventually, he found his voice. 'I could have told you that, you fools.'

'But you didn't,' Cwen noted.

'You didn't ask. I told you this was his conclave. Why wouldn't he be here?'

'Why then, but not now?' Wat asked. 'Why go to the trouble of making sure the place is ready for the Conclave and then not come to the Conclave?'

'We're told he fussed about the place,' Cwen said.

'Of course, he did. He fusses over everything. I did my best to avoid him.'

'What sort of thing was he fussing over? Cwen asked. 'Exactly.'

'What does this have to do with anything?'

'We won't know until we find out what he was up to.'

Gilbert shook his head. He gestured that they should walk down the corridor. 'I need to get to the Conclave, welcome the members.' Wat and Cwen followed in his wake.

'He wanted to see the main hall and confirm that it was suitable. He told Alan where the tables and chairs would go, and who would sit where.'

'Did he?' Wat asked. 'He actually said which person should sit in which chair?'

'Naturally. There's a priority to this sort of thing. You can't have Count Robert sitting next to some sheriff, can you?'

'Heavens, no,' Cwen said in mock horror. 'How awful.'

'Anything else?' Wat asked.

'Which chambers people would have.'

'Who would be sleeping in which room?'

'Their chambers are generally where they sleep,' Gilbert pointed out. 'What food should be served, How many men Le Pedvin would need. What the hours of the debate would be. Pretty much everything.'

'And he said your servants weren't good enough and

replaced them,' Wat said.

'No, that was mainly Leudric. Awful man, just like his master.'

'This really makes no sense, Wat mused. 'The man comes all this way and goes over every detail of the Conclave down to the tables the chairs, the food and the wine. Yet he doesn't turn up to the real thing to see if it's all being done as he instructed.'

'He sent Leudric?' Cwen suggested.

Wat shook his head. 'De Sauveloy is not a man to trust anyone else, is he?'

Nobody objected to that conclusion.

'So, why would he not want to be here?' Wat gave this careful thought as they walked. 'Or rather,' he said. 'Why would he specifically want not to be here?'

Cwen nodded to herself. 'Because he doesn't want to be caught up in whatever is going to happen.'

'Exactly. If he isn't here, he can't be held responsible, can he?'

'Responsible for what?' Gilbert asked in obvious frustration.'

'We don't know,' Wat said mysteriously.

'Well, that's very helpful, isn't it?'

'But it's something he's set up. He's arranged the whole thing. He knows where everyone is, where they're sleeping, where they're sitting, what they're eating.'

'And he's sent Hermitage into the middle of it all,' Cwen pointed out.

Gilbert was still looking confused, so Wat spelt it out. 'Something horrible is going to happen to someone during this conclave. Something set in train by de Sauveloy. And when it happens, he will be a hundred miles away, so it will all be someone else's fault.

'Definitely Hermitage's and probably yours, Lord Gilbert.'

Caput XV: Round the Square Table

No one said a word, which was somehow worse than if they had all burst into a tumult of complaint, waving their arms in Hermitage's direction while shouting their outrage at his presence.

And one or two of them really did look outraged. It was as if they'd asked for a goblet of their favourite wine, and someone had sat a dead badger at their table instead.

Others simply scowled with "What's he doing here?" written all over their faces.

Some were more neutral but did look as if there had been a mistake and someone had better tell this monk that he was in the wrong room.

A very few regarded him with disinterest, and this was because they seemed to be disinterested in everything.

One of them was Robert, Count of Mortain.

Hermitage had never met the man but knew who he was straight away. He sat in the most prominent position, was dressed in the very finest robes, had two attendants who stood at his back waiting for any need their master might have, and looked upon the whole conclave as if he was doing it the most enormous favour by being here.

He gave no more attention to Brother Hermitage than he would have done to the woman carrying his shoes.

The silence was getting unbearable until Leudric rang his bell once more, and everyone sat.

Another figure now appeared at the foot of the tables, down near Hermitage's end, and stepped through the gap with a solemn pace.

He was dressed in some sort of formal-looking robe, and he bowed to Leudric, who bowed back.

With the steps of a dance, the two men exchanged positions, and Leudric passed over his formal staff to the other.

'Walter de Arsic,' Aethelric whispered to Hermitage. 'The Conclave's attendant.'

Hermitage considered Walter, and he did have the look of a man who thought he was in charge when he wasn't.

Leudric walked out from between the tables and marched, in a phalanx of one, off to the far side from Hermitage, where he took up station.

De Arsic banged the staff on the floor three times. 'The Standing Conclave meets.' he announced in a voice heavy with self-importance.

Still, no one else spoke, which was making Hermitage shake with anticipation. He was sure that the first order of the meeting would be a proposal to have him excluded.

Walter de Arsic continued. 'By order of the king, we are gathered, here, in Nottingham, on this day, to consider the questions before us.

'Lord Gilbert, your host bids you welcome.'

He now bowed towards the bottom of the tables, and a much smaller figure stepped forward.

This one too, carried an air of entitlement, simply expecting that every eye in the room would be on them and that they deserved it.

Hermitage swallowed hard, as, looking straight ahead and walking with a very formal gait, Aveline entered the space.

She and de Arsic exchanged bows, after which she turned to Count Robert and bowed again.

Addressing him and those sitting closest, she spoke with a firm tone. 'My Lords, my lord bishops, barons, archdeacons, sheriffs and men of standing, on behalf of my father, Lord

Gilbert, I bid you welcome.

'I am Lady Aveline of Nottingham and I open my home to you.'

Hermitage thought that was a bit much as she had done her best to leave Nottingham and her father several times, and had done nothing but complain about her home.

He wondered why Gilbert wasn't here doing this himself, but thought that he probably didn't want to. Either that or Aveline hadn't told him.

She cast her magnanimous gaze around the room and acknowledged the respect that was simply her due.

Eventually, and inevitably, her eyes landed on Hermitage.

Well, they didn't land at first, they passed over, seemed to be surprised at what they thought they had seen, and came back for a second look.

This was a look of absolute fury. He recognised it in Aveline because she wore it so often.

He was slightly surprised at this, as she must have known he was on the list of attendees, and there couldn't be two Brother Hermitages.

Obviously struggling to contain the urge to take Hermitage by the ear and escort him from the room, she brushed down the front of her skirt.

'I wish you well in your deliberations,' she managed to get out before she walked, in a much less dignified manner than before, back out of the space in between the tables.

As she went, she kept her eyes on Hermitage all the while and he could tell she wasn't happy as he could see all of her teeth.

Walter de Arsic now resumed his position. 'I invite our eldest member, Bishop Aethelric of Selsey to pronounce the opening prayer.'

Aethelric stood from his chair and eyes turned to him. One or two, who hadn't been paying attention until now, spotted Hermitage and frowned. Perhaps they thought it reasonable that Aethelric had brought a monk with him, so took no more notice.

Aethelric said a beautiful prayer in Latin, exhorting all those present to put aside worldly thoughts and desires and let the spirit of truth and selflessness enter their debate.

Hermitage thought that half those in the room looked as if they didn't understand the Latin in the first place and the rest weren't listening, anyway.

Only one or two of the bishops nodded slowly in agreement, but even one of them looked as if he intended to do no such thing.

As he finished with Amen, he remained standing and paused for a moment.

'I follow the order of the Conclave,' he gave a nod to de Arsic. 'And I introduce a new member, here by gracious appointment of the king. I give you, Brother Hermitage.'

The continued silence was more insulting than an outcry of objection. Hermitage hadn't expected to be introduced.

Walter de Arsic was looking utterly confused by this, and Aethelric raised his hand.

'I know that it would normally be the role of our attendant to introduce new members and to enumerate those who have passed. However, as I am already on my feet.' He smiled all around and spoke as if he was doing everyone a great service.

'Under the precedent of the meeting in October of the year of our Lord ten thirty-seven, when the Bishop of Rochester introduced his own son, who, to this day, remains a most valued member.' He bowed to a cleric sitting on the far side of the table who looked as if he had started this very meeting thirty years ago, as he was sound asleep.

'Brother Hermitage is King William's own investigator of murder.' That did get a rumble of noise from the assembly.

'Many times has the loyal Brother uncovered wrongdoers in our midst.' That comment was clearly one intended for any wrongdoers in this midst. 'And served the king most assiduously.

'In return for this service, our gracious king has appointed Brother Hermitage to the Standing Conclave.' He bowed once more and sat.

'I thought I had better get in first,' he whispered to Hermitage. 'You never know what some of this lot have in mind. Mention of the king should keep them quiet for a while.'

Poor Walter still looked lost, as if he had been reading from a book and someone had suddenly reversed all the pages.

'Erm, erm,' he said.

A pronounced sigh from Robert of Mortain got him back on track.

'Those attending the Standing Conclave give heed,' he called. 'And announce your presence.'

'Robert, Count of Mortain attends,' one of Robert's attendants announced on his behalf, announcing himself clearly being beneath him.

Aethelric leaned close to Hermitage. 'Listen as each of them speaks, Brother. See if the voices you heard from that window are here.'

Hermitage thought that was a very good idea, and one he probably should have come up with himself.

Mortain's attendant was followed in turn by all the lords, lord bishops, barons, archdeacons, sheriffs and men of standing, who did manage to speak for themselves.

Hermitage was in such a state of worry that he couldn't keep track of all the names, even if he did recognise a few of them. There were twenty though, as he found that counting them calmed him somewhat. He did recognise Richard de Tunbridge, but that was only because he had the name in his head from Haimo.

Fortunately, Richard's voice did not sound familiar.

Unfortunately, none of them sounded familiar.

Once everyone had spoken, Hermitage felt a nudge in the ribs from Aethelric.

'Oh, erm, yes. Brother Hermitage,' he said to the room. It sounded so simple when most of the other members had announced their names, titles, lands and positions. All he had was "Brother Hermitage." 'The King's Investigator,' he added at a further nudge.

Walter seemed reluctantly content that all those at the tables had given their names, the reluctance being directed mainly at Hermitage.

'I now proceed to report those called from us since the last meeting.'

De Arsic then read a list of names that seemed to go on forever. Hermitage was familiar with the generations of Esau, but these seemed to be nearly as long.

Aethelric leant over. 'The last meeting was before the encounter near Hastings,' he explained. 'A lot of the Conclave's members were there. With Harold.'

Hermitage nodded that he understood. Perhaps it was fortunate that there were still twenty people available, although he had noticed that most of those present were Norman. They must have been appointed, as Haimo had said, simply to replace Saxons who were now permanently unavailable.

Hermitage's attention had really been on the people around the table, but the recollection of Haimo, who had not been announced, made him look around the room to the quite large number of people standing in the background.

Obviously, there were attendants and servants, but he did manage to spot Haimo, loitering near Robert's seat, and the figure of Le Pedvin, who was prowling around like a cat who has come across a conclave of mice. He was clearly considering them all with suspicion.

As Walter de Arsic droned on, people started to have their own conversations, low at first but increasing in volume. Hermitage thought this was quite rude while announcements were being made, but not even de Arsic seemed to mind.

'So, Brother, any voices you recognise?' Aethelric asked.

'I'm afraid not. Although hearing them here is different from out in the open. And it was only a few words.'

The bishop nodded. 'It could well be that they were not conclave members you heard.'

'Lord Le Pedvin seems to be looking at everyone as if they are up to something.'

Aethelric looked over. 'Yes, well, most of the people here have taken over positions previously held by Saxons. I don't know half of them.

'I imagine that many are not above taking over positions held by one another, should the opportunity arise.

'Just as our membership was depleted by Hastings, so these men are fresh from the field of battle. Le Pedvin probably knows them well, and what they're capable of.'

Hermitage considered this and it made an awful lot of sense. Of many things.

'Could that be why de Sauveloy sent me here?' he asked.

Aethelric looked at him thoughtfully. 'You think one of them might try to murder another? And you would be on hand to investigate?'

'It might be more cunning than that. Someone planning murder would think twice upon discovering that the King's Investigator was here. Watching them.'

Aethelric steepled his hands and considered this. 'In which case, why not simply have you sent? Like Le Pedvin or Haimo. There are many here who are not members. Why put you on the Conclave?'

It was a good question.

'And, without denigrating you in any way, Brother, would not Lord Le Pedvin provide a greater deterrence?

'You would investigate, surely, but he would do something much more direct, I suspect.'

That was a good point as well.

'There must be reason, though,' Hermitage said. 'And now that I sit here, I wonder what it can be. It cannot be genuine reward for service, I see that. These are important and influential people, I am none of those things.'

Aethelric looked thoughtful. 'Ranulph de Sauveloy is a man who probably schemes his way out of bed each day. There is nothing he does without reason.'

That did not cheer Hermitage in the slightest.

'Here's a plan, Brother. Now that you have been introduced and everyone knows you as a member of the Conclave, you can talk to people. Approach them. Engage with them. And listen. Those voices from the window must be here somewhere.'

Hermitage dreaded the thought of walking up to strangers and simply talking to them, but he could see that it might identify the speakers in Aveline's chamber.

Then, through devious interrogation and subtle, leading conversation, it might be possible to determine their intent.

No, he couldn't do that. But he might find out who they were.

'Which could be another reason why de Sauveloy sent me,' he said with some confidence. 'There is already some plot in hand, and I must uncover it before its deed is done.'

Aethelric did not object to this.

'Lord Le Pedvin would, as you say, be decisive, but perhaps only after the event. Has de Sauveloy caught wind of some plan that he needs thwarted?'

'It is possible, I suppose,' Aethelric admitted. 'But again, why not simply step in himself? I have never known any of the Normans fail to act if they thought something needed doing. Even if they were wrong.'

Hermitage could see that this was true. Even minor Norman nobles took matters into their own hands, even when there weren't any matters there in the first place.

He gazed around the room, wondering who here had been behind that window.

The space was crowded and he couldn't imagine anyone would miss the opening of the Conclave. There couldn't be many people left in the rest of the castle at all.

Apart from Gilbert, Wat and Cwen, who he couldn't see anywhere.

Walter de Arsic seemed to be coming to the end of his list, which only brought it home to Hermitage just how many Saxons were no longer here. It was no wonder the Normans had taken over so effectively; there was no one else left alive.

The chatter started to die down, the only area of calm being the head of the table where engagement in idle gossip was clearly for lesser folk.

'Robert,' Hermitage said.

'Yes,' Aethelric agreed. 'I'm not really sure what he's doing here. There can't be much of interest for him in the Standing Conclave. Probably wants to make sure we don't stray into matters that should be no concern of ours, as this is the first meeting after Hastings.'

'But he is the king's brother.'

'Half brother, yes.'

'So, he would be just the sort of person Ranulph de Sauveloy would have to tread carefully around. In fact, probably the only such person here.'

'You think he might be the subject of this plot?'

'Or the instigator of it.'

The two men looked at one another with obvious concern.

'And who better to send into a situation like this than a servant such as me, who might be found in Isaiah, chapter fifty-three, book seven.'

Aethelric looked grim and nodded slowly. 'The sacrificial lamb.'

Caput XVI: Exchange of Plots

'She's already done it,' Gilbert said as they entered the hall. 'I might have known she would.'

'Who's done what?' Cwen asked.

'Aveline. She's started the Conclave and bid everyone welcome.' Gilbert seemed resigned to this rather than upset by it.

'Aren't you supposed to do that?'

'Aye, but she's welcome. I'd rather not have anything to do with it, but she wants to be seen by all the important people. It's fine with me.'

'Anyone would think she'd arranged the whole thing, not de Sauveloy,' Cwen commented.

'Why is it here?' Wat asked. 'Leudric told us that Nottingham was a convenient part of the country, but London is probably the easiest place for anyone to get to.'

'I didn't volunteer,' Gilbert said glumly. 'When Ranulph de Sauveloy tells you you're going to host a conclave, you start hosting.'

'We know why it's here,' Cwen put in. 'It's so that Lord Gilbert can take the blame when the horrible thing happens.'

'Thank you very much,' Gilbert grumbled.

Wat shook his head slowly. 'Which means that de Sauveloy has been planning whatever this is for months. He even chose Nottingham specifically.

'It's quite impressive when you think about it. The man certainly puts his all into a scheme.'

'Oh, look, there's Hermitage,' Cwen pointed over to the other side of the hall. She stood on tiptoes and waved extravagantly.

Hermitage didn't notice, but several other heads turned

her way. From the looks on the faces, it was clear that no one waved at the Standing Conclave, let alone bakers.

She lowered her arm.

'We'd better have a word with him,' Wat said. 'Let him know what we've discovered.'

'I'm not convinced you've discovered anything.' Gilbert sounded weary. 'All you've got is a lot of assumptions based on the sort of thing that Ranulph de Sauveloy gets up to. There's still no telling that this is even one of them.

'He came here weeks ago to organise the Conclave and, having left his instructions, hasn't come back. He's the sort of man who expects his instructions to be followed.

'He probably can't conceive of anyone not doing what they're told.

'He appointed Brother Hermitage to the Conclave and that's that. This horrible thing that's going to happen is only in your head.'

Wat was grim. 'Ranulph de Sauveloy would not send us here if he wasn't up to something.'

'But he didn't send you here, did he? He sent Brother Hermitage.'

'He knows we go everywhere together,' Cwen said. 'He'd expect us to be here.'

'There you go, speculating again. You show me something horrible happening and someone doing it, and I'll stick my sword in them. Until then, I am not having you two being a nuisance to de Sauveloy's carefully planned conclave.'

Gilbert folded his arms to confirm that he was not going to be moved.

'Father.' Aveline's voice made them all jump, and Gilbert turned to see his daughter standing behind him. She didn't even spare a glance for the two bakers who were probably there to replenish the bread. The two bakers now slipped out of her eye-line and turned their backs.

'Aveline, my dear,' Gilbert replied. 'I assume you have done the welcome for the Conclave members?'

'I have. And do you know who is here? Sitting at that table?' She pointed towards the table concerned. 'Amongst the Conclave members? Do you know?' The words coming out of Aveline's mouth sounded as if they were pleased to be leaving. Each one was bitten off as it departed and was not going to be welcomed back.

'Erm.' Gilbert obviously didn't want to confess that he did know, had known for some time, but hadn't mentioned it to Aveline.

'That monk,' Aveline spat.

'Monk?'

'The monk. The same one who was impudent and disobedient before. The one who keeps turning up and making things go wrong.'

Gilbert made a play of looking over and considering the tables carefully. 'Oh, Brother Hermitage.'

'Yes, Brother Hermitage. I want him out of here.'

'I'm not sure it's that simple, my dear. If he's a member of the Conclave...'

'He cannot be a member of the Conclave, can he?' She stated this as a simple fact.

'Well, I don't know. If the king has appointed him, he could be. Is he on the list?'

'I don't have time to go over the list all the time,' she snapped.

'I'll have a word with him, see what's happening,' Gilbert said soothingly.

'Good. Now, I'm going to have another go at talking to

Robert de Mortain. His servants have seen that I'm the host and so can't continue keeping me away.'

Gilbert simply nodded at this and watched as she left, heading for the gaggle of men that comprised Robert's retinue.

'Is he on the list?' Wat asked with a grin as he and Cwen sidled back.

'Careful, Saxon,' Gilbert said with mock anger. 'Bakers and Weavers can be asked to leave the castle by the nearest cliff edge, you know.'

Wat held his hands up in surrender. 'At least she doesn't know we're here.'

'It'll be a nice surprise.' Cwen smiled and Gilbert sighed.

The chatter around the Conclave table died away and the man in the cloak, standing in the middle, banged his staff on the ground again.

'Those who are here, and those who are not, have been announced,' he cried.

'Which leaves?' Wat asked quietly.

'The Conclave will retire until tomorrow when the main question will be put.' The staff was banged once more, and that seemed to be that.

'Sounds exciting,' Cwen commented. 'What's the main question?'

'Why are these people doing this in my castle?' Gilbert complained. 'What their main question is, I have neither knowledge nor interest.'

'We can get to Hermitage now,' Wat said.

Several members of the Conclave stood from the chairs and pushed them back with a scrape on the floor. Others remained seated and talked to their neighbours, and the Bishop of Rochester's son was woken up.

Robert of Mortain stood, made an impatient gesture for everyone to get out of his way and made for the back of the hall, presumably to return to his chamber.

Aveline could be seen hopping up and down and waving her arms in his direction, but there were too many people in her way.

Wat and Cwen started working around to Hermitage, but before they had got very far, Gilbert was waylaid by Leudric, who, judging by the look on Gilbert's face, had something completely pointless to discuss.

Pulling their hats down, they managed to escape the man's notice and slipped around people, who helpfully took no notice of wandering bakers.

'Hermitage,' Wat said as he stood before him. 'And you must be Bishop Aethelric. We've heard all about you.'

Bishop Aethelric looked confused and worried as he was accosted by the staff.

'There you are,' Hermitage said with great relief. 'I was worrying where you had got to. And whether someone had got to you.'

'No, we're fine. We dressed as bakers.'

'So I see. Bishop, here are Wat and Cwen.'

'We're not really bakers,' Cwen explained. 'We're weavers. Of tapestry.'

'Aha.' The bishop did not seem comforted by this.

'We have all worked together on the investigations,' Wat explained. 'We, erm, have skills that Hermitage finds useful.'

Hermitage thought that was a nice way of putting it.

'Yes, I am aware of your history. It now includes dressing as bakers, I see,' Aethelric noted.

Hermitage looked around and gestured that they were probably best finding a quiet corner to talk in.

Several members of the Conclave were still considering Hermitage in an unhappy manner and looked as if they had several questions for him. He would be happy not to loiter here and have to deal with them.

'There's a small alcove here.' Aethelric indicated the wall behind them.

If the Conclave members considered Hermitage an anomaly before, seeing him in a corner with the bishop and two bakers was really going to give them cause for concern.

'Have you discovered anything?' Hermitage asked when he was sure they could not be overheard.

'It's all right,' he said in response to Cwen's glance at Aethelric. 'The bishop and I have discussed what de Sauveloy may be up to, and we have real concerns.'

'Good,' Cwen said. 'Us too.' She looked over her shoulder. 'He was here weeks ago.'

'Who was?'

'De Sauveloy.

'Oh, right.'

'Checking everything and issuing instructions. Who was to sit where, which chamber they would sleep in, what they'd eat and drink. He was obviously setting the whole thing up.'

'That is quite normal,' Aethelric put in. 'The organiser of the Conclave always goes to the site well in advance to check just those things.

'You would be amazed how upset people get if they're sitting next to the wrong person, or have a room that isn't as good as last time.'

'Oh,' Cwen said with obvious disappointment.

'We've also discovered that most of the servants have been replaced,' Wat added. 'Some from the castle remain, but others have been brought in.'

'Again, not surprising, really,' Aethelric said. 'Few establishments could manage the Conclave without extra staff. It is a great burden.'

'Right,' Wat too was somewhat dismayed to hear this. 'And then de Sauveloy left. All that trouble to arrange the Conclave, and then he leaves before it begins. In fact, he makes sure that he isn't here.'

Aethelric looked apologetic before he even spoke. 'The actual running of the Conclave is always handed over to the attendant. Organisation and delivery are very different things.'

Wat blew out slowly and looked to Cwen for any more ideas.

'Are you saying this is all perfectly normal and there's nothing to worry about?' Cwen asked.

'Oh, not at all. The process is reasonable, but there is still the question of Brother Hermitage.'

Hermitage looked on with interest.

'He is a fine fellow and has done some very worthy work in bringing the most serious wrongdoers to justice, but you have seen how the Conclave is made up. There are no other ordinary monks.

'There is a prior and couple of abbots, but they are in charge of large establishments. They do not have their feet on the ground, shall we say?

'Why did Ranulph de Sauveloy appoint him? Perhaps for this reason, but it is a puzzle. What is he supposed to be doing here as he is the only one? A clutch of appointments, I might understand, but not one.'

'And there's the priest,' Cwen announced.

'Oh, yes, the priest is here,' Wat confirmed. 'He must have wormed his way in somehow.'

'The priest?' Aethelric asked. 'What priest?'

'Ah, I should have mentioned that,' Hermitage said. 'But I never got the chance, somehow. There is a priest in Derby, well we think he's a priest, or rather, he says he's a priest.'

'I see,' Aethelric said, but he plainly didn't.

'And this priest, we don't even know his name, was very interested when he heard I had been appointed to the Conclave. He said he had connections with it and specifically asked that we give you his salutations.'

'Really?'

'Yes. He said to mention the priest who went to Derby.'

'Priest who went to Derby?' Aethelric repeated, and it didn't seem to mean anything to him.

'That's what he said.'

Aethelric looked thoughtful for a few moments before slowly shaking his head. 'I'm afraid it means nothing. What sort of fellow is he?'

'Awkward, difficult, rude, greedy, selfish,' Cwen said.

Aethelric raised his eyebrows. 'I know of such people, naturally, but try not to count them among my acquaintances. And he is a priest, you say?'

'No, he says he's a priest,' Cwen corrected.

'And what is his connection to de Sauveloy?'

'Oh, well, none, really,' Wat admitted. 'That we know of,' he added enthusiastically.

Cwen seemed despondent. 'Lord Gilbert said we hadn't really discovered anything at all. I'm beginning to think he may be right.'

'But I have,' Hermitage said, hoping to reassure them that something was going on. 'I overheard words coming from Lady Aveline's room. Two men speaking to a third. One said "Of course it can be done," and the second said "and during the Conclave.".'

'And what did the third say?' Cwen asked.

'Nothing that I could make out.'

'Erm,' Wat spoke up. 'Why were you listening at Lady Aveline's room?'

'I wasn't,' Hermitage protested. 'I was outside, walking around the castle when I happened to be under her window when they spoke.'

'How do you know it was her window?'

'Rablan told me.'

'And who is Rablan?'

'One of the chamber servants.'

Wat nodded that this sounded reasonable. 'I won't ask why you went for a walk around the castle. What do you think they were talking about?'

'It could be anything,' Cwen said. 'They could have been talking about a fresh supply of ale.'

'In Aveline's chamber?'

'A fresh supply of self-importance?' Cwen suggested.

'We further reasoned that this must have something to do with Robert of Mortain.'

'Why?' Wat asked.

'Ranulf de Sauveloy must have got word of some plot to be enacted at the Conclave, and so he sent me. We've agreed there is no sensible reason for me to be given the position.

'And, it was that plot I overheard from Aveline's room. If it was to do with anyone other than the brother of the king, de Sauveloy would simply have dealt with it himself. But no, he wants to keep his distance from it. So that any blame falls on me if it goes wrong.

'Either someone is planning to do harm to Robert, kill him even, or Robert is the killer. Either way, the king's brother is not a man to get tangled up with. Even de Sauveloy might not be safe from any retribution.'

'If someone kills the king's brother during the Conclave, William will be a very angry king,' Wat commented.

'So,' Hermitage continued. 'We need to find out who the people talking in Aveline's chamber were. I have listened to everyone on the Conclave speak, and I didn't recognise any voices.

'Apart from Robert himself, of course,' he said with some interest. 'He had people speak for him.'

'And there was the Bishop of Rochester's son,' Aethelric pointed out. 'But I don't think he could stay awake for long enough to plot anything.'

'So, you've got to go round listening to people?' Cwen checked.

'Or ask Aveline,' Wat suggested, which led to a painful silence. 'It was only an idea.'

'Are you going to question her?' Cwen asked.

'Me? God no. Begging your pardon, bishop.'

Cwen smiled rather disturbingly. 'I could ask her what men she's had in her chamber.'

'And get a reply in the form of a punch on the nose,' Wat said.

'She can try if she likes.'

'It seems to me,' Bishop Aethelric spoke up. 'That there are two routes to be followed. Brother Hermitage can walk amongst the attendees here, speak to anyone he has not heard yet, and see if he can spot the voices concerned.

'In the meantime, the Lady Aveline can be asked. People may have used her chamber without her knowledge, but she could have something to say.'

Cwen rubbed her hands.

'And I shall do that,' Aethelric said.

'Really?' Cwen didn't seem convinced that he would do it properly.

'I shall seek her help with the problem, perhaps suggest that there is some connection to Robert of Mortain. I have noticed that she seems most intent on meeting the king's brother, while his men seem intent on keeping her away.

'She might be tempted by such an offer.'

'Subtle persuasion and gentle encouragement, you mean,' Wat summarised.

'Just so.'

Wat turned to Cwen. 'You wouldn't like that at all.'

'Hm,' Cwen huffed. 'When that doesn't work, we'll try it my way.'

Caput XVII: Idle Chatter

'What do we do?' Cwen asked as they got ready to disperse.

'Look after the bread?' Aethelric suggested. 'I'm not sure that any of the Conclave members will respond well to being questioned by bakers.'

'We can check Aveline's chamber,' Cwen said.

Wat did not look keen.

'She's not there, is she? She's trying to get the ear of Robert of Mortain. We can be in and out in no time.'

'It's in the corridor with Gilbert's and Robert of Montain's chambers, towards the back of the castle,' Hermitage said.

'Hm. Which sounds like it's where we found the priest sweeping straw,' Cwen said.

'Sweeping straw?'

'That's what he was doing. Although we know he isn't a straw sweeper and we doubt that he's a priest.'

'And what do we hope to find in this chamber?' Wat asked.

'I don't know,' Cwen replied impatiently. 'There could be something. Evidence of the men Hermitage heard there would help. It would be something to question her over.'

'I think anywhere away from here would be best,' Aethelric said. 'People are starting to look at us. Probably wondering why we're talking to you for so long when you haven't given us any bread.'

A quick glance around confirmed that several faces were frowning at them huddled in their corner.

Wat tugged the peak of his cap and started bowing and backing away. 'Right you are, sir,' he said. 'Bread to your chamber, yes of course.' He nudged Cwen in the ribs and she followed him away.

'I say, you there,' a voice called across the room. 'Baker.'

'He means us,' Cwen tugged at Wat's arm.

'Yes, sir,' he replied in his rough voice.

'Bring me a loaf of that bread on the table.'

Wat looked over and saw the man who had called, standing about six feet away from the bread on the table.

'Help yourself, sir,' he called cheerfully. 'We can soon fetch more.'

'Help myself?' The man didn't understand what was being said to him. 'If I wanted to help myself, I wouldn't have called you, would I?'

'I suppose not, sir.'

'Our gracious Lord, the quality of servants these days,' the man complained loudly to a fellow he was standing with.

'Do you think he'd choke on a loaf if I gave it to him fast enough?' Wat asked Cwen quietly.

'Here we are, sir, here we are,' Wat said as he reached the table and extravagantly picked up a small loaf with his left hand, passed it to his right, and presented it to the noble.

The man broke the tiniest mouthful from the edge and handed it back.

Wat didn't move.

'What are you waiting for?' the man asked when he eventually registered Wat standing there.

'Just waiting in case you was wanting another bit, sir. What with it being all the way over on this table.'

The man considered him.

'Or shall I be off with myself?' Wat looked at the man closely. 'Right you are, sir, I'll be off with myself.'

Wat walked away with Cwen in his wake. 'If it turns out no one has planned a murder for this conclave, I might be able to provide one of my own.'

'That voice,' Hermitage said to Aethelric.

'Which one?'

'The one that just called Wat for some bread.'

'One of the voices from the window?'

'I think so.' Hermitage craned to see across the crowded room but couldn't get a clear view of the one who had spoken. 'If he would just say "of course it can be done" or "and during the Conclave", I would be sure.'

'If you asked anyone to say that specifically, I imagine you will get objections.

'Perhaps you could lead the conversation in the right direction. The tables are in slightly the wrong place, do you think it possible they could be moved?

'Erm, I don't know,' Hermitage wondered if Aethelric's mind had wandered.

'No, that's what you ask the fellow. And he replies, "Of course, it can be done" or something very close. And then you ask if it could be done during the Conclave.'

'Oh, I see. He might simply say "yes", or not reply at all, thinking I'm slightly mad.'

'All possible, but until we try..,'

Hermitage felt a slight push in the back and found himself taking a step towards the bread table.

'I shall find the Lady Aveline and see what assistance she can offer.'

And with that, Aethelric was gone.

Hermitage stood alone and felt that the bishop had left him exposed in this room full of people who either didn't want him there at all or didn't know why he was there.

He stood not doing anything at all for several moments, but eventually told himself that getting a bit of bread was perfectly natural. A lot of the other members of the Conclave and their staff were gathered around the table talking to one another, He could join. He was a member just like them.

All he had to do was walk up and say good day. Or Salve, or banjoor, which seemed to be what the Normans said.

But what if someone replied in Norman? He'd be lost straight away. Perhaps it would be best if he just waited for someone to come and talk to him.

Which looked very unlikely.

He told himself that this was for an investigation. He wasn't going to walk up and talk to perfect strangers in his own right. That would be unbearable.

His mind was made up, but his knees hadn't been informed and so he simply stood there for a moment. Eventually, they caught on, and he took shaking steps across the room.

As the bread table drew near, he still couldn't identify the individual who had spoken to Wat. He thought they had been to the right of the table, but there was a gaggle of people there, all talking at once. It could have been any of them. And they all looked alarmingly Norman. Not the sort of people to welcome a Saxon monk with nothing to say except, hello.

And why would a member of the Conclave be talking to someone else's servants anyway?

As far as he could tell, they all seemed familiar with one another, and he now saw that one of them was the man who had spoken for Robert. So, if they were all Robert's men, it may be his scheme that was being planned in Aveline's chamber.

Challenging the king's brother to explain himself was not something he was planning to do.

Four of the bishops were gathered a bit farther away, and

there was a good chance they were Saxon. Which probably explained why they had to talk to themselves.

He made it to the table and reached out to take a loaf. No one stopped him, and so he broke a small piece off and turned his back to the table to nibble it.

Everyone else seemed to be already in deep conversation with their fellows in groups of twos and threes, and he couldn't simply interrupt any of them.

'Wine, sir?' A servant appeared at his shoulder bearing a flagon in his hands, with goblets strung at his waist.

'Oh, erm, yes, I suppose so.'

The servant expertly unhooked a goblet, filled it from his jug and handed it over before walking off.

Even he seemed to think Hermitage was in the wrong place and didn't fit in.

He concluded that the best he could do was to simply stand here and listen intently. He may be able to pick up the voice once more, and at least see what the man looked like.

Just along the table, he noticed another man standing alone doing exactly as he was doing; nibbling a bit of bread and sipping occasionally from his goblet.

He recognised him from one of the seats around the Conclave table, but couldn't for the life of him remember the man's name. There had been so many that the moment he heard a new one, it pushed all the old ones out.

Hermitage sidled a little closer and his movement caught the other's attention. They looked at one another and nodded.

Well, it was a start. What to do now though? Say "Nice conclave, do you come here often?"

'Brother Hermitage, eh?' the other broke the silence and Hermitage was relieved that he would now be able to start a conversation without having had to start a conversation.

'Erm, yes,' he said, which wasn't very conversational.

Another painful moment of silence joined them.

'My, erm, presence here seems to be a surprise to everyone. Myself included.'

'Aye,' the man seemed to agree. 'They are a difficult lot.'

'Have you, erm, been a member long?'

The fellow was of a good age, so Hermitage imagined that he had been on the Conclave for some time. Perhaps he was one of the few Saxon survivors. He didn't have the look of a Norman about him. And the fact that none of the Normans were talking to him was another sign. He wasn't a bishop, though.

'Aye.' The man sounded quite despondent at the thought. 'I attended the Witan, under the old king.' He nodded to himself and leant closer to Hermitage. 'Too old to go to Hastings, you know. Officially, I am still Thegn of Boscombe, but not for much longer, I suspect. Alstan's the name.'

'Greetings, Thegn Alstan of Boscombe.'

'I wouldn't say that too loudly if I were you. Thegn is not a popular position under our new king. I've had word that some Norman called William of Eu is to be given my lands.'

'Really?'

'Of course, no one has told me. I just hear rumour. One day, the man will arrive and ask me what I'm doing in his manor.'

'But you keep your seat on the Conclave.'

'Only because no one has thought to take it away from me, I suspect. But you've been given a place, must be in good order with the king.'

'Hardly,' Hermitage said. 'He never remembers who I am, doesn't seem to think much of me when we do meet, and would hardly give me a reward if it rolled off his table.'

'Yet here you are.'

'And no one really knows why,' Hermitage confessed. He thought Alstan a safe person to confide in, obviously not being a friend of the Normans.

'Some Norman scheme or other,' Alstan said. 'They always have schemes.'

'It's possible, but I have no idea what it could be. Being on the Conclave is an honour. They certainly wouldn't give me an honour without good reason.'

'An honour?' Alstan asked. 'The Witan wasn't too bad. We discussed important matters and obviously appointed kings, when the need arose. But the Conclave? I wouldn't call this an honour.

'I attended a few in the old days, and you wouldn't believe the things we talked about. This conclave is one meeting I shan't be sorry to see go.'

'Go?' Hermitage asked. This was the first time he had heard this suggestion.

'Of course. William's already got rid of the Witan. Not surprising really, as the last one decided that Edgar Aethling should be king instead of him.

'I can't see him wanting the Conclave meeting and trying to decide things. I strongly suspect that Robert of Mortain is only here to tell us that this is the last meeting of the Standing Conclave.'

Hermitage's heart sank at that. He knew there was something going on. Of course, he didn't really belong on the Conclave, what with being a humble monk and not a bishop. Yes, Ranulph de Sauveloy was obviously up to something. But surely, they couldn't take the Conclave away from him now that he'd only just got here. It was so unfair.

Alstan didn't seem to notice Hermitage's distress. 'William does try to make us think he's listening to us and we have a place in his kingdom. He has to, really, it's the Saxons who still make the country work. But there are limits.

'He's not going to let me keep my land, and I suspect he won't let us keep our conclave.'

'Oh, dear,' was all Hermitage could say. This was to be his first and last conclave? 'Will there be objection?' he asked hopefully.

'I dare say there will. And it's possible that there will be every impression that such objections are listened to. Ignored, obviously, but listened to.

'They'll say that there are no plans to disband the Conclave, which will be true. Next, they'll go away and make some plans to disband the Conclave.'

'It all seems a lot of trouble to go to simply to cancel a meeting.'

'Has to be seen to be reasonable,' Alstan said. 'So we all think what a good ruler we have and don't rebel against him.

'And there are some influential people here that he won't want to upset too much. Your Bishop Aethelric for example.'

'My bishop?'

'Well, you seem to know him well.'

'We only met at the Conclave.'

'Really? He seems to have taken to you. I would stay close if I were you. He's well thought of.'

'Is he?' Hermitage knew that he was a kind and intelligent fellow, but that wasn't enough to make anyone well thought of.

'There's few who know the old Saxon laws like Aethelric. William will need him if he's not to rouse anger every time he tries to do anything.'

'Like take your land away,' Hermitage said sympathetically.

'Exactly. I'm not dead like most of the other thegns, so he'll have to do it properly. Within the law. Or at least show that he's trying to do it within the law.'

Hermitage's experience of the king was that he did what he wanted and woe betide anyone who got in the way.

Alstan obviously saw the thoughts on Hermitage's face. 'It's one thing to win a battle, quite another to win a country. At least to win one without having battles everywhere you go.

'William got himself accepted as king and everyone important submitted to him. He didn't simply chop their heads off.

'It may not feel like it, but he does need us.'

'But not our conclave,' Hermitage said.

'You have it.'

This worry about the Conclave had quite taken Hermitage's mind off the reason he had come over to the bread table in the first place.

'So, who are all these fellows?' he asked Alstan. 'They didn't sit at the table.'

'Mostly Robert's men, I think. At least, they flock around him like crows.'

So, it was one of Robert's men he had overheard. The plot, whatever it was, might be at Robert's behest.

If the man was here to disband the Conclave, did he intend to do it in some horribly violent manner?

And was de Sauveloy trying to upset some scheme of the king's brother? Is that why he had kept away but sent Hermitage instead?

Or, had those men at the window simply been discussing when to announce that the Conclave was to be no more. "Of course, it can be done," and "during the Conclave" could be perfectly innocent words.

Of course, the Conclave could be closed, and it would be done while the meeting was underway.

In which case, what was he doing here? De Sauveloy would not have sent him simply to witness an announcement.

Oh, it was all too confusing and he had nothing that he could put his finger on.

Apart from a few overheard words, there was no evidence of anything whatsoever. Even Alstan's assumption that the Conclave was going to end was just that, an assumption.

And now that he was here, and could be reasonably certain that one of this crowd of Normans had been in Aveline's chamber, what was he going to do? Ask him what he was up to?

Even if he engaged them all in idle and peculiar conversation and got them to speak the necessary words, what could he say? "Aha, you were in Aveline's chamber and you're planning something?"

They were Normans and he was a Saxon monk, it was hardly enough to generate a heartfelt confession and make them call the whole thing off. Whatever it was.

He had to be satisfied with the knowledge that at least one of the men in the chamber had been from Robert's party. He now needed information from Aveline herself, and anything from her chamber that Wat and Cwen might uncover.

'Aethelric said you investigate murders?' Alstan asked, sounding both interested and alarmed at the same time.

'I have done, yes. Not at my own behest, I assure you. They just sort of come to me.'

'I'd better not stand too close, then,' Alstan said with a smile.

'Still, at least you'll be in the right place at the right time for this one.'

'Which one?' Hermitage asked, worried that Alstan might know of something much more serious.

'The murder of the Standing Conclave,' he said. 'You'll be right here to see who did it.'

Hermitage shook under his habit. He knew that Alstan meant a sort of figurative murder, the demise of a meeting not requiring any actual death. But was there a truth under that? Was the whole conclave to be murdered? Very unfiguratively? Is that why he had been sent, so that he could be slaughtered with all the others?

He had heard that William had all the hostages at Hastings killed, so murdering a conclave might be nothing to him. It was an appalling thought. Surely, he would not be so evil? There were bishops here, after all. And it was suggested he needed Aethelric alive.

But it would send a message to the country. And had he sent Robert to do his bidding?

This was all too awful to contemplate, and he tried to tell himself that it was simply beyond reason. But the idea was in his head now, and it wasn't going to leave of its own accord.

Distracted by the foul images of fallen bishops and thegns littering the hall, he nearly missed the group of Robert's men drift away with loaves and wine in hand, chattering among themselves.

If they were going off to gather their weapons at this very moment, he would follow them and put a stop to it.

How he would stop a band of armed men bent on slaughter, he wasn't quite sure yet. And he wasn't even comfortable following people without them knowing, but things were getting desperate.

Perhaps he would catch the one voice he sought, or see

where these people were going and who they would meet.

Then, he could leap out and confront them. Or go and get Wat and Cwen. They'd probably be better at leaping and confrontation, come to think of it.

He tried to comfort himself with the recollection of Le Pedvin's rule of no weapons. But to Normans, no weapons probably meant some weapons, just not a lot of them. And how many would you need to murder a room full of bishops?

Caput XVIII: Aveline's Complaint

'Ah, Mistress Aveline, I wonder if I might have a word?'

Aveline turned her attention from one of Robert's attendants with obvious irritation. This man claimed to have access to the count and could make an introduction.

'What is it?' she snapped. She saw that this was Bishop Aethelric and simply sighed. 'I am a bit busy.'

'It won't take a moment,' Aethelric said.

'I'm sure it can wait.'

'It really won't take a moment, but it is a matter of some urgency.'

'I am talking to this gentleman,' Aveline insisted.

Aethelric smiled. 'Ah, this servant, yes, I see. And there's me, only a humble bishop.' He shook his head in disappointment. 'Strange how the world works.'

'I'm sure it is.' Aveline turned her back and returned her attention to the servant.

'A humble bishop with the ear of the king. A bishop who was just going to go and have a word with Robert, Count of Mortain. He wants to discuss a legal matter concerning some land, and it seems I am the authority.

'I suppose I could go and talk to him and then come back to you. Yes, that's probably best. You carry on with your servant.'

'What was it you wanted, bishop?' Aveline asked sweetly and she turned her back on the servant who had been in the middle of a sentence.

'Oh, you are free. That is good. Perhaps we can walk together.'

'Really?' Aveline didn't sound so keen anymore.

'On my way to the count.'

'Lead on.'

Aethelric strolled slowly away from the crowd, towards the back of the hall.

'It is a rather delicate matter,' he said. 'And one which will rely upon your utmost discretion.'

Aveline didn't look too happy about that.

'After all, it is connected to Count Robert, and Lord de Sauveloy and perhaps even the king.'

Aveline looked a lot more happy.

Aethelric spoke very carefully and annoyingly slowly.

'I fear that there is more going on at the Conclave than simply the matters for debate.'

'Oh, yes?'

'It is always the case at events such as these, that different interests pursue their own paths, shall we say.'

'Erm. All right.' Aveline didn't seem at all interested in this.

'People use the opportunity to advance their personal plans and schemes, instead of concentrating on the business of the Conclave.'

'How shocking,' Aveline said, although she didn't sound very shocked

'It is. And certain matters have been drawn to my attention. Discussions taking place. Words spoken in quiet corridors, that sort of thing.'

'Oh, yes?' This did sound a bit more intriguing.

Aethelric nodded. 'Of course, the ordinary attendee is of little interest. I am too old to be carrying on like this, but the more important members? Lord Robert himself, your father, perhaps, and Lord Le Pedvin is here, of course.'

'My father?' Aveline asked this not in shock that his name should come up in any mention of scheming and advancement of personal plans, but because she thought the bishop must be joking.

'You think not?.

'Absolutely not.' The daughter spoke with profound disappointment that such behaviour was beyond the capabilities of her father.

'That is good to hear.'

'My father?' Aveline actually laughed. 'Plotting his own advancement? He couldn't plot his way out of a vegetable patch.'

'Ah.'

'He's a soldier through and through. If you're looking for someone who wants a long march with a fight at the end of it, he's your man. But a scheme involving quiet words in corridors? No.'

'That is good to hear.'

'What on earth gave you the idea that he would be involved?'

'It wasn't so much a what, as a where.'

'Where?'

'Your chambers are all close, I understand.'

'Our chambers?' Aveline frowned deeply.

'Yours, your father's, Lord Robert's and Le Pedvin.'

'Erm, well, yes, I suppose so.'

Aethelric looked around to make sure no one was in earshot, despite the fact there was no one around at all now they had left the main hall. 'Have you heard anything yourself?'

'Such as?'

'Words spoken around your chambers. Drifting through the window, perhaps?'

'You think Robert is up to something?

'I cannot say. All I hear is rumour and circumstance. But

what makes you say Robert?'

'Well, we know my father wouldn't recognise a scheme if it came in a leather satchel with "schemes" written on the outside. And Lord Le Pedvin is a man after his own heart. Simple and straightforward.

'If it's beyond the reach of his blade, it's not worth worrying about. And if it's within the reach of his blade, it's probably dead already. Which leaves Robert.'

Aethelric nodded his appreciation of the argument.

'Because, if these words of yours were heard around my chambers, it can only have been him. Or to do with him, at least.

'I assume you're not going to tell me what the actual words were?'

'It might be safest.'

Aveline rubbed her hands with glee. 'Oh, this is more like it. The most interesting thing to happen around here in years. And I thought this conclave was going to be dull.'

'You seem to be in the centre of things,' Aethelric noted.

'Oh, yes, but that's just to meet people. Get to know them. Living with my father while he simply fought battles everywhere wasn't doing me any good at all.

'Paris was marvellous, but with Count Robert and the bishops and nobles coming here, I couldn't miss it.'

'The Conclave debate itself being of no interest?'

'That? Heavens no. Sorry, but no.'

'I can see that,' Aethelric agreed. 'It is not really for young people. Just old folk like me.'

'And now words being spoken, near my chamber. What do we do?' she asked enthusiastically. 'Go and talk to Robert?'

'Oh, no, no,' Aethelric urged. 'To involve the king's brother at this stage would not be wise.'

'I thought he wanted to see you?' Aveline asked with disappointment.

'About some land, yes, not about this.'

Aveline's smile was quite worrying. 'Is he up to something? Or is someone after him?'

Aethelric gave a non-committal shrug. 'Perhaps you have heard something yourself?'

'Me? Oh, that would be good. No, I've not heard anything.'

'Nothing at all? No words at your window, or door? No chatter heard in your chamber?'

'I wouldn't know, really,' Aveline said.

'You wouldn't know?'

'I've barely been in there. What with the Conclave to organise. That Leudric fellow is all right, but this thing needs to be done properly.'

'You have not slept?' Aethelric asked in surprise.

'Oh, dozed here and there. If you don't keep people at it, they'll slack. Can't have slack.'

Now that Aethelric had heard this, and considered Aveline a bit more closely, there was something about her of one who hasn't had enough sleep. A certain flickering of the eye, a twitch in the corner of the mouth said that she could really do with a lie-down.

'So, anyone could have been in your chamber?'

'I should hope not,' Aveline said with some horror. She blinked a bit too quickly. 'Who has been in my chamber?'

'Perhaps no one,' Aethelric assured her. 'It is simply a possibility. I am sure that no one would have.'

'They had better not. I've never heard of such a thing.'

'So, you wouldn't have been around to hear anything, anyway.'

'No.' Aveline sounded regretful that she hadn't stayed in

her chamber after all.

'And you've heard no chatter amongst the workings of the Conclave?'

'Well, there's been lots of chatter, but unless I know what I'm listening for, I can hardly tell, can I?'

This was a pretty blatant demand for more information and Aethelric considered it.

He lowered his voice lower than a low voice. 'There has been talk of something being done. During the Conclave.' Perhaps, as Aveline had been fretting about the Conclave, and not actually in her chamber, it was safe to confide this much in her.

'Something being done?' she asked.

'That's right.'

'During the Conclave?'

'Exactly.'

'And that's it, is it? Someone has overheard someone saying that something could be done during the Conclave. Are you serious?'

'Well, yes.'

Aveline shook her head. 'I think it's you who needs more sleep, bishop.

'This conclave has been nothing but a long list of things that had to be done, all of them during the Conclave. I'd be disappointed if there was anyone wandering the corridors who wasn't discussing what needed to be done during the Conclave.' She looked at him very hard. 'Have you got their names?'

'There is more to it than that,' Aethelric pleaded. 'These were words heard in the area of your chambers. A private area where only yourself, Robert, Lord Gilbert and Le Pedvin go.'

'And our servants. Who had better have a lot of things to do during the Conclave, or I shall have words.'

'You have not loaned your chamber to anyone else? Allowed use of it?'

'Certainly not.' She peered at him. 'Are you saying these words were heard from my chamber?'

Aethelric very carefully said nothing.

'Who has been listening at my chamber?' Aveline demanded. 'And then gossiping about it with a bishop?' She seemed to realise that there was something worse than that. 'And who has been in there?' she screeched.

She got no answer.

'Right. Come along.' Aveline marched away from Aethelric, heading in the direction of her chamber.

He hurried along after. 'My lady, Aveline,' he called after her. 'We must be careful.'

Unfortunately, there was no way he could catch up with her, let alone get ahead. And if Cwen and Wat were in there looking for evidence, things would not go well.

Wat and Cwen had quickly found the right place and had not been interrupted in their search.

''This dressing as a baker is really useful,' Wat commented. 'No one takes any notice of you at all. The other servants assume you're on your way to the bakery or something, and the nobles take no notice, probably because bakers are covered in flour and are only useful when you're hungry.'

'All very well until someone asks us to do some baking,' Cwen said. 'Now, which is her room?'

They stood in the corridor and considered the doors before them.

'Hermitage didn't say which one it was,' Wat said. 'We'll

have to check them all.'

'The ones with Gilbert, Le Pedvin and Robert of Mortain in?'

'We left Gilbert and Le Pedvin in the main hall.'

'Which only leaves the king's brother and any servants who might be at work.'

Wat screwed up his face at the problem. 'I've got an idea,' he said brightly.

'Why am I even more worried?'

Wat strode up and knocked on one of the doors. 'Bread service,' he called.

'Bread service?' Cwen asked incredulously.

Wat waved her to silence.

There was no answer from the door, so he turned the iron handle and pushed it open. 'Bread service,' he called again.

'No one here,' he said over his shoulder. 'This could be it.'

Shaking her head, Cwen followed him into the room and they considered the sight before them.

'Le Pedvin,' they both said together.

The bare wooden cot, the absence of warmth or comfort as well as of any servant tidying the place or making it pleasant, shouted the name of its owner.

'One down,' Wat said as he closed the door.

'Bread service,' he called as he knocked on the next door and opened it straight away.

'Get out,' a voice called from within.

'Bread service, sir,' Wat said meekly.

A Norman servant appeared at the door. 'What do you mean, bread service?'

'Would you like any bread?'

'What?' The man at the door clearly wondered what loons were doing in Lord Gilbert's castle.

'A service of Lord Gilbert, sir. Bread for the honoured guests, if they want it, of course.'

'Bread?'

'Yes.' Wat sighed slightly that the man couldn't understand something this simple.

Cwen sighed as well but for a different reason.

'Would you like any bread?' Wat asked. 'For the room?'

'Who is it?' A voice called from within.

'It's some baker,' the servant turned back and replied. 'He's asking if we want any bread.'

'He's doing what?'

'Make your stay more comfortable,' Wat explained. 'Bread for the room.'

'You're mad,' the servant said. 'Lord Robert does not want any bread. And if he did, I would fetch it for him. Bread service? I never heard the like. Now be off.' He closed the door in their faces.

'Two to go,' Wat said.

'Bread service,' Cwen repeated with her face in her hands.

'It's working, isn't it?' He walked up to the next door. 'Now we know where Robert is, this must be Gilbert or Aveline.

'We know it's Gilbert,' Cwen said. 'He came out of here earlier.'

'He could have been coming out of Aveline's room. You know, if he was having to explain something to her. Again.'

He knocked and opened the next door, 'Bread service,' he said more quietly.

'I'd like to see how you're going to explain Lord Gilbert's bread service to Lord Gilbert himself.'

'No one in,' Wat said as he stepped into the room.

'Gilbert,' Cwen confirmed.

This room was not quite so uncomfortable as Le Pedvin's,

but it was the chamber of a warrior. Everything was very neatly laid out and ordered, but it was all neatly laid out and ordered for battle.

Boots stood side by side under a chair that bore a chain mail shirt with helmet on top. To one side rested a sword, to the other an axe.

'Not Aveline's weapons of choice,' Wat agreed.

They closed the door and moved on.

'Aveline,' they both agreed at the next chamber.

'Although it doesn't look as if she's been here,' Cwen noted.

This room too was very neat, and it had a row of fine shoes at the end of the bed.

'How many pairs of shoes can she wear?' Wat asked.

'Never mind the shoes, they're hardly evidence of wrong-doing.'

'They're evidence of having too many shoes.'

'Unless she's planning to kick someone to death, we need something else. Look back there.' Cwen waved Wat towards the wall opposite the bed, where a large chest sat.

'It'd need four servants just to move this thing,' Wat observed.

He bent and put his hands to the lid and lifted. 'Dresses,' he said. Cwen came over to look.

For some reason Wat could not comprehend, all the breath seemed to leave her body. 'Oh,' she said in a tone he'd not heard her use before.

She reached into the chest and pulled out the top dress.

'Look at this,' she sighed.

'Yes, very nice,' Wat replied. 'There seem to be more below.'

'It's red.' Cwen held it up to herself.

Wat glanced up from the box. 'Ah, yes.' He frowned as he

saw that she was now stroking the dress.

'How does it look?'

'Erm, very nice,' Wat said absentmindedly.

Her face creased.

'Lovely,' Wat added quickly. 'No, I mean, really lovely. You should get one.'

'Me? I couldn't possibly.'

Fortunately, Wat recognised what this really meant. 'Of course, you could.'

'Do you know how much something like this costs?'

Wat swallowed. Hard. 'What does that matter?' He heard himself say.

'We'll talk about it later,' Cwen said as she lowered the dress, it being clear that the talk later would be about when she would get one.

'Oh, and there's a yellow one.' She reached into the chest and took out a beautiful yellow dress. She couldn't hold them both but didn't want to let go of either.

'Oh,' Wat said as he looked into the chest now that the dresses were gone.

'Is there another one?' Cwen asked with slightly mad enthusiasm.

'No, but there's this.' He stood back from the chest and held the object in his hands.

'Oh, great Lord,' Cwen forgot about the dresses. 'Where did she get that?'

'And what does she intend to do with it?'

They couldn't discuss the question any further as the door burst open.

Without looking, they both knew it would be Aveline.

'Thieves!' she cried. 'Robbers.'

Wat held his hands out to urge quiet.

She looked at them both and utter confusion spread across her face. 'Bakers,' she now said. 'Thief bakers.'

Then she considered them even more closely. 'Oh, my God, it's you two.'

Caput XIX: Weapon of Choice

'I might have known,' Aveline said as she threw her hands in the air and paced towards them. 'Once that idiot monk was here, I should have realised that you two would be skulking around somewhere.

'But in my chamber, of all places. Are you the chatterers the bishop has been talking about? I'll warrant you are. And what's she doing with my dresses?'

Cwen hastily dropped the dresses onto the open chest.

'Never mind the dresses,' Wat said. 'We're more interested in this.' He held his discovery out.

Aveline went silent and very pale. 'All right.' Her voice was nervous and thin. 'You can keep the dresses.'

'What?' Wat asked in confusion.

'Take them all,' Aveline begged. 'Just don't shoot me.'

'Shoot you? Who's going to shoot you? Oh, I see.' Wat considered the crossbow in his hand. 'It's not loaded,' he said. 'Anyway, I'd have to put it together first.' While the device was most obviously a crossbow, it was not assembled. The stock was one solid piece of dark wood, but the bow with its string was a separate piece, rather than being fixed in place.

'Easier to hide this way,' Wat observed. 'And we're not going to shoot anyone, you are.' He lowered the weapon.

'Me?'

'It's your crossbow.'

Aveline recovered herself quickly. 'It most certainly is not. I have never owned one of those horrible things. What would I do with it?'

'Shoot someone, like I said.'

'You're mad,' Aveline concluded. She took a step backwards, clearly convinced that this weaver, who was now dressed as a baker and was holding a crossbow in her chamber, was not someone to be meddled with.

She backed towards the door but only got as far as the threshold, where she bumped into Bishop Aethelric coming in.

'Ah,' he said, surveying the situation.

'These people are mad,' Aveline reported. 'I've met them before and they were mad then and they're mad now. One of them's even got a crossbow.'

'It's not my crossbow,' Wat insisted. 'It's your crossbow. It was in your chest.'

'Calm, calm, everyone' Aethelric said, holding up soothing hands. 'Let us consider the situation carefully and not leap to any conclusions.'

'I don't need to leap anywhere to see that he's got a crossbow,' Aveline complained.

'And Le Pedvin's orders were no weapons,' Wat tutted.

'Shall we perhaps close the door,' Aethelric said. 'I don't think we want to be discovered with that thing, no matter who it belongs to.'

Aveline opened her mouth to speak but seemed to accept this. She stayed close to the bishop as he closed the door.

'Now,' he said. 'Why doesn't everyone sit down? I know I need to rest my old bones.'

Slowly, as if Wat, Cwen and Aveline each suspected the other would make some sudden move, they found spots to sit.

'And perhaps put that back in the chest? In case anyone does walk in.'

Wat took the crossbow and put it in the chest, closing the lid on it and the dresses.

'Now then,' Aethelric rubbed his hands slowly. 'Lady

Aveline, you are obviously aware that Brother Hermitage is here. The King's Investigator.'

'The idiot monk, yes,' Aveline grumbled.

'He has been appointed to the Conclave.'

'Really?' Aveline seemed to think that the standards of the Conclave must have slipped. 'Father said it might be the case, but it seems peculiar to say the least. I mean, he's an idiot.'

'Would you stop calling our friend an idiot,' Cwen instructed. 'He is King William's own investigator, so perhaps you could tell the king that you think he's an idiot for appointing him.'

Aveline sulked.

'His companions, Wat and Cwen here are with him.'

Aveline opened her mouth to say something but clearly thought better of it.

'Can we confirm that this weapon here,' Aethelric gestured towards the chest. 'Is not yours?'

'Of course, it's not mine,' Aveline twittered. 'What would I be doing with a horrible thing like that? I wouldn't even know how to use it.'

'Nor even be able to load it, perhaps,' Aethelric suggested.

Aveline clearly had no concept that crossbows had to be loaded.

'It's in her chest,' Cwen muttered.

'It is,' Aethelric agreed. 'But Lady Aveline has hardly been in her chamber.'

'Oh, really?' Cwen asked with heavy insinuation.

'She has been working on the Conclave and has barely had time for sleep.'

'Hm,' Cwen snorted.

'I can always take crossbow lessons,' Aveline sneered at Cwen. 'Then I'd know how to shoot someone.'

'So, I think we can conclude that someone else put it here,' Aethelric continued. 'Or hid it, knowing that it would be in a safe place.'

'Or it is theirs,' Aveline countered. 'After all, he was the one holding the thing and pointing it at me.'

'I wasn't pointing it at you. It's in pieces. And in any case, it doesn't have a bolt.'

'Bolt yourself,' Aveline said rather cryptically.

'I don't think they can have brought it,' Aethelric said. 'They have only been here a short while and have spent most of that disguised as bakers.'

'Yes, why do they look like bakers?'

'It is part of a much larger tale,' Aethelric said.

'A tale which involves someone in this room being overheard saying something could be done during the Conclave,' Wat put in.

Aethelric nodded. 'And now we have a good idea what they were going to do it with.'

'Was it you listening at my chamber?' Aveline accused.

'No, it was not,' Cwen said firmly. 'It was the King's Investigator, who happened to be passing under your window. The window to the chamber whose door you leave unlocked so that anyone can come in here and hide their crossbows.'

'I wonder if that is what happened,' Aethelric mused. 'I don't know what your experience was, but when we entered the castle, our carriage was searched for weapons. Lord Le Pedvin's orders.'

'Us too', Wat said.

'But the castle must be full of weapons, anyway,' Cwen said. 'It's a castle, for heaven's sake. What good is a castle with no weapons?'

'The guards on the outer walls are equipped, apparently. The rest are locked away,' Aveline informed them.

'Why?' Cwen asked. 'Does this conclave often descend into armed conflict? Are bishops always drawing knives on one another?'

'It has never been the case,' Aethelric said. 'But this is the first conclave under the Normans. Perhaps this is their usual practice. And we do have word that the king himself may visit.'

'There's a man who would have his own crossbow,' Cwen commented. 'I can believe the Normans would settle mainly ecclesiastical questions on the point of a sword.' She sneered in Aveline's direction.

'Why do you think I went to Paris?' Aveline replied with a dismissive sniff. 'You can't have a feast in Normandy for Christ's Mass without someone getting stabbed. And they think it's roistering.'

'Which only gives more weight to the question of how this crossbow got here,' Aethelric said. 'Lady Aveline...,'

'It's not mine I tell you.'

'Just so. I was actually wondering what brought you to the Conclave. As you say, you were in Paris, far from the erm, conflicts of Norman rule.'

'Well, the thing was to be here in Nottingham, obviously. And full of important people. Rumour of the king, even.'

'And Robert, the king's brother.' Cwen put in.

'Among others. And if my father was host, then I should be here as well.'

'Showing everybody who you were,' Cwen said.

'Meeting important people,' Aveline bit back.

'But,' Aethelric interrupted the argument. 'How did you, in Paris, hear about the Conclave in Nottingham?'

'How did I hear about it? How does one hear about anything?'

'Someone tells you.'

'Exactly.'

'So, who told you?'

'Who?'

'Yes, who?'

'What, you mean precisely who?'

'That would be helpful.'

Aveline seemed surprised by the question as it was not one to which she had given any thought. 'Well, I don't know really. I mean, there are so many people in Paris talking about this and that, it could have been anyone.

'There are emissaries, you know. To the king. And messengers, and gatherings, and events.' She smiled to herself at the happy memory.

'No one in particular came to you and said that there was to be a conclave in Nottingham and that you should attend?'

Aveline frowned. 'Not that I can think of. It must have simply come up in conversation.'

'A strange conversation for Paris,' Aethelric observed.

'Robert is here already,' Wat said. 'There's talk of William coming. I imagine chatter of what the king and his relatives are up to is quite common.'

'So, you decided to come to Nottingham.'

'Obviously.'

Aethelric steepled his fingers. 'And you packed your chest.'

'Me?' Aveline seemed confused by that when it wasn't a difficult question.

'Yes. Did you pack it yourself?'

'No, of course, I didn't pack it myself.' She sounded quite insulted by the question. 'Who do you think I am?'

'Who did?'

'My maid.'

'Your maid. And what's her name?'

'What's her name?' This interrogation was challenging Aveline on a number of fronts.

'Yes, her name.' Aethelric managed to maintain a patient voice, but his eyes were giving him away.

'I don't know. Ethel. Margery. Something like that.'

'Something like Ethel or Margery,' Cwen commented. 'Which aren't at all alike.'

'When you have maids, you can learn their names,' Aveline bit back.

'So, someone else could have put the crossbow in your chest and you would never have known,' Aethelric suggested. 'And they used you because you would not be searched coming to your own home.'

Now, Aveline saw what he was getting at. 'Exactly!' she said happily. 'Hence it is not mine and I didn't know anything about it.'

'Which still leaves the question of why it is here,' Wat said.

'It's a lot of time and trouble to go to just to get a crossbow in,' Cwen said. 'Easier to go and steal one from the castle, I'd have thought.'

'Not with Le Pedvin prowling about,' Wat suggested.

'Which means it is probably here for someone important,' Aethelric said.

'Robert,' Wat concluded.

'Why is he here at all?' Cwen asked. 'I can understand all the bishops and the abbots, but Hermitage said this was all about ecclesiastical matters. And why would the king even think of coming?'

Aethelric nodded. 'William, if he does come, will probably

just pass by to give the meeting his blessing and authority. As for Robert, with all the manors that William has granted his brother, he is now one of the richest men in England.'

'Does that mean he knows about ecclesiastical matters?'

'I have had brief conversation with him and he does seem, erm, what can we say, light on ecclesiastical understanding. But, as I say, he is the richest man in England.'

'Which means his opinion on everything is now very important. Whether he knows anything about it or not,' Wat said.

'The only thing he's expert at is being given manors by his brother. If there was a conclave on that, he'd be fine. And other people only encourage him by fawning all over him and saying how wonderful and clever he is, purely so they can have some of his money.

'Or, because on a whim with no repercussions for himself, he can destroy someone's life.'

'Thinking of anyone in particular?' Cwen asked. 'An old weaving master of years gone by, perhaps?'

'Hm,' Wat grumbled.

'But in the case of our rich and rather stupid man, someone is planning to put him on the end of a crossbow,' Cwen concluded.

Aveline gasped.

'What did you think was going to be done with it?' Cwen asked shaking her head and sighing at Aveline.

'Why Robert, though?' Aveline asked.

'Got to be the most likely, hasn't he?' The king's brother. Richest man in England. Who else? No one is going to gain much from killing the bishop here.'

Aethelric nodded his agreement to that.

'In fact,' Wat said. 'This could be the very reason Le

Pedvin has imposed his no weapons rule. Some plot against Robert is known about and he has to be protected.'

'Or Robert is up to something himself?' Aethelric suggested.

'It's possible,' Wat agreed. 'But who here would he want murdered? Everyone's beneath him.'

'This is all fascinating,' Cwen said. 'But what do we do about it? Go and tell Le Pedvin we found a crossbow in Aveline's chamber?'

'No, you do not,' Aveline instructed. 'I didn't know anything about the wretched thing.'

'Doesn't stop it being here,' Cwen pointed out.

'You could go and tell him you were unpacking and found it in the bottom of the chest,' Wat suggested.

'He's not going to believe that, is he?' Aveline retorted.

'Don't see why not.'

'Me? Unpack my own chest. Don't be ridiculous.'

'All right,' Wat sighed. 'Your maid, Ethel or Margery was unpacking and they found it.'

'They're in Paris.'

'For heaven's sake, woman,' Wat snapped. 'You've got a crossbow in the bottom of your chest in your chamber. I don't know why we're helping you with this at all. We can simply go and tell Le Pedvin and leave you to deal with him.'

Aveline obviously wanted to say something cutting and demeaning, but couldn't come up with anything.

'We know so little,' Aethelric spoke calmly. 'If we tell Lord Le Pedvin about this, or even take him the crossbow for safekeeping, the plot, whatever it is, may simply proceed by a different route. It is that we need to stop.'

Cwen was shaking her head. 'I don't think this is something for us to get mixed up in. We're only three Saxons remember, and this is the king's brother. If he wants to kill, or is killed, the best thing we can do is get out of the way.'

'But Brother Hermitage was sent here.' Aethelric pointed out. And we can now think that it was precisely to investigate a murder before it has happened, and prevent it.'

'Or be on hand to deal with it afterwards,' Cwen said. 'And be blamed in some way.'

'Along with the two of us,' Wat added. 'Remember, we've had dealings with de Sauveloy before.'

'I left Brother Hermitage to see if he could identify the speaker at the window,' Aethelric said. 'He thought he heard the voice among a band of servants. Let us see what he has discovered and then make a decision about the next step.'

'You did what?' Cwen asked urgently.

'I left Brother Hermitage..,'

'You left Hermitage to follow some possible killer. On his own? Are you mad?'

'He is the King's Investigator,' Aethelric defended himself.

'And he's also Brother Hermitage. Come on. We've got to find him.'

'Surely, this is the sort of thing he has dealt with before?' Aethelric asked as they prepared to leave the room.

Aveline lifted the lid of the chest to consider the mess her dresses were in. She was clearly confused about how she was going to get someone to tidy them for her.

'Perhaps we had better move the weapon.' Wat took the crossbow from the chest once more and slid it under the bed. 'Don't want to be seen carrying one of those in a castle where Le Pedvin has banned weapons. And I don't think we want the one who knows it's there finding it again.'

'They're going to come back?' Aveline asked in some alarm.

'Of course,' Wat said. 'Unless they've got crossbows hidden

all over the place. But don't worry, they won't come if you're here.'

Aveline did not look comforted by that.

As Cwen left the room with Wat and Aethelric, she explained the situation. 'You are right, Hermitage has dealt with this sort of thing on many occasions. He's often confronted a killer or stepped into danger. And every time he's done it, he's been either captured, tied up, threatened with death, or all three. That's why we're here. You should never let him investigate on his own.'

Caput XX: The Chase

Brother Hermitage's approach to following suspects through the winding ways of a Norman castle was not, perhaps, the one most people would have adopted.

He began by walking so close behind them that it seemed he was part of the group.

When one at the back turned and gave him a very odd look, he realised that not being spotted while you were following someone was probably key.

He gave a smile and clasped his hands in front of him as if he were simply a brother pacing through the cloister contemplating some matter of great import.

'Is there something I can help you with?' the man asked.

It was quite reasonable that a servant should ask this of a member of the Conclave, but Hermitage felt there was something threatening in the manner of the asking. The question sent a shiver through his habit for another reason; this was the voice from Aveline's chamber.

'Oh, er, no, no,' Hermitage stuttered. 'I was, erm, just pacing and contemplating some matters of great import.'

The man frowned at him as if unsure whether this monk was very clever, or simply peculiar.

'Of course.' The man gave a bow of little respect and held his arm out to indicate that Hermitage should proceed through the gaggle and get on with his contemplation.

Hermitage gave a grateful nod of the head and stepped along. He tried to take a good look at the man as he passed but saw nothing of significance. Perhaps twenty-five or so, dressed as a servant and with the look of one, this was clearly not some mighty warrior in disguise. No chain mail peeped out from his jerkin, no dagger hung from his belt.

As he passed the last of them, Hermitage immediately realised that getting in front of the people you are following made following them a bit tricky.

He paced on in what he thought was a contemplative manner, all the time trying to see out of the back of his head. Fortunately, the servants' conversation resumed once he was through. It was all in Norman French and was obviously being kept low in case he could hear them, but at least it gave him an indication that they were still there. He just needed to not get too far ahead.

When he felt they were slipping behind, he stopped, looked to the ceiling, stroked his chin and nodded to himself. His contemplation had obviously resolved one of the matters of great import. Once they drew closer, he set off again.

When their chatter subsided, he thought stopping for another look at the ceiling might be a bit obvious. Instead, he came to a halt and adjusted the cincture around his waist, putting it back into place as if it had shifted uncomfortably. Twisting left and right allowed him a quick glance back down the corridor.

Where there were now no servants.

With a sense of panic, he stopped fiddling with his clothes and looked urgently all around. He even glanced at the ceiling once more, but didn't really expect them to be up there. They must have taken some turn while he was distracted. He would have to retrace his steps.

Maintaining his contemplative pace, albeit a quick one now, he went back up the corridor until he came to a branch off to his right. This was a smaller passage, looking like one servants would use to get from the main body of the castle to their own area.

Not being able to think of anywhere else they could have

gone, he wandered on, prepared to say that he was lost should anyone ask.

At the end of the way, a small and simple door blocked his path and presented a dilemma. If he opened it, he was sure that he would walk straight into a gathering of murderers, all sharpening their weapons and growling at one another in a generally murderous manner.

Upon seeing him appear, they would all, quite naturally, get on with some murder straight away, and that would be that.

He bent to the door and put his ear as close as he dared, to see if he could detect what was going on within.

Hearing nothing at all, he took a step back and considered the door. It really needed to be open if he was to make any sort of progress, and so he really needed to open it. Perhaps he could do so in an absent-minded manner. Distracted by his contemplations he had wandered down the wrong corridor and simply opened the door that stood in his way.

He wondered if "sorry, wrong door" was the sort of excuse bands of murderers accepted.

With a deep breath and half-closed eyes, he reached out to the simple latch, lifted it and opened the door.

Well, that was a disappointment. Or a relief, one or the other. No murderers, no people at all. In fact, simply another passage leading onward.

Briefly wondering what the point of a door in the middle of a corridor was, he moved on.

He was now well beyond any excuse of going the wrong way, being lost or having taken a wrong turn. Trying to tell himself that he was a member of the Conclave and so could go where he liked, did not help. When asked what he was doing, replying "Mind your own business" was simply not in him.

Could it be that, outside of the Conclave, he was a monastery designer and was examining the castle for any interesting features? Yes, that sounded entirely believable to his own ear.

The corridor twisted away to the left now, and he was starting to wonder what purpose this route served as there was no one using it. The castle was filled with members of the Conclave, and their servants more than doubled the number. How could any part of the place be empty?

Unless all of the servants were in on the murder, of course, and were even now massing for their attack.

As he turned a sharp bend, he heard noise from ahead, and he thought it sounded like the normal clatter of a kitchen. Voices were raised, but it was above the clash of pans, and they sounded like simple instructions, rather than calls to arms or battle cries.

He slowed his pace and reached the end of the corridor, which did, indeed, open out into the kitchen. He remained unnoticed at the threshold and quickly scanned the place, looking for his quarry.

The room was abuzz with activity around the fire and the tables, as food was prepared. The whole scene appeared to be perfectly harmless and no one was doing anything suspicious. They weren't even cooking in a deceitful manner.

Had those he pursued moved on? In which case, where had they gone?

Over in one corner of the room, which only caught his attention because it seemed quiet and empty, he saw a number of figures gathered in the shadows of a stack of barrels and sacks.

He couldn't make out who they were, but they obviously

didn't have anything to do with the activity in the room. Or if they did, they were hiding from it.

From his resting place, he thought he might be able to make it across the back wall of the room without being noticed. Then, he could come up behind the barrels and sacks and listen to what was going on.

The whole idea was quite shocking, really, and alarmed him with its fundamental dishonesty. Trying not to be seen so that he could eavesdrop on someone's private conversation was not the sort of thing he should be doing.

But then they shouldn't be planning to murder people, which was much worse. He would need to have a long think about ends and means when he got out of all this.

This time thinking that he would say he had come to bless the food if he was stopped, he walked as calmly as he could across the back wall. Everyone seemed so busy, that no one took any notice at all.

He thought one young man stirring a pot of something or other had noticed him, but the look on his face said that the last thing he wanted to deal with was some monk in the kitchen. He looked quickly away and took a great interest in his pot.

Once at the sacks and barrels, Hermitage found himself tiptoeing along, his head tipped over to see what snippets of conversation he could catch.

This wasn't just disgraceful behaviour for a monk, it was disgraceful behaviour for anyone, but it was too late to stop now.

Squatting down by one of the barrels, the gap between it and its neighbour provided the perfect space for his ear.

Knowing that he needed an explanation for his action in advance, as he would never be able to make one up on the spur of the moment, he decided that the bread had disagreed with him, and he was squatting here to let its effect pass.

No self-respecting cook would want anyone squatting in their kitchen letting anything pass, but he couldn't think of anything better.

The voices from the other side of the barrels came to him, and he just hoped that this wasn't a simply band of lazy servants avoiding their duties.

He also hoped it wasn't a band of murderers discussing their plan. Something in the middle would be fine.

'He'll be in the main hall at dusk,' one of the men said in heavily accented Saxon English.

'I know, I know,' another replied, and he was a native speaker.

With a sharp intake of breath, Hermitage realised which native speaker it was; Haimo.

'So you'll be ready,' the first said.

'Yes, yes.' Haimo was sounding impatient, as if he had been given these instructions several times over and was wondering why people had to keep repeating themselves.

'You've got to see this through, Haimo,' another voice said, and this was the one from Aveline's chamber.

Hermitage rather wished he wasn't hiding behind a barrel so close to these people now. He had been right. The voices in Aveline's chamber had been plotting some foul deed, and he now knew that Haimo was the one to do it.

The question was, what should Brother Hermitage, the King's Investigator, do about it?

He could stand up, stride into the group and declare that they had been discovered and their plan was now in ruins. Whatever it was they had been planning to do could not now happen, and they had better confess to someone in authority.

As the King's Investigator, he thought that he might be the one in authority, but didn't really want to deal with confessions from doers of foul deeds. He supposed that he could go to Lord Gilbert, or even Le Pedvin, but say what? He'd overheard some people planning to do something? He really knew no more now than he did when he was outside Aveline's window. Apart from the fact that it was Haimo who was going to do it. He must have been the other person in that room.

If he strode boldly forward and confronted them before they'd actually done anything, they could simply deny it. They could claim they were planning to give a gift to someone and that Hermitage had now spoiled the surprise.

And if they hadn't done anything, they couldn't be held responsible, or punished for it. But he couldn't wait for them to do whatever it was they planned. If it was murder, that would be unthinkable. He couldn't let someone die simply because it was a bit awkward to confront the plotters.

He had to find out what it was they were plotting. What was this thing that Haimo was going to do at dusk? And who was he going to do it to? Once he knew that, he would be able to stop them. Well, he could quickly go and get Wat and Cwen and together they could stop them.

He turned his ear back to the conversation.

'Of course, I'll see it through,' Haimo replied, although, to Hermitage's ear, he didn't sound sure.

'You don't sound sure,' the other voice commented, and Hermitage nodded his agreement.

'I have to see it through, don't I?' Haimo said.

'You're right there. You know the consequences of failure. When our lords and masters set their minds on something, they get very upset if it doesn't come to pass. And this particular master has ways of dealing with failure that don't bear thinking about.'

'You think I don't know that?' Haimo sounded somewhat hopeless. 'And I don't really need you two watching over me night and day and saying the same thing over and over again.'

Hermitage hoped they might reveal what it was that was planned, by way of a reminder to Haimo of his duty. And if they could mention the name of the master while they were at it, that would be helpful. He craned closer to the barrel to catch any low whisper that might be exchanged. If he could hear the plot first-hand, that would give him reason to step in. Or go and get someone else to step in.

At least he now knew that Haimo was in the middle of all this. And he could identify the other man as well. The third was still a mystery, but could probably be discovered once the whole business was exposed.

Unfortunately, and Hermitage knew that there had to be an unfortunately as things seemed to be going quite well for once, the barrel against which he leaned was not stacked with being leaned against in mind.

He felt it shift beneath his shoulder, and the one stacked above that moved quite noticeably. So noticeably that the people on the other side of it noticed, unsurprisingly.

Standing quickly, Hermitage got away from the barrels as fast as he could, the young man at the pot looking up with some gratitude that the monk seemed to be leaving the kitchen quite quickly.

As the crash of falling barrels resounded behind him, Hermitage looked back and was grateful that those hiding behind it had managed to get out of the way.

He only briefly thought that if they had all been crushed to death this whole plot problem would have gone away.

Haimo, the servant from Aveline's chamber, and another stood looking at the mess the fallen barrels had made. The other still had his back to Hermitage, so was unrecognisable, but there was something familiar about him.

The three appeared to be quite alarmed that they had escaped a dangerous situation, and were perhaps concerned that they had been discovered, and the attack with the barrel was deliberate.

Hermitage slipped away back up the corridor, pleased that they had not looked in his direction for the source of their trouble.

The sound of their trouble came loud and clear as some screaming cook shrieked demands to know what the devil they had done to her salt. And what they were doing in her kitchen in the first place. And who they were anyway and did their masters know they were skulking about down here? And how she would personally crack barrels over their individual heads if they didn't clear the mess up and look sharp about it.

Hermitage hurried back down the corridor, anxious to find Wat and Cwen and let them know what he had discovered. At last, they would be able to take action. Haimo was their man, he was now sure. He had been given instruction by the servant and the event they planned was to take place at dusk in the hall. And there was a master behind it all.

It was all very well apprehending the doer of this deed, but the one behind it was the most important. The servant seemed to be Robert's man, and Haimo was Odo's, so which of them was issuing the orders? And what were the orders for?

He had to admit that this could still be some completely harmless scheme. Had Haimo been selected to bestow an honour on someone? Or had he been delegated to make the announcement that the Conclave was to be no more?

That last option was unlikely as Haimo seemed to be poorly thought of by all who had an opinion of him. He was not a member of the Conclave and only seemed to be here to argue for some land.

There really was no evidence that he was going to do anything drastic or even unexpected.

Hermitage chuckled to himself as another thought entered his head. He had been carrying out these murder investigations for too long. Every tiny event in life was not the precursor to murder. He told himself not to be ridiculous. It wasn't as if Haimo had a crossbow or anything.

Caput XXI: Plot of Plots

With Wat and Cwen looking for Hermitage, and Hermitage looking for Wat and Cwen, the chances of them actually meeting were strangely diminished.

When Hermitage had left them, they had been going to visit Aveline's chamber, so that is where he would go, blissfully unaware that was the one place they would not be.

Aethelric had left him planning to wander the main hall, listening to people to spot the voice from Aveline's chamber and then follow them. They would head to the main hall. Where Hermitage would not be, either.

In the course of their journeys, they actually passed very close by one another, but, almost as if they were in a tale that was dragging itself out for no very good reason, they didn't look in the right direction at the right moment.

Arriving at Aveline's door, Hermitage hesitated for a moment. If Wat and Cwen were in there, it would be safe to simply walk in. If they were not and Aveline was alone, simply walking in would not be at all sensible. He knocked.

'What is it now?' Aveline's voice demanded.

'It is Brother Hermitage,' Hermitage announced hesitantly but politely.

There was an audible sigh of frustration from within, so loud that it cut through the thick oak door. Footsteps followed and the door was opened. Aveline stood there with a dress over her arm.

'What are you doing here?' the lady of the castle asked, the question clearly implying that Hermitage should be somewhere else completely.

'I am looking for Wat and Cwen?' He tried to make it sound like a harmless enquiry.

'Well, they're looking for you, aren't they?'

'Are they?'

'Of course, they are.'

Hermitage felt embarrassed that he didn't know this, as Aveline obviously thought he should. Even though there was no way that he could.

'I see.'

'That bishop said you were following someone.'

'Bishop Aethelric,' Hermitage reminded her.

'I suppose so,' Aveline replied, and Hermitage briefly wondered how many bishops she had been talking to about him.

'Do you know where they went?'

'I just said,' Aveline huffed. 'To find you.'

'Ah, yes.' He wondered just how much Wat and Cwen might have told Aveline, and whether he could question her about the presence of Haimo in her chamber.

'They were here, then?' he checked.

Aveline now added an annoyed frown to her demeanour. 'They'd have to have been, wouldn't they? If they left here to find you?'

'I suppose they would.'

Aveline rolled her eyes. 'If there's nothing else?' she said. The clear instruction being that there was nothing else.

'Did they, erm, tell you anything about why they were looking for me?'

'Don't you know why they'd be looking for you?' Aveline now closed the door slightly, as if worried that Hermitage was the sort of monk who could do something unexpected.

'Well, yes, I do. I'm wondering if you do.'

Aveline considered him carefully. 'Are you ill?'

'Ill?'

'Yes, Or peculiar in some way?'

'No, I don't think so.'

'Hm. You might want to think about that some more. Well, I must get on.' She made to close the door.

'No, no,' Hermitage pleaded. 'I mean, if you know what is going on, I can tell you more, or perhaps ask you a question or two.'

'I'm not sure I want to know what's going on. Having you lot coming in and out of my room is bad enough.'

'Did Wat and Cwen tell you about the voice I heard?' Hermitage thought that he had to say something direct before she slammed the door in his face.

'You hear voices?'

'At your window,' Hermitage plunged in as he was in danger of confusing things.

'Oh, that. Yes. That bishop was going on about it. They said it was you listening at my chamber. And you a monk.'

'I just happened to be passing outside.'

'And you shouldn't be doing that, either.'

This was not going well. 'Do you know a fellow called Haimo?' Hermitage asked.

'Know him?'

'Yes, do you know him?'

'Hardly.'

'Hardly?' Hermitage asked, getting thoroughly confused. 'What does that mean?'

'It means that Haimo is not the sort of person I know.'

No, that didn't help.

Aveline obviously saw his confusion. 'This Haimo fellow is simply on the list of those attending the Conclave. No one really knows why, and as far as I can tell, no one has a good word for him.'

'He is Sheriff of Kent.'

'Is he, really?' Aveline sounded conflicted. She obviously thought little of the man, but more of the title.

'Bishop Odo's man.'

'The King's Brother?' Haimo had suddenly become much more interesting.

'And he is here to try and discuss some land, apparently.'

Aveline frowned. 'But the Conclave isn't about land.'

'Just so. Yet he is here. Perhaps Bishop Odo saw an opportunity for Haimo to simply meet the right people.'

Aveline nodded as she obviously agreed that the Conclave was perfect for that sort of thing.

'Or..,' Hermitage prompted.

'Or what?'

'He is here for some other purpose.'

The puzzlement on Aveline's face slowly lifted. 'Doing the something that is going to be done at the Conclave.'

Got there in the end, Hermitage thought.

'He was the man you overheard in my chamber?' Aveline now sounded quite disgusted that someone like Haimo might have been in her room.

'Not exactly,' Hermitage said. He looked up and down the corridor. 'Do you think I might come in? You never know who could be listening.'

'That's certainly true,' Aveline agreed. 'No one's chamber is safe from eavesdroppers these days.' She gave Hermitage a very pointed look but did open the door wide and close it behind him once he was inside.

She turned to face him with arms folded.

'Haimo was not the man I heard in your chamber.'

'Then what does he have to do with anything?'

'But I think he was in here, being given the instruction to

do this thing, whatever it is.'

'How do you know that?'

'Because I did find the one with the voice I heard. And he was repeating the instruction to Haimo in person.'

'And who was he?'

'The one with the voice?'

'Yes, the one with the voice,' Aveline snapped. 'I want to know who has been coming into my chamber without permission.'

'Well, I don't know exactly.'

'You said you found him.'

'Yes, but I don't know his name. All I know is that he is one of Robert's servants.'

'Robert?'

'Count of Mortain.'

'Yes, I know who Robert is, thank you very much.' Aveline turned away from him and paced up and down the room. 'This makes it very awkward.'

'It is difficult,' Hermitage agreed.

'On the one hand, I can't have servants wandering in and out of my chambers as they please, but on the other, he is Robert's man, and I wouldn't want to offend him.'

'And we still don't know what instruction Haimo has received. What is it he is going to do?' Hermitage said.

'Well, he's going to shoot someone, isn't he?'

Hermitage blinked while he checked that he had heard what he thought he had.

'He's going to what?' Even though he was clear about the words, he wanted to hear them again.

'He's going to shoot someone.'

No, they were the same words.

'What makes you think he's going to shoot someone?'

'Look under the bed,' Aveline instructed.

Hermitage couldn't immediately connect this instruction with any part of the conversation thus far, but Aveline was the sort of person whose instructions were instinctively obeyed. He got down on his knees.

'Oh, my,' he said as he saw what was under there.

'Quite. And it's not mine before you get that idea in your head.'

'I didn't think it was.'

'Your weaving friend did.'

'Oh, my, oh, my,' Hermitage repeated as he stood. 'He's going to shoot someone.'

'Do you think so?' Aveline asked sarcastically.

'It all makes sense now. Haimo was in your chamber being instructed to carry out the deed because this is where they hid the crossbow.'

'Yes, we had worked that out already,' Aveline said. 'We just didn't know that it was going to be Haimo. Now we do, it can all be dealt with, can't it.'

'Oh, erm, can it?' Hermitage asked.

'You are this investigator, thing, yes?'

'Well, yes.'

'Well, you've got a man who has a crossbow in a conclave where there are supposed to be no weapons. So do something about it.'

'I suppose I should.' Hermitage still wasn't sure what he was going to do about it.

'You suppose you should?' Aveline asked clearly incredulous that there should be any doubt.

Obviously, Hermitage could go to Le Pedvin and say that a crossbow had been found and that the servant of Robert had been in Aveline's chamber issuing instructions to someone, who was, in all probability, Haimo.

It was all very suspicious and improper, and would doubtless lead to the servant and Haimo being punished in some way, but it still didn't lead to the motivation behind this plan, or whose plan it was.

'There was also talk of a master,' Hermitage said.

'A master what?'

'No, I mean a master who was behind the whole scheme.'

'And who was that, then?'

'I don't know.'

Aveline sighed. 'You don't know much, do you?'

'There are still gaps, it's true,' Hermitage admitted. 'I could have this servant of Robert and Haimo taken by your father or Lord Le Pedvin, but that might not reveal what is behind all of this. Who has instructed that a shooting be done, and who are they going to shoot?'

'Robert.'

'Robert?'

'Your weavers said that he was the most important person at the Conclave and so would be the one to get shot.'

'By his own servant?' Hermitage asked. 'I suppose it is possible that someone in his retinue conspires against him.'

'And you said Haimo is Odo's man,' Aveline pointed out.

'Odo would have his own brother killed?' Hermitage couldn't believe that.

'Richest man in England, so they say. Can't be rich when you're dead.'

'And his riches might go to Odo.' Hermitage grimaced at the awful thought.

'Well,' Aveline said brightly. 'I'm glad you've got it all sorted out now.' She moved over to the door and opened it. 'You can be on your way and take the horrid crossbow with you.'

Hermitage hadn't got that far in his thinking about what to do next.

'Oh, erm...,' he started as another thought occurred to him.

'It can't stay here. You know what is to be done and who is doing it, what more do you want?'

'No, I was thinking that this reveals why Lord de Sauveloy sent me here,' Hermitage said with some disappointment.

'Does it?' Aveline asked with little interest.

'Yes. It wasn't that I have anything to contribute to the Conclave, or even as a reward for my service.'

'That is a shame.' Aveline held the door even wider.

'He must have got wind of this plan, or that there was a plan of some sort, and sent me to uncover it before the deed could be done.'

'Yes, that sounds nice. Off you go and tell someone all about it.'

'It was just lucky I happened to be passing your window at the right time.'

'Yes, wasn't it,' Aveline said with increasing impatience.

'Of course, if I hadn't overheard anything, and the murder had been committed, Lord de Sauveloy would probably have blamed me for not finding out in time.'

'Yes, I'm sure he would. Can you go now, please?'

'Oh, erm, yes. Of course.'

'Thank you.'

'Hermitage, there you are,' Cwen said as she appeared at the door with Wat and the bishop.

'Oh, not again,' Aveline wailed. 'If you lot have more chattering to do, go somewhere else and do it. I've got dresses to tidy.'

'Have you been taking lessons in that as well as crossbow?'

Cwen asked.

Aveline pointed a finger. 'I can have you thrown out of the castle, you know.'

'Please do,' Cwen replied. 'Then you can sort out the crossbow yourself.'

'You know about the weapon now,' Wat said to Hermitage. 'Someone is going to get shot. We thought Robert.'

'Yes,' Hermitage replied. 'Aveline's been telling me. And I've discovered that it was Haimo who was being given the instruction.'

'Was it? We have the man and the method, then.'

'And that instruction came from one of Robert's own men, can you believe?'

'Conspiring against his own lord?' Wat nodded appreciatively at that, which didn't seem at all appropriate.

'But even that instruction came from some master or other,' Hermitage added.

'And Haimo is Odo's man,' Bishop Aethelric pointed out.

Hermitage nodded. 'A scheme to get Robert's riches, we thought.'

'Being the richest man in England has made him a very large target,' Wat observed. 'Brother killing brother, eh?'

'And this must be why Ranulph de Sauveloy sent me here,' Hermitage said. 'He wanted me to stop the plot, or, if I failed at that, take the blame for not stopping it.'

'Why not simply tell Le Pedvin?' Cwen asked.

'You know how those two get on,' Wat pointed out. 'I don't think de Sauveloy would tell Le Pedvin if the sky was falling. God forbid he should risk Le Pedvin getting any credit for stopping a murder. Sorry Hermitage,' Wat apologised for the unwarranted blasphemy.

'But if Lord de Sauveloy knows about all this, why not

come himself and stop it?' Aveline asked.

Everyone laughed heartily at that.

'What?' Aveline asked in some anger at the mockery.

'Lord de Sauveloy does not, erm, how can I put it?' Aethelric pondered.

'Get his hands dirty?' Cwen suggested.

'Something along those lines, yes. He would set events in motion, issue instructions, hints and directions, but never get too close himself.'

'In case someone blamed him personally,' Cwen explained. 'That would never do.'

Aveline shook her head at all this. 'Whoever is doing whatever, you can now get this crossbow out of my room and begone, the lot of you. Take it up with my father or Le Pedvin. I want nothing to do with any of it.'

'It's still not straightforward though, is it?' Wat said. 'We've may have Odo trying to have his brother murdered. They stand above even Le Pedvin. It's only the little men who will get punished.

'Even if we get Haimo to confess this instruction comes from Odo, he'll be dismissed as a liar trying to save his own skin. And Robert's man will probably deny the whole thing and say how loyal he is to his lord.'

Thoughts of how appallingly these people behaved to one another disturbed Hermitage deeply, and he hoped that there might be some means by which their behaviour could be exposed. If word could be put in the right ear about who had been doing what, some action might be taken against those who actually deserved it.

As he speculated about this, a new possibility occurred to him and he clamped a hand to his mouth as a wave of hideous realisation swept through him.

'Hermitage?' Cwen asked. 'I've got a nasty feeling that you've just come up with something we are not going to like.'

All eyes turned to Hermitage, and he dearly hoped that his speculation was just that. Idle fancy from the midst of a web of deceit and duplicitous dealing.

He managed to get his words out and hoped that giving them air would see them wither as the others dismissed such nonsense.

'Haimo is Odo's man, we know that.'

'Aye,' Aethelric agreed.

'And the man issuing the instructions was Robert's.'

'You saw him,' Wat confirmed.

'So, between them, they are plotting a murder with the weapon we have found.'

'Yes,' Cwen prompted.

Hermitage swallowed. 'What if the two brothers are not conspiring one against the other?'

'Who then?' Wat asked.

'The third brother,' Hermitage said.

The room was silent and even Aveline paled as this realisation came to them all.

'My God,' Bishop Aethelric breathed. 'They're going to murder the king.'

Caput XXII: Word Spreads

'Now we really have got to tell Le Pedvin,' Cwen urged.

'If he isn't part of it,' Wat said quietly.

'A plot to kill the king?' Cwen frowned. 'Funnily enough, I don't see him as the type. If he wanted to stab someone in the back, he'd do it from the front.'

Hermitage was still too horrified by his own ideas to think straight, but the suggestion that Le Pedvin might plot to murder the king did not sound right.

'He may not be involved, ' he said. 'In fact, I agree with Cwen that this is not the way he would go about things, but that doesn't mean he's innocent. He may know about it and is simply letting it happen.'

'De Sauveloy?' Wat suggested. "There's a man who probably schemes his way into his shoes in the morning.'

'Not to kill the king, I think,' Aethelric said. 'Without William, Ranulph de Sauveloy is nothing. In fact, there are many who would like to see Lord de Sauveloy at the wrong end of a crossbow. The king is his protection.'

'And this plot does explain why I was sent here,' Hermitage put in. 'De Sauveloy heard of it and sent me to stop it.'

'Rather than get in harm's way himself,' Cwen observed.

'It was a bit of a long shot, wasn't it?' Wat asked. 'I mean, we only know what we know because you happened to be passing Aveline's window when the conspirators were, you know, conspiring. Even De Sauveloy couldn't scheme that into being, surely?

'If he did want you finding things out, he might have mentioned it. You know, simply send you to Nottingham with instructions to uncover a plot. Why appoint you to the

Conclave?'

Hermitage could see the problem. 'Maybe he didn't know much? Just had hints that something was going on and wanted me here just in case.'

'To find out who did it after they'd killed the king,' Cwen suggested.

Hermitage grimaced at that possibility. 'My appointment to the Conclave could simply have been a disguise. Sending me as the King's Investigator might have put the plotters off.'

Wat nodded very slowly at this. 'That could make some sense. If Odo and Robert are in this together, they could be removed from the picture by being exposed as the killers.'

He was looking at Hermitage as he said this, which was very worrying. Accusing murderers at any time was bad enough, but Bishop Odo and Count Robert? It didn't bear thinking about. If the brothers were prepared to murder their own kin, killing an interfering monk would take very little effort.

'Who gets to be king if William isn't around and his brothers have been executed for murder?'

Bishop Aethelric looked quite appalled by the question. 'Well,' he stuttered. 'Erm, his son, I suppose. William.'

'At least the name is convenient,' Wat commented.

'He's a strange boy,' the bishop shook his head.

'All of this is very interesting,' Cwen said. 'But never mind worrying about the next king down the line, what do we do now? If we confront Haimo and this man of Robert's, they'll simply deny everything.'

'Lord Gilbert,' Bishop Aethelric said decisively. 'He is an honest man who would not scheme against anyone.'

'Not even for his own daughter's benefit,' Aveline mumbled.

Everyone scowled at her.

Hermitage saw Gilbert as a sensible way forward. 'We tell Lord Gilbert what we have discovered and take his advice. He knows much of what has happened so far, this new information puts everything in its place.'

'Agreed,' Aethelric said. 'Mistress Aveline, do you know where we might find him?'

'As far away from the Conclave as possible,' Aveline replied. 'Probably with the horses or in the stores.'

'I left him in the main hall,' Hermitage said. 'But the Conclave was breaking up.'

'Sounds like the perfect time to check supplies,' Aveline snorted. 'A few hours away from everyone counting the wine and the ale again.'

'Back to the stores, then,' Wat said. 'I'm sure the victualler will be pleased to see us again.'

'We had better hide the crossbow,' Aethelric said. 'We don't want the plotters coming back to take it.'

'The suggestion was that the deed would be done in the main hall at dusk,' Hermitage said. 'Obviously, they would have to wait for the king to arrive before killing him, and no one has actually confirmed that William will come. It's only been suggested that he might.'

'It could be these plotters have better information than we do,' Wat said. 'And they might wait until the time to collect the weapon, but then again, they might want it early. Let's get it out of harm's way.'

'And where would that be?' Cwen asked.

Wat frowned. 'Gilbert's chamber? I think just putting it under the bed again won't be much good. It's the first place they'd look.'

'I'm not sure my father would like the murder weapon of

the king put in his room.'

'It hasn't murdered anyone yet,' Wat replied. 'Well, no one we know of. It's the only place I can think of. We certainly can't carry it around.'

'And we'll tell Lord Gilbert what we've done with it,' Cwen assured her.

Aveline still wasn't happy, but obviously didn't have an alternative to offer.

...

'You've put it where?' Gilbert virtually exploded when the last detail of the tale was told.

'We couldn't leave it in your daughter's room, could we?' Wat pleaded.

Gilbert calmed a little and sat back down on the sack of grain in the victualler's cave, the man himself having been dismissed with the helpful instruction to "take a walk somewhere".

'I suppose not,' Gilbert accepted. 'It is a real crossbow, is it? Not some toy?'

'Oh, it's real,' Wat assured him. 'Not assembled and no bolts with it, but they could be anywhere.'

'And someone got it into the castle in Aveline's clothes?'

'In the chest with my clothes,' Aveline specified, clearly not wanting anyone to think she could hide a crossbow in her dress.

'This is unbelievable.' Lord Gilbert seemed to sag under the weight of the information. 'Murder the king? Are you sure?'

'Well, no, we're not sure,' Bishop Aethelric gave him some comfort, 'But the facts of the situation seem to point in that direction. Robert and Odo's men conspiring, with a crossbow at a conclave the king is due to attend. A deed to be done at dusk in the main hall, when the king might arrive. What else would they be up to?'

'We have to stop them,' Gilbert announced.

'Well, yes,' Wat stated the obvious. 'I think that would be for the best.'

Gilbert scowled at him.

'Being Saxons, we've no great love for William, but he is king.' Wat explained. 'And while kings generally get to be kings by killing one another, I'd rather not be in the vicinity when it happens. Let alone at the same conclave.

'Look what happened at Hastings. If this is Robert or Odo's plan for the throne, they may decide to get rid of all the witnesses after they've done their brother.'

Cwen nodded agreement at this. 'Do you think they'll try to kill one another after they've done William? After all, you can't have two kings at the same time.'

'Good point,' Wat said. 'Who is the eldest?'

'It's not too clear,' Aethelric said. 'I have heard that both claim to be the elder, but the general view is that Robert is younger. But not by much.'

'King Odo it is, then,' Wat said. 'And Robert carries on as the richest man in England. Until he gets bored and wants to be king. In which case, poor old Odo.' Wat made the traditional slicing gesture across his throat.

'None of which will come to pass,' Gilbert said firmly. 'Because it will be stopped, won't it.' This was not a question.

He stood from the grain sack. 'First of all, we remove this crossbow from the castle.'

'What, throw it out of the window?' Cwen asked.

'No.' Gilbert was now struggling to control himself. 'We

take it to Lord Le Pedvin and it goes under lock and key. At least you were right about him. The man gave his eye in service of the Duke. There is no more loyal or trustworthy servant.'

'Or violent and murderous,' Cwen muttered.

Gilbert pointed his finger at her. 'I didn't say he wasn't violent and murderous, I said he was loyal and trustworthy. Gods, to think this is all happening in my castle. The weapon brought in with my daughter's property and the king murdered in my home. Le Pedvin must be told, or he'll think I had something to do with it.

'Men have had more than their castles taken away from them for less than this.'

He gestured that the door to the store be opened again, and they found the victualler outside, clearly fretting about what was being done to his victuals while he was away.

'Where is Lord Le Pedvin?' Gilbert demanded.

'Erm, I don't know, my lord,' the victualler replied, unprepared for a question that wasn't about stores.

'Should we find Haimo and this man of Robert's and take them?' Wat asked. 'Then, we can present Le Pedvin with the whole problem.'

Gilbert shook his head as he walked back towards the castle. 'This needs very careful handling. If William's own brothers are scheming against him, the likes of you and I will be easily dealt with.' He considered Wat for a moment. 'Well, the likes of you will be easily dealt with. The bishop and I might be a bit more difficult, but could still fall in the midst of all this. No, we need Le Pedvin. He's as close to the king as there is.

'If anyone is going to deal with the plotters and explain what his brothers are up to, it must be him.'

Hermitage didn't like the idea of working with Le Pedvin at all. The man looked at everyone as if they were already dead, but just hadn't stopped walking around yet. To say that he had no love for Hermitage was a statement considerably further down than an understatement.

He tried to think of one, but couldn't recall an occasion when Le Pedvin hadn't referred to him as an idiot. Sometimes even the idiot. As if he were the Platonic archetype of all idiots.

When they found him, Hermitage would make sure he was standing behind Lord Gilbert.

Back at the main hall, the guards stood aside for their master and one of them opened the door, scowling their confusion as Aveline, a monk, two bakers and a bishop were hard on his heels.

'Have you seen Lord Le Pedvin,' Gilbert turned and asked one of the guards.

'Oh, yes, my lord,' the guard replied, while his fellow nodded. 'Thin fellow. Eye patch.'

'I don't want to know what he looks like. I want to know where he is. Now.'

'Oh, erm, sorry, my lord. I think I saw him prowling, erm, that is, patrolling the outer wall.'

'How long ago was that?'

'Just after all that chatter in the hall finished,' the guard explained.

'The Conclave?'

The guard nodded.

'Right. Down to the wall,' Gilbert instructed.

He strode down the hill and everyone else had to keep up. Except Aveline and Bishop Aethelric. Aveline was clearly not going to walk down the muddy track to the outer gate and it would be too much effort for the bishop. 'You can tell us what he says,' she called after her father, who waved a hand in acknowledgement.

'It's probably best to talk to him down here,' Gilbert explained to the others. 'Less chance of being overheard.'

At the main gate, the guards seemed to be particularly alert and stood stiff and respectful before their lord.

'Lord Le Pedvin just passed by?' Gilbert asked.

One guard simply nodded and Hermitage noticed he had a somewhat haunted look about him.

'He went that way,' the other guard said, his voice breaking.

Gilbert nodded and led the way along the palisade. Guards were posted every so often, each in sight of the one on either side. Most of them were visible from this spot by the gate as the outer wall of the castle circled around in each direction.

The next two guards off along the wall to the right stood as if ready for action at any moment. Weapons were in hand and the first sign of any threat would be dealt with in an efficient and deadly manner.

The next guard along was leaning against the wall, his sword was stuck in the earth and he was using the handle as a rest for his helmet.

Prowling towards him, and Hermitage agreed with that guard at the hall, there was no better word for it, was Lord Le Pedvin.

The slovenly guard had no idea what was about to hit him, and probably wouldn't for some considerable time afterwards.

'My Lord,' Gilbert called as he hurried along.

The resting guard looked up from whatever it was he had been doing with his hands, and quickly saw the situation. He sorted himself out in very short order and stood alert.

Le Pedvin glanced back and looked disappointed that his quarry had been snatched from him. Nevertheless, he waited for Gilbert and his party to catch up.

He considered the group with his singular eye. 'A problem?' he asked.

'Aye, my lord,' Gilbert confirmed. 'And one I think best discussed out here.'

Le Pedvin took a long deep breath. 'I suppose it was to be expected with the idiot and his two weavers skulking about the place.'

Hermitage took some perverse comfort from the fact that he was still an idiot.

Le Pedvin turned his gaze to Wat and Cwen. 'You didn't think putting a smock and a hat on would stop me recognising you, surely?' he asked. 'I could have had you taken at the castle door, but I thought it might be interesting to see what you were up to.'

'We were up to uncovering a plot to kill the king,' Cwen said. She then coughed as Le Pedvin had taken one step forward, grabbed her by the jerkin under her throat and lifted her from the ground.

'Here,' Wat complained. 'Put down my wife.'

'My lord,' Gilbert said placatingly. 'We believe we have uncovered a scheme of some sort. Men overheard talking about doing some deed at dusk. And we have found a crossbow hidden in the castle.'

Le Pedvin slowly lowered Cwen but continued to glare at her in a very alarming manner for a man with only one eye to do the glaring with.

'And why would this be aimed at the king?' Le Pedvin asked.

'One of the schemers is Odo's man, Haimo, and the other is a servant of Lord Robert.'

Le Pedvin stood in silent thought for a long moment. 'I suppose it was you overheard them?' he asked Hermitage.

'Erm, yes. My Lord, erm.'

'Yes. I thought it might be.'

'I overheard words from, erm, one of the chambers in the castle, but couldn't see who it was. Then, I heard the voice again and followed the man to the kitchen. Once there, he discussed the plan with Haimo and another, and I saw them both.'

'You overheard them, followed them and identified them?'

'Erm, well, yes.'

'You surprise me. I didn't think you were that useful.'

Hermitage thought that might be a compliment, but he wasn't sure.

'Show me this crossbow,' Le Pedvin instructed.

'Aye,' Gilbert replied. 'I have had it secured in my chamber.' He raised an arm towards the castle and Le Pedvin led the way back up the hill.

'Well,' Wat said as he Cwen and Hermitage brought up the rear. 'I thought that went as well as could be expected.'

Caput XXIII: A Plan For The Plot

The guards at the main castle door couldn't have stood more upright or looked more guard-like, as Gilbert and Le Pedvin approached.

Their sighs of relief were audible and they seemed to sag into their armour as the two Normans entered the castle without a word, and a ragged band of Saxons followed on.

'Where do you think you're going,' the first guard asked as he stepped in their way.

Cwen simply glared, leaned around him and called into the castle. 'Lord Le Pedvin, this guard is holding us up.'

The man vanished as smoke on a breeze.

Once through the door, they stepped along quickly as Lord Gilbert led the way to his chamber. There was no one in the main hall to be brushed aside, but if there had been, they would have been. A couple of the bishops from the Conclave were talking by the fireplace, but everyone else must have retired to their chambers.

They looked over as the Normans passed by, seemingly pursued by a monk and a couple of bakers. Eyebrows were raised, but that was the only interest as if this sort of thing were commonplace.

Winding through the castle, they soon arrived at the corridor to Gilbert's chamber.

'This is my room,' Le Pedvin noted, sounding somewhat confused as they passed his door.

'Aye,' Gilbert confirmed. 'The best chambers in the castle. Mine, yours, Count Robert's and my daughter's.'

'You, monk,' Le Pedvin said turning to Hermitage.

'Me?' Hermitage asked.

Le Pedvin's sigh was short and to the point. 'I think you're the only monk here. Where did you overhear this plotting? You said it was in a chamber, was it one of these?'

'Erm, well, yes. I was outside and heard it through the window.'

'And where was the crossbow found? The same chamber?'

'Yes, I suppose it was.'

'You suppose it was?'

'Yes, it was.'

Le Pedvin nodded at this and Hermitage grimaced as he knew that the moment had come when Aveline's name would be connected to the plot and the weapon.

'And Robert's chamber just here, eh?' Le Pedvin said thoughtfully.

Just as Hermitage was sighing his own quiet relief, the door to Aveline's chamber opened and she stood on the threshold with Bishop Aethelric behind her.

'Mistress,' Le Pedvin gave her a curt nod. 'Bishop,' he added with a bit more of a frown.

'At last,' Aveline said, stepping into the corridor. 'We're going to get this nonsense sorted out.'

Hermitage desperately wanted to stand behind Le Pedvin and make the sort of gestures that tell a third person to shut up as they are about to cause no end of trouble. Instead, he just closed his eyes and screwed up his face in that expression people use in the moment between a jug falling from the table and it hitting the floor; as if the look will stop the inevitable destruction.

'Nonsense?' Le Pedvin asked.

'Aveline is concerned about the crossbow,' Lord Gilbert stepped in quickly. 'To have such a thing close by when it may be intended for the king is most alarming.'

'How does she know about it? Does the whole castle

know?' Le Pedvin was clearly going to be very disappointed if that were the case.

'Oh, no, no. Just us.'

Le Pedvin looked at everyone. 'Let's see the thing,' he said. 'Then you can tell me exactly how it was found.'

Gilbert gestured Le Pedvin to go first, and as he did so, the father turned to the daughter and made a far more explicit "shut up" gesture than Hermitage would even have thought of.

Aveline looked quite shocked.

As they gathered in the room, Gilbert nodded hard at Wat, indicating that the crossbow could now be recovered.

Going down onto his knees, Wat reached under Lord Gilbert's bed and emerged with the parts of the weapon in his hands.

'The weaver knows where it is, then,' Le Pedvin observed, taking it and turning it over for a closer examination.

He expertly slotted the bow section into the front of the stock and secured it with a leather thong that was attached there for the purpose. Once content, he put the back of the stock against his thigh and pulled the string until it dropped over a small ledge cut into the top of the stock.

As he did so, a lighter piece of wood rose up on top, levered up by the string on its far end.

Aiming at the wall, he depressed the near end of the light wood. It, in turn, released the string from its constraint and it snapped hard forward, pulled by the tension of the bow.

'Oh, my.' Hermitage had seen a crossbow before but had never been so close to one in action. It was so simple, yet so horrifying.

'Not much good for battle,' Le Pedvin observed. 'Takes too long to reload. Good for one accurate shot at one person, though.' He cast his gaze around the room, primarily at the people in it. 'I think it time for the full explanation.'

Everyone looked very briefly at everyone else to see who was going to take the lead in this.

Hermitage thought it only fair that he should begin, as it was his overhearing of the conversation that had started all this.

'Shall I begin?' he asked.

'I wish someone would,' Le Pedvin said.

Hermitage took a breath. 'While I was waiting for the Conclave to begin, I took a walk around the outside of the castle.'

Le Pedvin opened his mouth, clearly intending to ask why anyone would do such a thing out of choice, but decided to say nothing.

'And it was while I was outside one of the windows at the back that I heard the conversation. It was an instruction that something was going to be done and that it would be done during the Conclave.'

'Whose chamber was it?'

'Well, erm, I didn't know. Not being familiar with the layout of the castle. That was something I would have to find out.'

'And you did.'

Hermitage opened his mouth.

'It was mine,' Aveline spoke up.

'Aveline!' Lord Gilbert hissed through clamped teeth.

'He's got to know sometime.'

'Yours?' Le Pedvin was obviously surprised.

'I have been organising the Conclave with Leudric, and have barely been in my chamber at all,' she explained.

'How did you find out it was hers?' Le Pedvin asked

Hermitage.

'Oh, well, er, that is, I sort of came into the castle and got one of the servants to show me the rooms. I looked out of the windows and saw that Aveline's was the one.'

'Hm,' Le Pedvin frowned. 'Maybe not such an idiot after all.'

Now that really was a compliment.

'And the crossbow?' Le Pedvin asked.

'In the chest with my clothes,' Aveline said.

'Hermitage told us it was Aveline's chamber,' Wat said. 'So Cwen and I went there, looked around, and found the crossbow.'

Le Pedvin nodded and turned to Aveline. 'Just to be sure, you're not plotting to kill the king, I suppose.'

'No, she is not,' Gilbert snapped. 'We'd hardly come and tell you, would we?'

Le Pedvin held his hands out to urge calm. 'I didn't think so, but everything has to be checked. So, the men are plotting in your empty chamber, they hide their crossbow there and are overheard again by the monk.'

Hermitage wondered if he might take this moment to remind Lord Le Pedvin of his name. On balance, he'd rather the man knew him as simply "the monk".

'They aren't very good at this, are they?' Le Pedvin said. 'Overheard twice and their weapon discovered.'

'We think they must have used Aveline's chest of clothing to get it into the castle as it wouldn't have been searched.'

Le Pedvin nodded grim agreement to this. 'Not a mistake I will be making again.'

'If this is Odo and Robert plotting against their brother...,' Gilbert left the consequences to everyone's imagination.

'They must be stopped,' Bishop Aethelric said. 'I have been

giving this some consideration, and I think we should apprehend the conspirators now.'

'Who will only deny everything and we won't get to the bottom of it,' Gilbert replied.

'Better that than risk the king's life.'

'No one is risking the king's life,' Le Pedvin said.

Aethelric nodded that he was happy with this.

'But Lord Gilbert is right. Haimo and this man of Robert's are only the fleas. We want to catch the dog.

'Do we know if they have come looking for their weapon?'

'No one has been in my chamber that I know of,' Aveline said. 'And I have been there most of the time.'

Le Pedvin rubbed the patch over his missing eye. 'Then we put this back where it came from and leave the chamber clear. Mistress Aveline, you must go back to your duties with the Conclave, and try to make it clear that you are busy about the castle. Not in your chamber.'

'We're going to give them the weapon back?' Aethelric asked in obvious horror.

'Not exactly,' Le Pedvin replied.

He removed the bow from the stock once more and went on to take a small wooden pin from the stock. With this gone, the lever that fired the string came free and Le Pedvin held it in one hand. With the other, he took his dagger from his belt and whittled away at the wood until he had removed a significant section of it.

Reassembling it and putting the pin back he considered his work. 'Still looks the part, but the first time someone tries to use it, the firing lever will snap.'

'You sound like you've done this before,' Wat observed.

Le Pedvin made no reply to that. 'We know who we are watching, and we know what they are going to do.'

'Do we know that William is even coming?' Cwen asked. 'No one has said for sure.'

'He is,' Le Pedvin confirmed. 'He was always coming, but there is more trouble in the north that he travels to deal with. He will stop here for the night.'

'Who would know those plans?' Hermitage asked.

'A good question,' Le Pedvin said.

Hermitage was finding it hard to get used to this.

'But it is no secret,' Le Pedvin added. 'Certainly, Robert or Odo would know, along with half the court in London.'

'We try to catch the men in the act,' Wat said.

'We do. If the king is to be presented with a tale of his brothers' treachery, he will want the evidence.'

Hermitage hesitated to raise the question that was in his head, but, like Aveline's confession, he thought Le Pedvin finding things out later, would be much, much worse. 'We did wonder if this was why I was sent to the Conclave in the first place,' he said nervously.

Le Pedvin frowned at him. 'To overhear a conversation at a window and then find a crossbow hidden amongst dresses?'

'Well, not that specifically, obviously. But if Lord de Sauveloy heard word of a plot?'

'He should have told me,' Le Pedvin said very plainly. 'More likely, you are the scapegoat in the event the plot succeeds. After all, this is his conclave. God forbid the king should be murdered during it. If the King's Investigator is here, he can be hanged instead.

'De Sauveloy can't have thought there was a serious plot, or he would have done something serious about it.'

'Or he's erm..?' Wat was trying to sound innocent.

'In on a plot to kill the king?' Le Pedvin did that laughing noise again. And it wasn't any better the second time around.

'Without the king to protect him, I would give de Sauveloy half a day before some noble he's insulted has his head off.

'I will grant that Ranulph de Sauveloy is a deeply unpleasant, scheming, deceitful and dishonest man. But, if there is one thing all his manipulation is aimed at, it is advancing the interests of Ranulph de Sauveloy. And that can only be achieved with William as king.

'Robert would throw him to the wolves, and Odo would have him tied down and invite the wolves in.'

'Not in on the plot, then,' Wat concluded.

'Not in on the plot,' Le Pedvin confirmed. 'Now, you put this back where you found it, exactly as you found it, yes?'

Wat nodded as he took the disassembled crossbow.

'Mistress Aveline back to work and the rest of us as we were. Once the king arrives, we know that the attack will be in the main hall.'

'And I know where it's going to come from,' Cwen said.

All eyes turned to her.

'Alan's little gallery.'

'Alan's what?' Gilbert asked.

'Little gallery. The one overlooking the main hall. Where Alan is hiding.'

'Is that where he's gone?'

'What little gallery?' Le Pedvin interrupted the domestic discussion.

'There's a small gallery above the main hall,' Cwen explained. 'You can get to it from the upper floor. Only big enough for one or two people. Lord Gilbert's servant, Alan, is staying there while Leudric takes the castle over.'

'It's for the minstrels,' Aveline said, sounding quite defensive.

'What minstrels?' Gilbert asked. 'We haven't got any

minstrels.'

'You think I don't know that?' Aveline snapped.

'Then..?'

Aveline was looking very agitated. 'Agh,' she huffed and turned away.

'Wouldn't get many minstrels in that,' Cwen observed. 'One man and a lute and that would be about it. Gallery of the minstrel would be a better name. And preferably a fairly small minstrel.'

Aveline turned to Cwen and her features were frozen. 'Shut up.' she instructed.

Gilbert opened his mouth to speak, but Wat held his hand up and gave a shake of the head to indicate that no words should be spoken at this moment.

'Very well,' Le Pedvin said. 'I will set my guards but will have to attend the king when he arrives. Gilbert, you watch the gallery. You, weaver girl, show me where it is.'

'Cwen,' Cwen said.

'Don't push your luck, Saxon.'

Ah, there was the old Le Pedvin. It was a bit of a relief, somehow.

Waving his arms at them all like a flock of sheep, Le Pedvin herded everyone out of the room.

Wat peeled off and returned to Aveline's chamber with the crossbow.

'Exactly as you found it,' Le Pedvin instructed.

'Oh, let me,' Aveline went as well. 'You'll ruin the dresses,' she accused Wat who shrugged.

'Bishop and monk, back to the Conclave, whatever it's getting up to. Lord Gilbert, you're with me. The weavers had better carry on pretending to be bakers. It seems to have worked so far. Keep your ears open in case you hear anything else.'

'Oh, glad to be of service,' Cwen said sarcastically and bowed sarcastically as well.

'When we get this all sorted out,' Le Pedvin said in a warning tone. 'There had better not be any weavers here at all. Baking ones, or not.'

Before she could come up with a reply, Wat and Aveline reappeared.

'All set,' Wat reported.

'They had better not crease my dresses,' Aveline warned. 'Plot to kill the king or not.' It was clear where her priorities lay.

As they walked on away from the chambers, Gilbert came to the back and took Wat by the arm.

'Was I supposed to get some minstrels?' he asked quietly.

'Oh, yes,' Wat confirmed the most obvious fact in the world.

'She never said anything about minstrels.'

'You should have known. And if you didn't know, she wasn't going to tell you.'

Gilbert released a heavy sigh. 'I think I'd rather deal with plots to kill the king.'

Caput XXIV: Ready

It was very clear that news of the king's arrival had spread.

When they returned to the main hall, Hermitage and Bishop Aethelric found the place thronging with people, every one of whom seemed to think it was their place to stand closest to the door. By this means they would catch William's eye and become known to him. They might even find favour.

'I'm too old for this business,' Aethelric said as he and Hermitage loitered at the back by the fireplace. 'And I've had enough to do with kings for one lifetime.'

'I'd be quite happy if William didn't know I was here at all,' Hermitage added. 'I've only met two kings, which is more than most, I suppose, but neither provided happy experiences.'

Aethelric considered the crowd. 'I suppose many of these men see their livelihoods threatened by the whim of the king, and so need to take some sort of action.'

'Ah, Brother Hermitage.' Alstan came over and joined them. There seemed to be a slight slur to his voice for some reason.

'Greetings, Alstan,' Aethelric said. 'Not joining the throng to make obeisance to the king?'

'I'm beyond that,' Alstan said with almost cheerful resignation. 'It's quite refreshing to know that my fortune is already gone, so I don't have to kiss the royal, erm, toe.' He seemed to choose "toe" for the sake of the bishop and Brother Hermitage.

'Your fellows on the Conclave do not share your happy position.' Aethelric nodded towards the main door where one or two of the sheriffs were starting to barge the bishops, who, for holy men, were giving as good as they got.

'I hope he arrives soon, or there could be an unseemly brawl.'

Hermitage was saddened to hear that. The Standing Conclave descending to violence? Surely these men were better than that?

Of course, the other person absent from the throng was Count Robert. Being William's brother, he had no need to fight to be close to the king. But, Hermitage wondered what his plan was, if he thought his murderous plot was proceeding.

Would he be here in the hall, just to show that he was not firing the fatal bolt himself? Would he rush to the king's side and demand the killer be found and brought to justice? Perhaps he would even point to the gallery and shout something along the lines of, "There he is, get him".

Hermitage felt sorry for Haimo, briefly. Did the poor fellow think that his masters would defend him, or spirit him away? Reward him, even? More likely, they would kill him to stop him from talking.

Feeling suddenly quite sick that the brothers of William could get away with this, he tugged at Aethelric's arm.

'Hm?' Aethelric asked.

'Just a brief word bishop, if I may?' He nodded an apology to Alstan, who waved it away as he spotted a servant carrying a tray of goblets and a jug of wine. Hermitage suspected that this would not be the first goblet of wine Alstan had taken this day.

'Something amiss?' Aethelric asked.

'I think Haimo's life is in serious danger,' Hermitage whispered.

'I would think so,' Aethelric agreed quietly. 'Trying to kill the king will not go unpunished.'

'More than that. There are probably orders out to murder Haimo as soon as the deed is done. Murdered by his fellow conspirators, most likely.'

Aethelric nodded. 'Stop him from talking.'

'Exactly. Robert and Odo cannot leave him alive to tell his tale. If the king is dead, they must not have it known that they had anything to do with it. And if he survives, it will be even more important. I think that everyone involved in this scheme is under a sentence of death, whether they know it or not.'

Aethelric glanced up at the small gallery above the hall. 'You think Haimo will be murdered up there?'

'It has to be done quickly before Haimo can say a word to anyone. There may even be someone up there with him who will do the deed as soon as the bolt is fired.'

'But we know that the bolt won't fire. Lord Le Pedvin has disabled the crossbow.'

'But Haimo will still be up there pointing the thing at the king. He still has to go.'

'And his fellow makes a pretence of discovering the would-be killer and taking his life.'

'Exactly.'

Aethelric thought about this. 'The killer is killed, but then who kills the killer of the killer?'

'Oh, erm.' Hermitage worked his way through that. 'Someone who knows nothing of the plot. One of Robert's men who just kills who he's told.'

'Until all who know of the plot are gone,' Aethelric concluded. 'Except for us, of course.'

Hermitage didn't like to think about that. 'There would be little for me to investigate if the killer of the king is dead.

With my knowledge of the plot though, I might have to be eliminated.' His voice trembled.

Aethelric lay a reassuring hand on his arm. 'You and me and Lord Gilbert and Le Pedvin and Wat and Cwen. The list is overlong, even for Robert or Odo's reach.'

Hermitage tried to breathe normally.

'But it will be a hard tale to tell without Haimo,' Aethelric said. 'Robert and Odo will simply deny it, saying that Haimo was a madman acting alone, or at worst, in connivance with the man of Robert's, who will be the next sacrifice.'

'We have to save Haimo,' Hermitage said, not thinking he would have to say that.

Aethelric nodded sharply. 'Doubtless, Lord Le Pedvin will be by the king's side, but Lord Gilbert should be keeping watch near the gallery. Go and find him, quick now.'

Hermitage must have looked surprised at this order.

'Your young legs will find him quicker than mine.'

'Of course.'

'Leaving so soon, Brother?' Alstan asked, and it sounded as if the goblets of wine needed rapid replenishment. 'You'll miss the king. You've got to stay and see the king.' Yes, Alstan was drunk. And he must have devoted most of the day to the task.

'I've seen him before,' Hermitage said. 'I just have an errand to run.'

'I hope you catch it,' Alstan said and started looking for more wine.

In the kitchen, the furore that had previously existed seemed but a pale memory of quiet times. The cook had obviously had word that she was now going to feed the king, and if that was a great honour, she didn't seem very pleased.

It was only to be hoped that she didn't speak to the king with that mouth.

Wat and Cwen had got back into the kitchen without being noticed but worried that there would be a screamed demand for a dozen loaves if they were spotted.

'Time for a change of trade, I think,' Wat said as he took off his apron.

Cwen did likewise and they looked for an alternative occupation. Simply standing still and not doing anything, or keeping out of the way and hoping not to be spotted were unrealistic options. The cook seemed to be everywhere at all times and was shouting at everything and everyone.

'Wine,' Wat said.

'I hardly think this is the time,' Cwen replied.

'No, no. We serve wine. Look.' He nodded towards two slightly better-dressed servants who were leaving the kitchen with jugs in each hand.

'Anything to get out of here.'

They moved over towards a gathering of barrels that stood against the back wall, in front of which, servants were queueing to get their jugs refilled.

'Bit of a mess,' Wat observed as two barrels lay broken on the floor, surrounded by a scattering of salt.

'The cook probably shouted at them too loud and they went to pieces.'

'Ho, ho,' Wat chuckled. 'Here, take a jug.' He took jugs from a store of them on a shelf to the right. 'And be serious,' he whispered. 'Someone is trying to kill the king, you know. This is no time for jokes.'

'I'll wait till he's dead,' Cwen nodded.

With their jugs filled by a very harassed individual whose sole function seemed to be to pass the shouts of the cook down the chain, they wound around and out of the kitchen.

Once clear of the place, Cwen put her wine down on a table.

'What are you doing? We've got to serve the Conclave their wine.'

'What? I'm not doing that.'

'What are you here for, then? In a room the king is about to visit. The one with all the guards looking around for someone who shouldn't be here and who might cause trouble.'

Cwen snorted and picked the wine up again. 'I'll carry it around, but I'm not giving any to anyone.'

'Looking at this crowd, it makes you wonder how Haimo thought he was going to get away with it,' Wat speculated as they stood against the side wall and tried very hard not to be noticed by anyone who wanted wine.

'He will be in the gallery,' Cwen said. 'Everyone else is down here.'

'They won't be for long, not once the bolt comes flying.'

'Which it isn't going to do because the crossbow has been broken.'

'Even so, he must have had an escape plan. If the king's guards got hold of the man who's just shot the king, he'd wish he'd shot himself.'

'The other conspirators get him away?' Cwen suggested. 'Through an upstairs window. Bit of rope? Ladder?'

'Could be. Which means he would have to move quickly once the shot is fired.' Wat glanced up at the gallery. 'Which also means they'll all be up there, ready to go.'

'And when the bow doesn't work?'

'They won't know that until he tries the shot. It's not the sort of thing you can practise.'

'So, what do we do about it?'

Wat took a breath and screwed up his face in thought. 'I think we see if anyone on the upper floor needs wine.'

Lord Gilbert, as host of the Conclave, was in the main hall, talking amicably to the attendees, accompanied by his daughter. Anyone who thought that Aveline was talking amicably to the attendees accompanied by Lord Gilbert, who seemed very distracted, had clearly misunderstood the situation.

Le Pedvin had left Gilbert in charge of the hall while he went down the main gate to await arrival of the king. Keeping half an eye on the gallery at all times, Gilbert was happy to let Aveline engage in all the pointless chatter that seemed to be required at this sort of thing.

For some time, he had been thinking that if Aveline was happiest in Paris, and the conquest of England was going to continue with only the odd skirmish or rebellion here or there, he might head to Sicily. He'd heard that the Norman conquest there required pretty much constant battle; which was the way he liked it.

Of course, he was at William's command and couldn't simply leave, but being a tenant of the king and a responsible landholder was not in his nature.

'Isn't that interesting, father?' Aveline was saying.

'Oh, yes,' Gilbert agreed with a nod and a glance for the man she was talking to, who looked vaguely familiar. 'Very interesting indeed.' He'd find out later whether it had been interesting, whatever it was. Or not.

Aveline took him firmly by the arm and steered him away from the conversation he hadn't been taking part in anyway.

'Father,' she hissed at him. 'That was Richard de

Tunbridge.'

'Really?'

'The son of Gilbert, William's guardian when he was young.'

'Oh, that Richard,' Gilbert said, still not having much of a clue.

'The one who was rewarded by the king with land in Normandy. He fought at Hastings and now has even more land.'

Gilbert frowned. 'Richard, did you say?'

'Yes.' Aveline was clearly unhappy at her father's lack of engagement.

'Not Richard de Bienfaite?' Gilbert did now look over to the man.

'Yes, I think that's his Normandy land.'

'Well, why didn't you say? I know old Richard, we fought at Hastings, you know.'

'Oh, God!' Aveline said for some reason.

'Once this is all over, we must find him again.'

'Once this is all over.' Aveline shook her head in disappointment.

'We have got a plot against the king to worry about,' he whispered in her ear.

'I know that. I also know that Richard is now talking to Walter Giffard.'

'Oh, I know Walter as well.'

'And you know his daughter, Rohese? About my age?'

'Erm, no, I don't think so.'

'No, of course you don't.' She looked him in the eye. 'You know, when this is all over, perhaps you'd better ask the king if you can go to Sicily.'

'How do you know about that?' Gilbert asked in surprise.

'You mutter it under your breath whenever you have to do something you don't want to, like deal with the tenants.

'I shall go back to Paris and have to sort myself out, won't I?'

'Sort yourself out?' Gilbert puzzled over this. Then he looked again at Richard in conversation with Giffard, before coming back to his daughter. 'Oh.' he said as he thought he might have realised what was going on.

'Precisely,' Aveline confirmed. 'I'm seventeen, father. I'm not getting any younger.'

'Ah, right, well. Let's, erm, see how all this goes and then we'll talk.'

'We will,' Aveline confirmed. 'In the meantime, you had better go up to the gallery, hadn't you?'

'Really?'

'You're not much good for anything else with that weighing on your mind.'

Gilbert gave her a crooked smile, leaned forward, kissed her on the cheek, and left.

'Ah, Lord Giffard,' Aveline called, hurrying over to interrupt the conversation.

If the expectation was that Haimo, in his gallery hiding spot, could be sneaked up upon, the small crowd that was now making its way to the upper floor made that rather unlikely.

Hermitage had spotted Gilbert heading towards the stairs, and with a wave to Aethelric, had followed.

From the other direction, Wat and Cwen were weaving their way through the crowd, jugs in hand, refusing to give wine to the several people who tried to stop them.

The timing was such that they all met halfway up the

stairs.

'Why have you brought wine?' Gilbert asked in a hushed tone.

'I thought we could have a drink after we've captured the killer,' Cwen replied with a heavy sigh.

'I can't get to Sicily fast enough,' Gilbert complained.

Bishop Aethelric now reached them and looked at the gathering. 'Aren't we going to be spotted if we all go?' he asked.

'We thought we'd better get up there,' Wat said. 'It occurred to us that Haimo's accomplices are probably planning his escape. We can't let him get away.'

'Really?' Hermitage asked. 'I thought they'd be planning his murder.'

'Hermitage, really?' Cwen said.

'Well, yes. If he's dead, he can't reveal the secrets of the plot, can he?'

'It's a bit harsh, isn't it?'

"They are plotting to kill the king,' Hermitage pointed out. 'What's one more murder after that?'

'I suppose so,' Cwen admitted. 'But I wonder if you've been dealing with murder a bit too long.'

'I know I've been dealing with murder a bit too long. But no one will let me stop.'

'Never mind whether he's going to escape or die, we need to get him after he's tried to fire the bow,' Gilbert said. 'If his accomplices are in the area, the only people they wouldn't attack directly are me or the bishop.'

Aethelric acknowledged this with some reluctance.

'So, I think it had better be me.'

No one objected to that.

'Do we know if Haimo is in position yet?'

'It's hard to see into the gallery from below,' Cwen said. 'And he may not go there until the king arrives. We don't want to scare him off.'

A clatter from below caught their attention, and they looked over to see the main door pushed wide.

A very proud and haughty-looking Leudric proceeded into the room, with Walter de Arsic following, the ceremonial staff being held very ceremonially.

Behind them, a troop of guards marched, pikes in hand and helmets gleaming.

In the midst of their ranks, King William and Le Pedvin walked side by side, in quiet conversation as if no one else was in the room at all.

Hermitage almost sank to the steps when his legs gave way having seen, walking behind the king and appraising the castle with a look that said it wasn't a very good castle at all, came Ranulph de Sauveloy.

Caput XXV: Action

'Oh, my. What's he doing here?" Hermitage wailed. 'I thought we agreed that he wouldn't come.'

'We did,' Wat said. 'But we didn't let him know.'

'Perhaps he has come to see if this scheme he sent you to resolve has come to pass?' Gilbert suggested.

'More likely he has come because the king told him to,' Aethelric put in. 'Even Ranulph de Sauveloy has to do what he's told sometimes. And he really does need the king alive, so best to be on hand for the possibly fatal moment.'

'What do we do now?' Hermitage asked.

'Exactly as we were going to,' Gilbert said urgently. 'Now that the king is in the hall, I need to be near the gallery.' He stepped quickly away.

Wat sucked air in through his teeth. 'Always assuming Haimo is in there. We've got nothing to say that he will be.'

'Apart from the fact it's the best place,' Cwen said firmly. 'If I were going to kill the king, it's where I'd go. And where else? Stand in the middle of the hall with a crossbow and point it at the king? I can't see that lasting long.'

'Let's just hope Gilbert gets him. If he gets away or gets murdered, we'll have nothing to tell anyone.'

Lord Gilbert crept quickly but silently up the final steps until he was on the upper level, where he crouched and looked about. He drew a dagger from his belt. This was more like it. Yes, it was his own castle and he was trying to prevent the murder of the king, but it felt good to be in action again. He really would have to have a word with William while he was here.

Looking ahead towards the gallery, he couldn't make out

anything unusual, but then, if Haimo was already in there, he wouldn't be visible. He crept forward in a low stoop, prepared for an attack to materialise out of the gloom.

As he drew close to the corner around which the entrance to the gallery was, he thought he detected movement off to his right. If there was anyone there, they managed to keep completely still now or had slipped away. On to the gallery, then.

Moving slightly away from the wall and out into the corridor, he swung around so that he could get a look into the gallery before coming upon it. If accomplices were present, they might be with Haimo, ready to defend his position.

It was particularly dark just here, and he felt both vulnerable if anyone was watching him, but also comforted by not being seen.

Just as he was going to take the final step into the right position, his foot struck something in the way and he nearly fell forward. Struggling to maintain his silence, he reached out with his free hand and felt the shape of a body in front of him. His hand had found a leg, and he wondered who had fallen here. Had someone stumbled upon the plot and had to be silenced?

He drew in a breath as he thought of Alan. Had his poor servant been in the wrong place at the wrong time, occupying the gallery as his refuge when it was wanted by assassins? Had Haimo mercilessly killed the man and left him here? He supposed that if escape was planned, it wouldn't matter if another body was left lying about the place. All attention would be on that of the king.

He knew that it took a strange sort of courage to kill at close quarters, and from what he had heard of Haimo, he was not a man of courage. Shooting someone from a distance with a crossbow was one thing, a hand-to-hand struggle, or even a silent killing from behind, was something else altogether.

Now kneeling by the body, Gilbert worked his way up to the head, where his hand, questing in the dark, came to rest on the face. It was still warm. There was no way he could tell whether this really was Alan or not, but whoever had dealt with his man in this manner would pay the price.

Just as he reached further to close the eyes, if they were open, the face snored on Gilbert's hand. This was followed by a belch and Gilbert waved the reek of wine away.

He would have words with Alan in the morning. He couldn't think who else would have got drunk and lay down just where the murder of the king was about to take place.

Carefully stepping over the body, he worked his way around until he had a clear view into the gallery.

There was a figure in there, and it appeared to be holding the crossbow.

Any last, lingering thought that this whole business might be idle fancy or ridiculous speculation, was sent on its way. Brother Hermitage had been right, there was a plot. And Wat had been right that the crossbow was the weapon. And Cwen had been right that the attack would come from the gallery.

He briefly wondered what his own men had been up to. Did it really take three Saxons to uncover all this? Had no one been suspicious of anything, or overheard nothing? Why had Aveline not checked her dresses? It was the sort of thing she did all the time.

But the castle had been disturbed. As Alan could bear witness. That wretched Leudric had come in and thrown everything out. No one knew what they were doing anymore, even if they were allowed to do it at all. New servants ran about the place and it was no wonder no one was paying attention to the details.

Was Leudric part of this, he wondered? Had the distractions been part of the ploy? This plot to kill the king could run far wider than he had imagined.

Enough of that, though, the man in the gallery was raising the crossbow. From behind, there was no telling if this really was Haimo, but it wouldn't matter in a moment or two. At least Gilbert could be confident that the crossbow would fail, he didn't need to leap forward and tackle the man.

He took his last step and stood directly behind the assassin, looking down the stock of the crossbow as if he were firing it himself. Which made him frown.

He even closed one eye and moved his head so that he could line up with the target. And frowned some more. If this Haimo was ill-thought of generally, he'd been even more ill-thought of if he did manage to get the shot off. He was going to miss the king by a barn's width.

Gilbert was no crossbowman, but he knew how to use one, and even he could do a better job than this. The murderer's hands were shaking, which was understandable, but that didn't account for the hopeless way he was shooting. It just showed that if you wanted a king murdered, you should use an expert.

Down on the floor of the hall, the members of the Conclave had been unceremoniously pushed to one side to give the king space, which meant that William stood exposed in the middle of the room.

The moment came, and the man in the gallery pressed the firing lever, which, as promised, snapped before it could release the string.

'Oh, God's holy...,' the man swore, and it was Haimo. 'What's wrong with the bloody thing?'

Haimo lifted the bow to his face and examined the two parts of the firing lever.

'What did they give me this pile of dung for?' He complained, shaking the thing as if it would meld the bits of wood together again.

Gilbert sat back on his heels and smiled. He thought that he would wait until Haimo gave up and turned to escape, before announcing his presence and the fact that he had seen everything.

Haimo shook the crossbow some more, but nothing happened. He even aimed it down into the hall again and pressed the already broken lever. Unsurprisingly, nothing happened again.

He now tipped the thing up and examined it more closely. He seemed to work out that the lever should have pushed the string of the bow up from the ledge that held it, allowing it to snap straight and fire the bolt.

Clamping the end of the stock under his right arm, he used both thumbs to see if he could dislodge the taught string himself.

He found that he could. The string leapt over its ledge, was whipped rigid by the bow, and hurled the bolt - straight into his own foot.

The scream from the gallery got everyone's attention and all eyes turned upwards.

Faces then frowned in puzzlement as Lord Gilbert of Nottingham's prolonged and genuine howls of laughter rang around the chamber.

A few moments later, everyone was gathered at the foot of the stairs as Lord Gilbert half-carried, half-pushed the limping and bleeding Haimo into the hall. He was still chuckling and held the crossbow in one hand.

Obviously, Haimo was limping because he had shot himself in the foot, but his position was rendered even more uncomfortable by the fact that the crossbow bolt was still in it. It protruded below the sole of his foot and made walking a virtual impossibility.

'You missed, then,' Cwen observed.

'Assassinated his own foot,' Wat noted. 'Clever. I bet the other one will watch what it's doing from now on.'

'The other one will be on its own if someone doesn't take that bolt out soon,' Cwen added.

Haimo had no words for anyone.

'What's amiss, Gilbert?' King William stood before them all. He glanced around at those nearest and peered at Hermitage, Wat and Cwen. 'I've seen those three before somewhere,' he said.

So much for the Standing Conclave being Hermitage's honour from the king.

'A sorry tale, majesty,' Gilbert said. 'And perhaps one we had best discuss in private.'

William looked to Le Pedvin who stood to his right, and who nodded sharply.

'I see. A man shoots himself in the foot with a crossbow in a room with the king,' William mused. 'I don't think too much explanation is required.' He stepped forward and looked at Haimo's bleeding foot. He leaned forward and gave it a gentle kick as if checking that it was still attached.

Haimo entertained the hall with another scream.

'Many people have tried to kill me,' the king said amicably.

'They even started when I was still a child. But I don't think anyone has done it as badly as this.'

'We discovered the plan and disabled the bow,' Gilbert explained. 'But even if he had managed to fire the weapon, he would have missed. The man couldn't even aim straight.'

'Who on earth would employ a useless assassin?' William enquired.

Hermitage thought that as well. These were the king's brothers, Robert and Odo, both hardened fighting men. Granted, Odo was a bishop and so could not, in all decency, carry a blade, so he used a club instead.

Surely, if they plotted to kill their brother, they would have it done properly. What possessed them to use Haimo if the man couldn't even shoot a bow?

'Haimo was going to miss?' he asked Gilbert.

'Aye, by a long margin. I was right behind him and he was aiming far too far to the left. Perhaps he can't even see properly.'

Now that really would be a poor bowman to choose.

'Oh, yes.' Recognition came to the king. 'You're that monk who does all the murders.'

'Oh, well, erm, something like that, majesty.'

'King's Investigator. That's it. You're my investigator.'

Hermitage bowed, extremely disappointed that William had remembered.

'I might have a job for you.'

Hermitage wanted to sit down on the steps again.

Wat and Cwen had been right, he should never have come. He should have known it would end up like this. The place had been rife with a plot to kill the king, and now the king had been reminded who he was. It was a disaster. Even the murder plot he'd uncovered had been a very bad one.

He looked at all the faces in the vicinity. Even that of Ranulph de Sauveloy, whose fault this whole sorry situation was. If only the man had known a bit more about the plot and told Hermitage what was afoot, he could have dealt with it a lot more easily.

Oh, that was a thought.

He put a hand to his chin. 'Lord Gilbert, you said that Haimo was not aiming properly?'

'That's right.'

'Off to the left?'

'Aye.'

Hermitage cast his mind back and pictured the scene just before the first of Haimo's howls.

He then considered his invitation to the Conclave and the organisation that had gone into the whole thing. Leudric and Thodrum had brought the news and then virtually took over Nottingham Castle. And Aveline, she had had word of the Conclave and come from Paris, with her chest of clothes that would go unsearched.

'Aha,' Hermitage said before he could stop himself. He tried to swallow the word back, but it had already escaped.

'Oh, yes,' King William pointed a finger. 'That's what he says before he tells us who did it. It all comes back to me now.'

'But we know who did it; Haimo,' Cwen said. 'In the plot to kill the king, which we need to talk about in private.'

Just at that moment, Robert, Count of Mortain appeared from a corridor.

'Ah, greetings, Brother,' he called to William. 'Have I missed something?'

'This man tried to kill me.' William nodded at Haimo.

'Not very well, by the look of things.'

'Not very well at all,' William agreed. 'Not like the old days, eh?'

'Ha, ha, yes,' Robert agreed enthusiastically.

'Anyway, monk, you were going to say something.' William prompted.

Hermitage had hoped that Robert's arrival would have driven that from everyone's minds, and he could go back to the moment before he had let that "aha" slip out.

'Oh, well...,' Hermitage tried to make it sound as if it was nothing, really.

'No, no. Go on. Aha, and...,'

Hermitage took a deep and slow breath and looked to Wat and Cwen with as apologetic expression as he could manage.

'I don't think Haimo did try to kill you, majesty.'

'Really?' The king sounded strangely disappointed that no one had tried to kill him.

'No. Lord Gilbert says that he was aiming far off to the left.'

'Only because he's not very good with a bow.' William kicked Haimo in the foot again. 'We can all see that.' He looked to the rest of the crowd in the chamber, clearly expecting everyone to laugh at his humour. They duly did so. Apart from Haimo, who was now crying.

'But we have to ask ourselves about the Conclave, majesty,' Hermitage said.

'Do we?'

'We do. Your arrival here seems to be generally known, but was it planned many months ago when the Conclave was first mooted?'

'Aye,' William confirmed. 'It is the first meeting since the usurper, Harold was deposed, so I said I would attend.'

'Of course.' Hermitage said. 'And I had an invitation to

join the Conclave, and Master Leudric brought it to me. The venue of Nottingham was chosen and the operation of the castle, as well as its security, was taken out of Lord Gilbert's hands. As you were attending, a rule of no weapons was imposed.'

'It is quite common,' William said. 'A lot of people do want to kill me.' He obviously considered this a matter of pride.

Hermitage continued 'Mistress Aveline, residing in Paris, somehow got word of the Conclave and all the important people who would be there, and so she packed her chest and came home. Or rather, had it packed for her.'

'Quite right,' Aveline put in with a polite bow for the king.

'The point of all this is?' William asked.

Hermitage closed his eyes so that he would not have to look at the faces. 'Haimo was not trying to shoot you, majesty. He was trying to shoot the person to your left. Lord Le Pedvin.'

Caput XXVI: That's Clear, Then

'Me?' Le Pedvin said with some surprise. 'Who would want to kill me?' He thought for a moment about his own question. 'Well, quite a lot of people, probably. But who here would want to kill me?'

All eyes turned to Hermitage, and he sincerely hoped that they would work this bit out for themselves. The last thing he wanted to do was give a name to his suspicion.

'Did Haimo have a personal hatred?' Gilbert asked.

'How would he have got the crossbow in Aveline's luggage?' Hermitage asked politely. 'He is Sheriff of Kent, I don't think his influence spreads that far.'

'We know Lord Robert's man is in on it,' Bishop Aethelric put in.

'He's what?' Robert asked with more disgust than anything.

'One of your retinue was overheard planning this with Haimo, I am sorry to say.'

'Was he, indeed? Well, you point him out to me and he won't be in a state to be in anyone's retinue by morning.

'I certainly have no interest in seeing Le Pedvin shot. Other than entertainment, perhaps.'

'I think that's right,' Hermitage said. 'Neither Lord Robert nor Bishop Odo would gain from Lord Le Pedvin's death.'

'Odo?' the king asked. 'What's he got to do with this?'

'Haimo is his man,' Gilbert replied.

'I suppose so,' William accepted. 'But my brothers do not stoop to scheming such as this.'

'And there is a third man,' Hermitage said. 'In the conversations overheard, one voice I discovered, Haimo I recognised eventually, but the third I had never heard before.

But I thought there was something familiar about the man when I saw him in the kitchen. Now, I wonder if I might guess who it was.'

'Guess away,' Wat prompted.

Hermitage prepared himself. 'Thodrum', he said.

'And who is Thodrum?' the king asked.

'He came with Leudric to appoint me to the Conclave. But he never said anything. I never heard his voice.'

'What makes you think it's him, then?'

'If I might ask a question instead, majesty?'

'Oh, go on then. But I must say, you're making this whole business far too complicated. Why don't you simply tell us who is behind it all?'

'It should become clear. Why am I on the Conclave, majesty?'

'Why? I don't know. Why are any of these people here?'

'They are the great and good of the land. Bishops, sheriffs, nobles, and me.'

'And you're not a bishop?'

'No, majesty.' Hermitage was rather alarmed to hear that William thought he might be. Did the king know nothing of his subjects? 'I am a simple monk. So what am I doing here? Who appointed me?'

'It wasn't me,' the king said. 'De Sauveloy dealt with all that. Didn't you?' He turned to de Sauveloy, who was looking rather bored as he gazed around the room.

'He organised the whole event,' Hermitage confirmed.

'It was even his idea,' William said. 'Get the old Conclave together and show the Saxons that they can still have a say in things. Nothing important, obviously, but it gives them something to do.'

Le Pedvin took this in with a nod and smiled. It was as

revolting a sight as his laugh was a sound. He took a step over to de Sauveloy and laid a heavy hand on his shoulder.

'And he has the connections to get word to Paris,' he drawled. 'Once he'd heard that I would make the Conclave no weapons.

'And his man Leudric has virtually taken over the castle and replaced all Gilbert's loyal men. I wonder what he has promised this Haimo and Robert's man.'

'I think there was something about land,' Hermitage prompted. 'Haimo said that was why he was here, but the Conclave does not decide on land.'

'I should think not,' William said.

'And Robert's man has probably been promised advancement if not simple money,' Le Pedvin added. 'I must say,' he patted de Sauveloy on the shoulder quite hard. 'This is an awful lot of trouble to go to. Why didn't you simply hire a killer in London? There's lot's of them about.'

William was frowning. 'De Sauveloy did this? Just to kill Le Pedvin?'

Hermitage gave an awkward look. That was not a question he wanted to answer out loud.

'Then why did he send you, Hermitage?' Cwen asked.

'To get Haimo discovered and dealt with quickly, I imagine. If the scheme had worked, Lord Le Pedvin would be dead, I would identify Haimo as the killer, as the King's Investigator and Lord Gilbert would deal with him.

'Aye,' Gilbert confirmed. 'A quick execution for that.'

'Oh, what?' Haimo complained.

'Any complaints that he had been sent by, erm, Lord de Sauveloy would be dismissed as lies to save his life,' Hermitage said.

'And if that didn't work, one of the other men in the plot

would simply kill Haimo directly,' he added. 'In fact, that might have been the plan, come to think of it. Haimo shoots Le Pedvin, sorry, Lord Le Pedvin. One of the conspirators then murders Haimo on the pretence that he was discovered just a moment too late. I confirm that Haimo did the deed, as he was found dead with the crossbow, and no one would ever know why.'

'Oh, come on,' Haimo wailed.

Hermitage sighed.' 'I was not appointed to the Conclave as any sort of reward. I was not even sent here to prevent a murder or uncover a plot. I was simply thought of at the last moment as someone who might confirm Haimo's guilt. Hence only being appointed the week before.'

King William appeared to be thinking about all this carefully, and he was gently nodding to himself as he considered the situation and its implications. No one in the room made a sound.

Eventually, with horrible intent, he turned to face de Sauveloy and Le Pedvin and shook his head slowly from side to side sighing heavily.

'How many times do I have to tell you two to behave? You don't have to like one another but you do have to be loyal to me.

'Le Pedvin, you've been my man for as long as I can remember. We have fought side by side on more battlefields than this lot will ever have seen.' He extended his arm to take in everyone in the hall.

'De Sauveloy, you are a key adviser. The manipulations and schemes of kingship are second nature to you. You do not defeat enemies on the field but in the corridors and chambers.

'You are both vital to me, so enough of this.'

He pointed a regal finger at de Sauveloy's face. 'It was a cunning scheme,' he said with a grin and a push for the man's shoulder. 'But never again, do you hear me?'

'It's my turn, next,' Le Pedvin said with disturbing relish.

'Enough,' the king repeated. 'It stops now. If I find de Sauveloy with a knife in his back, front, or any other part where there shouldn't be a knife, I will simply know who did it and have them dealt with. Old friend or no.

'Have I made myself clear?'

After the briefest moment of deliberation, de Sauveloy and Le Pedvin nodded.

Was that it? Hermitage thought in more outrage than he had felt since Prior Athan locked him in a cell and accused him of murder.

A simple reprimand? For attempted murder? For the manipulation of the entire conclave, for the deceit of Aveline, a young woman who only wanted to get on in the world? For the lies to Haimo and Robert's man? For the dishonesty towards Gilbert? Don't do it again? Seriously?

He glanced to Wat and Cwen who were looking equally disappointed with the way the world worked these days.

'Get on with this conclave thing, then,' the king instructed the room. 'I gather you have some important question to consider. I give you all my blessing. There you are.

'Come Le Pedvin, I'd discuss this problem in the North. If this lot can be left alone.'

Hermitage had to ask. 'Shall I, erm, stay, majesty?'

'You?' William considered him. 'You'd be no good to me fighting rebels in the north. You've been appointed to the Conclave, so you're on it, as far as I'm concerned.'

Ranulph de Sauveloy sighed.

'That'll teach you to fiddle about, won't it?' the king said to him.

The people in the hall seemed to realise that they could relax now that the awkwardness of shooting people and murder was out of the way.

Hermitage felt a nudge at his back and turned to see a figure crouched low, pushing his way through the crowd. When he got to Hermitage's side, he reached out and tugged the sleeve of Bishop Aethelric who was standing next to him.

'Bishop, it's me,' the priest of Derby said. 'Thank God I've found you.'

Aethelric looked down and started away in surprise which rapidly turned to horror. 'Good God,' the bishop said. 'It's you.'

'It's him,' another voice called out, and this was Le Pedvin.

Hermitage had never heard a priest scream before, but he did now. The man looked over, saw that Le Pedvin had spotted him, and jumped in the air with a piercing shriek. He immediately turned on his heels and made for the stairs.

'Come back here,' Le Pedvin called. He stepped forward and snatched the crossbow from Gilbert's hand.

In one flowing movement, he took a long pace forward, swung the crossbow to his waist and reached down to snatch the bolt from Haimo's foot.

Haimo's face reacted to this experience before his frame could give it voice. The distortions of his features said that having a crossbow bolt unceremoniously ripped from your foot, was a far worse experience than it going in in the first place.

His shout of pain was prolonged, heartfelt and continued until he had fallen to the floor, where he grasped the top of his leg, clearly fearful of going anywhere near the injured part itself.

Ignoring all this completely, Le Pedvin expertly cocked the crossbow once more, slipped the bolt into place, took aim at the departing priest, and only then remembered that he had broken the firing lever.

'God's teeth,' he swore as he threw the crossbow to one side and set off after the priest. 'I said at Hastings that if I ever saw you again I would shoot you in the back. Come back here.'

Hermitage thought that was hardly a motivational call, and he watched as Le Pedvin disappeared up the stairs. Whatever the outcome of this, he doubted that they would be seeing the priest of Derby again.

'That's not really an explanation, is it?' Wat observed. 'But at least we know where our priest made his enemies.'

King William watched with mild interest as Le Pedvin disappeared, but then turned to discuss something with de Sauveloy.

The rest of those in the hall started to disperse and go about their business. Doubtless, there would be a lot of gossip about what had just happened.

'Oh, monk,' the king said. 'While I remember. After the Conclave is over, get yourself to Northantone.'

'Northantone, sire?'

'You know where it is?'

'Erm, yes, sire, it is not far.'

'Good. There are monsters murdering people there.'

Hermitage can't have heard that right. 'Monsters, majesty?'

'That's it. Sort them out, would you?

'Erm.'

'Good.' And that was the end of the conversation.

'Oh, Lord,' Cwen said. 'We know where we're going next, then.'

'There are no monsters,' Hermitage said. 'This is nonsense.'

'Won't take long, in that case.'

'Erm, yes,' Wat did not sound keen.

'You don't believe in monsters, do you?' Cwen asked.

'No, no. It's just that, well, Northantone is a bit of a difficult spot for me.'

'So, there are monsters in the town, eh? Or at least there have been,' Cwen arched her eyebrows.

'The king has confirmed my place on the Conclave,' Hermitage said. 'That could go on for some time. Northantone will have to wait.'

'Hermitage,' Cwen sounded surprised. 'That doesn't sound like you.'

'Well,' Hermitage complained. 'I thought the Conclave was a reward for all those murders I had to deal with, and then I found it wasn't. Just another horrible, murderous plot.

'Two plots, in fact. Odo's and Robert's to kill the king, which didn't exist, and De Sauveloy's to send me here as part of the one to murder Le Pedvin. Unless they were all part of the same thing? It's too much to think about.

'I'm not saying that I deserve a reward, it's just that I am choosing which of my duties to do first.'

'Good for you,' Cwen nodded. 'Do you know what the Conclave is going to talk about?'

'Oh, well, no. No one has mentioned it yet.'

'You might be glad to get away.'

Hermitage was used to his hopes being dashed, but he would keep this one alive for one more night, at least.

The next morning, the Conclave gathered with sombre formality under the instruction of Walter de Arsic. Leudric was nowhere to be seen, which Hermitage thought was probably for the best.

The king, Le Pedvin and de Sauveloy had also gone, along with a lot of the soldiers.

'Some peace at last,' Lord Gilbert noted when he met them in the hall. 'This is just the sort of thing that makes you want to go to battle. You don't get people plotting to murder one another on the battlefield. They just get on with it.

'I asked the king if I could go to Sicily.'

'Is it nice there?' Cwen asked.

'They have a lot of battles,' Gilbert said wistfully. 'But William said no.'

'Bad luck.'

'I shall just have to stay here and do my best to get Aveline a good match.'

'That's good of you, she'll appreciate that.'

Gilbert sighed. 'Aveline told me I've got to stay here and do my best to get her a good match.'

'Ah.'

'Just make sure her match doesn't meet her too soon,' Wat said. 'Or at all.'

Gilbert grumbled to himself and wandered off.

'Right, Hermitage, we'll get back to Derby and see you after the Conclave,' Cwen said. 'You're all right to walk? We've got to get the horse and cart back to the tanners or there'll be more to pay. Don't get in any more murders while we're gone.'

'I hope all the murderous people have departed. Haimo is still in a chamber somewhere, but only because he can't walk.'

'And Robert's man? I see the count is still here.'

'Ran away, apparently.'

'Very wise. I wonder if he's caught up with the priest.'

Walter de Arsic rang his bell at that moment and the members of the Conclave took their seats. Everyone seemed to be present, except Count Robert, who had another of his servants standing in for him.

Wat and Cwen waved a last goodbye and slipped out of the door.

'The Standing Conclave is in session,' de Arsic announced.

Bishop Aethelric was back next to Hermitage again. 'What a day,' he said. 'Perhaps we can get on with some normal business now. Do you have to put up with this sort of thing all the time?'

'It does seem to happen quite often,' Hermitage confessed.

'You poor fellow. Still, the business of the Conclave will take your mind off it.'

'What is the subject for discussion?' Hermitage asked.

'Oh, a matter of great import,' Aethelric said seriously. 'It has been debated before, but we never reached a satisfactory conclusion. It's absolutely vital that the truth of it be established once and for all.'

Hermitage thought that sounded rather dull if he was honest. A matter of great import to the king was likely to be something about titles, or the jurisdiction of the church, or some such.

'The question before the Conclave,' Walter de Arsic intoned. 'Is presented once more.' He took a breath. 'Is the shrine at Walsingham superior to that of Saint Winefride?'

Finis

As King William has just told us, Brother Hermitage will next have to deal with the murderous monsters of Northantone.

Printed in Great Britain
by Amazon

57584964R00169